THE LOVE SUCKS CLUB

THE LOVE SUCKS CLUB

BETH BURNETT

SAPPHIRE BOOKS

SALINAS, CALIFORNIA

The Love Sucks Club
Copyright © 2014 by **Beth Burnett** All rights reserved.

ISBN - 978-1-939062-50-5

Cover Design by Christine Svendsen
Editor - Lee Fitzsimmons
Book Designer - LJ Reynolds

Sapphire Books
Salinas, CA 93912
www.sapphirebooks.com

Printed in the United States of America
First edition – April 2014

This and other Sapphire Books titles can be found at
www.sapphirebooks.com

Dedication

Dedicated with great love to everyone who walks their own path no matter how twisted the road gets.

Acknowledgements

I have been absolutely blessed to have the love and support of so many people in the writing of this novel.

First, I want to thank the amazing Erin Saluta, my beta reader. She did an incredible job of whipping this manuscript into shape. My editor Lee Fitzsimmons was the next piece of the puzzle, and again, I thank her for her attention to detail and her always kind, yet accurate feedback.

Thank you to Aschlie Lake and Donna McArthur who read and critiqued my feeble attempt at writing a stunning back blurb.

Thank you to my Tally Hoes, Renee, Chris, Jen, Kathy, and LK, for so much love and bliss and energy and joy. It is not even close to possible to express my love for you.

Thanks to Dad and Robbie who helped me out of a tight spot.

Thanks to my mom who constantly buys me things that she thinks look "authoreseque."

Thanks to the adorable butch who gave me a place to live, among other things, while writing this book.

Thanks to my friend and current roomie, Sandy Balzer, who is letting Brutie and I stay in her spare room.

Thank you Sapphire Books, Isabella and Schileen, who run this whole crazy ship and do it with aplomb.

Thank you to my BFF Kim for being awesome in every way.

Thank you to the whole online lesfic community, some of whom I have met and adored in real life.

Lastly, I want to thank all of my fest sisters. Nisey, Barb H, Jenny, Yvonne, and so many more, who keep me entertained, make me think, make me laugh, and remind me above all else, to nourish my spirit.

Chapter One

A storm is rocking my windows as I claw my way out of sleep. An invisible hand wraps around me, squeezing all of the air out of my body. Clutching the side of the bed, I pull as much air into my lungs as I can. It's not enough. Heart pounding, I drag myself to a sitting position, arching my back to make more room in my chest. With one hand pressed against my heart, I force another deep breath. The pain in my jaw moves down the left side of my neck and into my left arm. Concentrating, I focus on making myself breathe steadily. The shadow voice from the dark place in my mind is convinced that I'm having a heart attack. My rational voice diagnoses a panic attack. It's been years since I've had one. Even when I was trying to extricate myself from my last shitty relationship, I was able to keep the anxiety at bay for the most part. Now suddenly, out of nowhere, I'm either having a panic attack or a heart attack and I'm torn about whether to call 911 or just try to breathe through it.

Several minutes of deep breathing dulls the panic enough to let me stand up. Stumbling into the kitchen, I stick my head under the faucet and let the cold water run over my head. The coolness brings me back to the real world and my heart slows down. Afternoon naps always seem like a good idea when I think of them, but sleeping in the heat always seems to give me nightmares. It isn't even storming. The sun is shining, as usual, and the day looks balmy. It seemed so real, but a glance out the window assures me that the ground is completely dry. It must have been part of my dreams.

Staring at the wall, I cast my mind back, searching for the memory of the nightmare. I'm not sure what I was dreaming, but I think Annabelle might have been part of it. I think I've survived as long as I have by avoiding thoughts of Annabelle. I lean back against the counter, opening a bottle of water. A few sips brings my head back to normal. I glance at my computer, debating whether to try to get some work done. Fuck it. I can't stay here all afternoon; I'll go crazy. Dropping a quick text to my buddy, Sam, I head down the hill to mingle with the general population at The Grill.

We have a small population and after a while, everyone starts to look and act exactly the same. There are really only three kinds of ex-patriots on this island. There are the drinkers; the ones who consider themselves on permanent vacation. My ex-lover falls into that category. I met her right after I moved to the island. Despite having come here to be alone, I was miserable and lonely. I had bought and moved into my awesome house, but I felt so alone there. My ex was a bright light. She seemed fun and full of life, but without the deeply imbedded craziness that came from Fran. For a time, our relationship was actually kind of blissful. I was new to the island and living it up. After all, the weather is amazing and the Caribbean water is clear and warm. My ex was fun while we were dating, but she moved in with me way too quickly. Once we were living together, the partying got to be too much.

I mean, she fell into drinking her first beer at breakfast and doing shots at lunch, and I found myself in the ridiculous role of the harpy. I mean, I was constantly counting how many shots she drank and anticipating when she would either fall into alcohol-induced hypoglycemic tremors or pass out. My best friend Sam and I would sit together, watching her get drunk. Eventually, she would launch into a slurred argument with someone at the bar about how much more she knew about whatever the subject was than the other person did and it was time to herd her out to the car and get her home.

The drinkers on this island are a pretty tight group, as long as they are drinking together. My ex has plenty of people she calls friends. That is, she has a lot of people who will sit at the bar and get drunk with her or come over to her apartment and get drunk with her, but no one who will just pick her up and take her to K-mart or go for a picnic on the beach. The drinkers are on permanent vacation. They work as many hours as they have to in order to keep themselves in booze, which is, fortunately for them, extremely cheap on this island. They meet up in the various bars along the beach and they spent long hours drinking and laughing and clinking glasses together and buying shots and talking shit about whoever passes out first.

The other group on this island is the water people. They're generally athletic. They came for the diving and the snorkeling and the beach time. They tend to be younger than I am and extremely fit. They may also overlap into the drinker's group from time to time, but they spend the bulk of the time on the water, so drinking is a secondary activity for them.

The third group is the outcasts. They may all

be here for different reasons, but the basic feeling is the same. They lost someone, or they're hiding from something, or they somehow fucked up their real lives so badly that moving to a barely populated island in the middle of the Caribbean somehow seemed like the only option left. Some of them have money and some of them are flat broke. They can be young or old. Most of them are white and male. Really the only common denominator is a pervading sense of gloom underlying the forced hilarity that comes when an unhappy person moves to an extremely beautiful place.

Sam and I didn't really fit into any of these groups, which is probably why we found each other. We became friends the moment we met. I'm pretty sure we were sisters in a past life. Honestly, I can't explain it any other way. We had that kind of "eyes met across the crowded room" kind of moments, but there was never any sexual chemistry. We simply knew, instantly and with utter surety, that we were destined to be friends.

Sam is perpetually single. She's been in love with some bitch back in the States for years, but the woman is supposedly straight. Every once in a while, she drunk dials Sam and promises her that underneath it all, she's truly in love with Sam. They talk sexy to each other for a while and Sam hangs up the phone believing that it is only a matter of time before Josie leaves whatever guy she's doing at the time.

Sliding into a chair at my favorite table, I glance around the restaurant. Every place around here is part restaurant, part bar, but this place seems to attract people who are more interested in having a meal and watching the waves than those who want to slam booze until they projectile vomit. Sam and I hang here for the excellent food and the view of the water. Our island doesn't get a lot of tourists, and the ones that do come are more hippie than hottie. Every once in a while, a hot chick in a bikini saunters past our regular perches, but for the most part, the denizens of this beach are families with children or young men throwing tennis balls for dogs. Sam has just wandered across the beach from the water and plopped onto the chair next to me.

"The sea is like bath water today," she says, shaking her head like a dog.

Wiping off the stray drops that land on me, I look out at the water. "Well, it is almost ninety degrees."

"The locals say that when the sea water is this warm in June, it means a bad hurricane season."

"The locals say everything means a bad hurricane season."

Sam grins and sips her beer. "There's a new woman on the island," she says.

"I heard."

"Heard she's pretty cute."

"Is she a dyke?"

"Who knows?" Sam shrugs, grinning. "If she's straight, I might have a chance with her."

Laughing, I toast her with my iced tea. "Straight women and gay men," I chuckle. "They just can't resist your charm."

"It must be my gregarious personality."

"Or something."

I flag down our waitress and order a veggie pizza. Sam asks for another beer. She's not a drinker the way the drinkers are, but she does enjoy a good buzz now and then. I, of course, don't drink at all.

That figures, doesn't it? I lived with an alcoholic for ten years and I don't touch the stuff. I suppose if I had ever been tempted to become a drinker, living with my ex would have cured me of that idea. Sam waves over Karen, a friend of hers from work. I don't really know what to think of her yet. I'd like to say that if Sam thinks she's cool, she must be cool, but I have to admit that sometimes, Sam is friends with the most useless women in the world. Karen is kind of sexy, in a culottes and polo shirt sort of way, so I've mostly written off their friendship to the possibility that Sam wants to sleep with her.

I give Karen a smile and a quick hello before turning my attention back to my notebook. I'm a writer. I always fancied myself as a cross between Robert Heinlein, without the nipple fixation, and Kurt Vonnegut, without the politics. Sam says I'm more like Danielle Steel for dykes. She's a bitch, but dammit, she's probably right. I've actually written several romancey type novels under my own name and they've done pretty well for dyke drama. The only book I've written that I considered serious was published under an assumed name and did shit for sales.

"Hey, Dana." Karen pokes me in the arm. "Check out the new woman."

I hear the guys at the other end of the bar muttering to themselves, but I don't pay much attention. As I said, a new woman on the island is worthy of a press release. If she's cute, every single lesbian and most males on the island perk up. If she's not that cute, we still check her out. You know, there's not that much excitement here and we have to entertain ourselves somehow. I shake myself out of my writing and look across the restaurant.

A tall, skinny woman is shaking water off herself at the top of the stairs from the beach. I don't know if I'd call her beautiful, but she is cute. There's something about her that I find appealing. Watching her throw a cover up over her bathing suit and lope over to the bar to place an order, I'm entranced. Her legs are long and on the verge of too skinny. Her elbows seem to poke out at ridiculous angles and as I look at her, one of them knocks into a bottle of ketchup and sends it flying across the bar. Sam is chuckling softly under her breath. We meet eyes and grin. The woman has short hair that falls over her face in the front and sticks up in little chunky spikes in the back.

"She looks like a teenage boy," Sam whispers.

Watching her move, I shake my head. No, she doesn't look like a boy. She's slim and gangly, but there is something beautifully female about the curve of her jaw, the shape of her small ears, and the length of her neck. She turns from the bar with a bottle of water and for a second, our eyes meet. Hers are a rich hazel and I swear they have flecks of gold. Her lips curve into a warm smile, but I keep my face impassive and lower my eyes back to my notebook.

Karen doesn't miss a beat. "Why don't you go talk to her?"

"I'm happy here."

"You never talk to anyone," she answers.

"That's not true." Rushing to defend myself, I hold up my hand, marking off a list on my fingers. "I talk to my sister. I talk to Sammie. I talk to people. I buy groceries, I order stuff. Sometimes I even have to go to the office supply store and buy, you know, office supplies. That involves a lot of conversation because they never have exactly what I need."

Sam and Karen are laughing. "Forgive me," Karen mocks. "I had no idea you had such a rich, full life!"

Chuckling, Sam takes another sip of her beer. "Such an exciting life," she intones. "Going to the grocery store. Buying kitty litter. Someday, when you go on the Oprah show, you'll regale them all with the fascinating tales of your life in the Caribbean."

"Fuck off." I'm laughing, but a little irritated. I've only been single for nine months, after all.

"Oh come on, Dana." Sam's laughing, too, though she can tell she's hit a nerve. "You know I'm just messing with you. It took me six years to tell Josie that I'm in love with her."

"And look how well that turned out," Karen said, dryly.

I'm saved from answering by the approach of the new woman to our table. Sam smiles and Karen says hello, but her eyes are on me. I was right; her eyes are hazel and flecked with gold and lit with amusement and vitality. Her mouth is full and smiling. I keep my face impassive. There's no point in encouraging anyone into thinking I'm a nice person.

"I'm Esmé," she says, holding out a hand. I shake it briefly and nod. She shakes hands with both Sam and Karen before turning back to me.

"The men at the bar told me not to talk to you," she grins.

"They're probably right," I return. Holding my pen, I look pointedly down at my notebook before looking back at her. She doesn't take the hint.

"Do you mind if I join you?"

Sam moves over and pulls up another chair. "Please, sit down," she says. Traitor. It's bad enough

I have to deal with Karen at my table. Now I have to make small talk with a stranger. I glare at my best buddy for a moment before begrudgingly inching my chair over to allow Esmé space at the small table. Now we're crammed in and I have to move my notebook to my lap to keep it out of the small puddle of condensation from Sam's beer and Karen's vodka and whatever.

Esmé crosses her legs and takes a large sip of water. I try not to notice Sam noticing Esmé's legs.

"Where are you from," Karen asks.

"Chicago."

"My kind of town," Sam sings and the three of them laugh.

Grinning, Esmé sings along for a second. "Have you been to Chicago, Sam?"

"I have," Sam responds. "I've been everywhere. But I'd happily go again if you want to show me the sights."

"Chicago is an amazing place," Esmé laughs.

"And I am an amazing woman," Sam says. "We're meant for each other."

Sam is such a flirt; sometimes it drives me crazy. She says the most outrageous things sometimes and people just respond with laughter and joy. On the rare occasions when I try to flirt, women either look at me as if I am a psycho, or they laugh politely and change the subject. I don't know if I'd call Sam smooth, it's just that in comparison to me, she comes off like Barry White.

Karen interrupts. "So Esmé, did the guys at the bar tell you why you shouldn't speak to Dana?"

Kicking Karen under the table, I glare at her. "Honestly, who gives a shit what they think?"

"I don't," Esmé answers. She pauses as the waitress comes around to bring refills and snacks. When the woman has moved on, she looks directly at me. "They said you're crazy."

"They're right," I say, at the same instant that Sam states, "They're wrong."

Karen and Esmé laugh.

Frowning, I shake my head. "It doesn't matter. I don't care what anyone thinks about me."

"They said you believe that your dreams can tell the future," Esmé says. "Do you?"

"It's none of your business what I believe."

"I'm not prying. I don't think you're crazy."

"As I said, I don't care what anyone thinks about me."

She looks out over the water for a second. "I read *Annabelle Lies*," she says after a moment.

Sam and I both pause, looking at each other. Karen looks from one to the other. "What's *Annabelle Lies*?" she says, finally. "Is that one of your books?"

Sam nods. "It was written under an assumed name."

"For a reason," I growl.

Holding her hands up in a gesture of peace, Esmé nods. "I really don't have any interest in outing you. I just wanted to let you know that I read it and it spoke to me."

"Yeah, well, you're one of probably about six people. One of whom was my publisher."

"I read your other books, too, but I didn't like them as much."

"Well, as fascinating as this conversation has been, I've got things to do, so..."

She stands up. "I just wanted to introduce

myself."

Looking up at her for a minute, I'm almost tempted to smile. Instead, I ask, "How did you know that I wrote *Annabelle Lies*?"

She pauses. "Annabelle was my ex-girlfriend."

Sam exhales sharply. I grab my notebook and open it, trying to lose myself in my own work. I can feel the three women at the table looking at me. Worse, I can feel the eyes of everyone in the bar on me. A tunnel comes over my vision and I focus on my breathing. The words on the page blur together as I concentrate on just breathing in and breathing out. A loud hum starts to fill my ears and my head. I feel as if I can feel the eyes of everyone in the bar and everyone on the island. It feels as if they're all looking at me, they're all talking about me. My eyes close as a pressure fills my sinuses and the front of my brain. I'm half sure that I'm going to pass out.

"Dana. Hey. Dana." Sam has her hand on my arm.

Lifting my head, I blink at her. The humming is dissipating. My vision is still a little blurred but I can make out the concern on her face. Her dark brown eyes stare into mine. We have the same eyes. It's another reason that I'm sure we are somehow related. I never really considered us as looking alike. Sam is taller than me by about four inches. She has darker skin than I do thanks to some Native American ancestry. Her hair is dark brown with ever-increasing flecks of gray, just like mine, but hers is cut extremely short, almost buzzed, and mine is long and wavy. We're both outdoorsy types; we like hiking and swimming and such, so we're both pretty stocky. Sam is broad in the shoulders and slim in the waist and she works as a maintenance woman for a living, so her biceps are hard and kind of big. I don't work out and I make my living sitting on my ass with a notebook, so I'm a bit softer and rounder than she is. Still, one day when we went on a hike to an abandoned lighthouse, she took a picture of the two of us with our faces close together, and later, looking at the picture, I realized that we had the same eyes, the same nose, the same mouth, and the same basic facial structure. Trying to work it out, we both determined that while our fathers would probably have stepped out on their marriages, neither of our mothers were the type. Of course, we're both from Ohio, so maybe there's still a chance of some cousinery there somewhere. At any rate, even without a blood relation, Sam is my sister and the only non-blood I trust anymore. She's worried about me, so I make an effort to pull myself out of my state.

"I'm fine, I'm fine," I mutter. I give her a half-smile and look away.

She squeezes my arm one more time. "Thought you were taking off for a second there."

"No, I'm fine. Just a bit of a headache for a moment."

Karen pushes some water toward me. "You're probably dehydrated," she says. "I usually get headaches when I haven't had enough water."

Sam knows that I don't have a headache, but she takes the water from Karen and puts it into my hands. "Drink it."

As I take a big gulp, the last of the blurriness retreats from my vision and the hum in my head passes completely. Esmé is still standing over me. "I guess I should leave."

"Yes, you definitely should," I agree.

Karen holds out her hand. "It was nice to meet you."

"It was. I hope we meet again soon."

"Absolutely," Karen replies. "In fact, my husband and I are having our end of the summer blow out soon. Maybe you could come to that. It'll be a good chance for you to meet all of the other ex-patriots on the island."

"I'd love to." Esmé smiles at Sam, and turns to me. "I don't have any ill feelings toward you."

"You should."

She pauses for a moment. Leaning down to whisper in my ear, she says, "My dreams come true sometimes, too."

She walks away. Karen and Sam watch her go, but I keep my eyes on the table. Oblivious, Karen says, "Do you think she was surprised that I have a husband?"

"Why would she be?" Sam asks.

"Well, I'm hanging out with a couple of known homosexuals."

"Lesbianism is contagious," Sam laughs.

"You do look like a dyke," I say.

"How so?" Karen is affronted.

Sam snorts into her beer. "Sometimes it's hard to tell the difference between soccer moms and LPGA."

Chuckling, I give Karen the once over. With her plaid culottes and her pale yellow polo shirt, I have to say that she does kind of have a lesbian golfer thing going on. The ever-present visor just adds to the image.

"Whatever." Karen takes her visor off and squints against the sun. "Lesbians always want everyone else to be gay."

"Hardly," Sam scoffs. "We only want the hotties to be gay."

"Calm down, Karen," I say, seriously. "I never said you were gay, just that you look gay."

Snorting again, Sam gives me a high five. Karen shakes her head in disgust and puts her visor back on.

"You two can have your little jokes. I need to get home anyway. Rick should be home soon and I want to cook him a nice meal tonight."

"Happy housewife," Sam chirps.

"I'd rather be a happy housewife than a miserable, lonely dyke who uses sarcasm to cover her sadness," Karen retorts before tossing a couple of dollars down on the table and walking out.

"Wow," I say, watching her go. "So which one of us is the miserable, lonely dyke?"

Sam shrugs. "Well, I'd guess it would be you. I mean, sure I use sarcasm as a defense mechanism and I haven't had sex in six months and I'm in love with someone who'd rather give a blow job than be with me, but hey, I'm not miserable."

"I'm not miserable. I live alone by choice."

"Yeah, but you haven't had sex in three years."

"Sad since I've only been single for nine months."

Laughing, Sam pops open another beer and reaches for some fries. "You do have an awesome best friend."

"The best."

"And you live in a cool house."

"With a cool cat."

She nods. "You have enough money to pay the mortgage, buy cat food, and occasionally rent a movie."

"I live on a beautiful island."

"Which only gets the occasional hurricane."

"And I only run out of water in the cistern a few

times a year."

"And sometimes, the broccoli at the grocery store is actually green."

Nodding, I smile at her. "So how bad can my life actually be?"

"I mean, just because we started a group called The Love Sucks Club."

"Well, love does suck."

She nods, "I'm not saying it doesn't. I'm just allowing as to how some unenlightened people might consider us bitter because of the name of our club."

"Karen has the best husband in the world. She can't possibly understand."

"I think Karen is just frustrated because she's a closet lesbian."

"You really do think everyone is a closet lesbian. You need to focus on dating actual lesbians and you'll soon be able to tell the difference."

She waves her hand in the direction of the door. "Drinkers, ten 'clock."

Since I like to watch the beach, my back is to the street entrance. Pretending nonchalance, I keep my eyes on Sam, resisting the urge to look over my shoulder. "Is Voldemort with them?"

She scans the group quickly. "Nope, but her new girlfriend is. Maybe we should go."

"Fuck that. They're not scaring me off."

"I didn't say anything about being scared. I just don't want to have to deal with she-who-shall-not-be-named today."

Grinning, I roll my eyes. "It's so mature to call her Voldemort, isn't it?"

"Mature or not, it's hilarious, and totally appropriate."

"Remember that time I was talking about her to Barb and I referred to her by her actual name and Barb was like, who the hell are you talking about?"

She shakes her head. A shrill scream from the bar catches my attention and I finally have to look. A group of the drinkers are doing shots at one end of the bar. The bartender, Dave, is doing a shot with them. The bartenders on this island are a strange bunch, too. Some of them are just doing their jobs and trying to make a living. Some are just doing it to get as many free shots as they can possibly get. Although The Sunrise Grill usually hires competent bartenders, Dave is the latter, obviously. Now that the drinking crowd is here, he is going to be absolutely worthless in an hour. We might as well head out before the service goes completely downhill. Voldemort's new girlfriend, a chubby woman with humongous breasts that always seem in danger of falling out of her shirts, is doing a dirty dancing slide down some dude's body as he chugs a beer. A couple of the other drinkers are cheering her on. One guy is standing behind her, spanking her ass as she gyrates against the other dude.

Sam snorts again. "Did you ever wonder how someone can go from being involved with you to being involved with her?"

"No, but I do wonder how one body can support that much weight in makeup and still carry those breasts around."

"Nice. I still can't picture them together."

Watching Mandy, the new girlfriend, I shrug. "All Voldemort ever wanted was to drink and have fake, alcoholic fun with other people who want to drink and have fake alcoholic fun. I think she got exactly what she wanted this time."

Sam hands some cash to the waitress and stands up. "Come on, I'll drive you home."

We walk out past the drinkers who call out to us as we pass. Mandy turns as I walk by and wiggles her fingers at me. "Oh, hi Dana," she simpers.

I give her a fake smile and turn away. Sam puts her arm around me as we hit the door and leaves it there until we reach the parking lot.

At the car, I wriggle out from under her arm and cross my arms. "What the hell was that about?"

She grins. "Voldemort has told the whole island that you two broke up because you were having a fling with me. Might as well let her keep believing it."

"Voldemort and I broke up because she's a raging alcoholic who can't do anything but drink and argue about how superior she is to everyone in every single way."

"I know that. You know that. And probably most of the sane people on the island know that."

"Are there any?"

"How anyone could believe that we're lovers is beyond me anyway," Sam says.

"Yeah, butch on butch–totally weird."

"It's your long hair. Throws 'em all off."

I toss my hair in an exaggerated hair model pose and bat my eyelashes. "Do I look feminine now?"

"Yeah, about as feminine as Chuck Norris."

"Glad you didn't say Chuck Heston."

"Soylent Green is people," she yells, shaking her fist in the air in a lovely Charlton Heston impersonation.

Sam sees me into her beat up pickup truck and drives me home. Most of the money from my royalties went into this house. It sits up on a hill, high above the village and the beach. The house itself is kind of small.

It has two standard sized bedrooms and a decent kitchen. The living room area is rather large. The defining feature of the house is the wall of windows that looks out over the hanging deck and consequently, the ocean. When the weather is nice, I can sit in my favorite chair for hours, mesmerized by the waves. Sometimes, when they crash hard enough, I can hear them all the way up here. After Sam leaves, I plant myself in my chair, and stare out at the ocean. I'm trying to focus my thoughts on my latest novel, but for some reason, Esmé keeps popping into my head. Even if she knew Fran, the woman on whom Annabelle was based, how could she have known about me? As far as I know, Fran didn't talk about me to anyone. Fran certainly never mentioned Esmé while we were together. Hell, she never mentioned anyone from her past. It was only after she died that I realized how little I had known about her while we were together.

I pop back inside to make myself some hot chocolate and retire back to the deck to watch the waves. Frank, my huge Maine Coon cat jumps onto my lap, nearly causing a muscle spasm in my thigh. I push him into a prone position and pet his massive head. He chirps at me and goes to sleep. Trying to clear my mind of thoughts of Esmé and Fran and Voldemort and Mandy, I have to laugh a little. How does a self-proclaimed loner find herself having to deal with so many women at one time? I take another sip of cocoa and force my thoughts back to my latest novel. Maybe I can just hibernate up here for the next couple of years. Sam can bring me groceries and cat food. Sighing, I give up trying to focus on my work and let my head fall back against my chair.

Chapter Two

I'm a hermit. It isn't that I don't like people; it's just that I don't like them a lot. So I had to set some boundaries when it came to my time. Mainly, don't expect me to show up at every function, don't be surprised if I don't answer my phone, and don't ever come to my house without calling first. With those rules firmly in place with everyone in my life, I am pretty much guaranteed privacy whenever I want it. Except now. My doorbell is ringing and I haven't invited anyone over. That can only mean one thing. Susannah.

I moved to an island to become a full-fledged hermit. Unfortunately, it didn't work. Not only did Sam follow me, my sister decided that she couldn't live without me. After our mother died, she did her time trying to take care of our dad, but eventually she decided that she needed to be closer to me. Now, she's leaning against the wall outside my front door. I give her a fake snarl before hugging her with one arm and relieving her of a bag of doughnuts with the other. Susannah doesn't believe there should be boundaries between sisters. She thinks our blood relationship means she can show up at my house whenever she wants, eat the food out of my fridge, raid my closet for something new to wear, and hang out all day.

She waves in the direction of the herd of peacocks that live in my yard. "Peacocks are so cool."

"They're not cool. They're a nuisance."

She shrugs and caws at the birds before stepping inside.

"Come in," I say, ushering her to the kitchen. "But you can't stay long. I have a story due soon and I want to finish it today."

Waving her hand, she dismisses me. "I'll be quiet when you start working. You won't even know I'm here."

"I will know. That's the point."

"They're working on the street in front of my apartment. The noise is unbearable. I'm just going to hang on your porch and get some sun."

Sighing, I gather up some papers and offer her a seat at the counter. "Why don't you go hang at the beach and get some sun?"

"Because I won't have a comfortable place to take a nap when I'm tired of it?"

Giving up, I pour water for both of us and sit down across the island from her. "Is that my shirt?"

She looks down at herself. "Uh, I guess. Yours or Olivia's."

"Please, we hardly have the same fashion sense. And that isn't pink."

"Don't be so judgmental. Not everything she owns is pink."

She's successfully sidetracked me once again. I don't get it. My straight sister, who is about twenty pounds thinner than I am and about a million times more girlie, still manages to steal my clothes on a regular basis. Her boobs are a lot bigger than mine, so maybe it evens out. At any rate, she's got that new man glow that I've seen so many times before. "So, who's the new man?"

She grins. "His name is Thomas and he's very sweet."

"Married?"

She pauses. "No, definitely not."

"Definitely not as in you know for sure, or definitely not as in you don't know for sure?"

"Jeeze, Dana. Give me a break. He's not married, okay?"

"I'm just sayin'."

"Jack told me he was single. How was I supposed to know?"

My sister has a habit of dating the world's most obnoxious men. Jack was actually a pretty good one in comparison to most of her boyfriends. The one before that was a wanted felon.

"Anyway," she ignores my pointed silence. "Thomas is a sweetheart. He works at the bank and he's friends with Lori's brother."

"Aw well, I didn't realize he came with a pedigree."

She ignores me to answer her cell phone. Giving her privacy, I go back to the porch and position myself in front of my computer. With Susannah around, I have to take every moment I can possibly get. She follows me out a few minutes later and stands awkwardly in the doorway. Pretending that I don't realize she's there, I continue to type, letting her squirm. Finally, she clears her throat.

"What, Susannah?"

"Olivia blew a tire on the Frank Court Highway. We need to go help her."

Tapping my fingers on the side of my keyboard, I count to ten. Olivia Parker is the very embodiment of everything I dislike about human beings. She is filled with nothing but drama. Everything that happens is cause for horrific tears and weeks of bitter complaint. She and Sam had sex once, many years ago, and to this day, she still complains that Sam didn't call her after. In Sam's defense, she said that Olivia complained so much during the act that Sam almost called it off at the midway point. I still have vivid and terrifying memories of the time that she twisted her ankle on the beach in front of The Cottage. The horrified owner probably still has nightmares about her berating him about the slippery rocks in front of his restaurant. Suppressing a shudder, I try to reason with my sister.

"Go get her. Take her to that tire place on Front St. Tell Hank that you need to buy a new set of tires, but you don't know how to put on a spare to bring it in. I'm sure he'll send someone back with you."

"Come on, Dana. You know she doesn't have the money to buy new tires now. We just need to go put the spare on so she can take the old one in to get a patch."

I don't know why I'm bothering to put up a fight. Somehow Sam and I have become the handymen for every single woman on this island. Not for the first time, I'm lamenting the shortage of capable men in our lives.

"Wait a minute. What about your new beau?" I'm grasping at straws because I really don't want to leave my house today.

"Please. I just met him. I can't call him to fix my best friend's tire. Not until we've been dating for a couple of months at least."

As a last ditch effort, I pick up my cell and call Sam.

She answers sounding happy. "Hey-O!"

"Sammie. I need a favor."

Suddenly leery, she pauses for a hit of her cigarette. "What?"

"Our mutual friend Olivia has a flat tire and is in need of assistance."

"Aw shucks." She feigns disappointment. "If only I wasn't in the middle of a project at work, I would so do it. Gosh, I wish I could be there for you on this."

"Whatever, ass."

"I'd love to help."

"And I'd love to be able to pawn her off onto you."

Laughing, she says goodbye and I follow Susannah out the door.

Sliding behind the wheel, she glares at me. "That wasn't very nice."

"What wasn't very nice?"

"Making fun of Olivia with Sam."

"I'm not a very nice person."

"Olivia is a wonderful woman and you and Sam are always assholes to her."

"Olivia is not a wonderful woman and Sam are I are not assholes to her. We simply choose not to be in her company for longer than is absolutely necessary."

She ignores me as she starts maneuvering the dirt road from my house. With a deep rut on one side and overgrown brush on the other, my road can be damn near impassable in some cars. During the rainy season, Sam loads cement into the back of her truck, and even then, it doesn't always make the hill. It has been inconvenient at times to have to trek two miles up a mud road on foot, but it's worth it to me to live in a place that discourages visitors.

When we make it to the paved road, Susannah sighs. "I really wish the government would pave your road."

I watch her guide the jeep over a particularly huge rut in the road. "Why would they? I'm the only one at the top of it and I don't raise a fuss. Why spend the money for one quiet taxpayer?"

"There's shovel guy," Susannah says, laughing.

"The road is paved most of the way to his driveway. Plus, I don't think he really cares that much about modern conveniences."

"Either way, it's a pain in the ass."

"You have a jeep."

"Yeah, and it used to look pristine before I had to drive to your house."

"I moved to the top of a hill to discourage visitors."

She smiles. "Nothing can keep me from seeing my loving sister. Even if I sometimes have to drive you to the grocery store."

"Small price to pay for me paying your cell phone every month."

She nods. "Yeah, good point."

Stopping behind a herd of goats that are blocking the road, Susannah grimaces. "Sometimes I think about moving back to the States."

"Hey ladies." A group of men in a pickup truck swerves around us and pushes forward into the goats. One of the goats is hit by the truck and the rest run, bleating, to the sides of the road. The truck roars through and a beer can hits the hood of the jeep as the truck roars off. Susannah flinches as the can bounces up onto the windshield and off the side. She looks at the goat in the road in front of us.

"Dana, go see if it's dead."

There's no point in even arguing. Stomping toward the possibly dead goat, I pause for a moment to glance back at my sister. She's staring straight ahead, blinking furiously. I know what that means. She's on the verge of tears and if this goat is dead, the rest of her day will be ruined. Approaching the goat cautiously, I stare at it for a few minutes trying to see if it is breathing. Another goat, embolden by curiosity or perhaps hunger walks up to me and starts chewing on my shorts. I yank the fabric out of its mouth and reach down for the other goat.

"Meh!" It rears its head up and bleats in my face. Half-screaming, I fall back, tripping over the other goat. Sitting on my ass in a pothole filled with mud, I glare back at the jeep. Susannah is indeed in tears, but this time, it's because she's laughing too hard to hold them in. Both of the goats have run back to join the herd at the side of the road making their annoying little goat noises. I make a mental note to stop sending money to PETA. This is all Olivia's fault. I yank myself up and angrily brush as much mud off my shorts as possible. Fuck it, anyway. If Susannah's jeep seat gets ruined, I won't shed a tear.

She's still laughing as we pull past the goats and onto the main highway in town. Of course, when I say highway, I really mean a big paved road with a high speed limit, several traffic lights, and potholes that are only slightly less dangerous than the ones on my road. Susannah tools along watching the side of the road until she sees Olivia's little red Ford Focus. A Focus. Seriously. She might as well just drive it off the side of the road and leave it there. Half the potholes are as big as the car.

We pull up and Olivia tears over to Susannah. She throws her arms around my sister, crying.

"Oh thank Gawd you're here. I thought I'd be stuck on the side of the road forever."

"Yes," I intone. "I can't imagine the terror of being stuck on the middle of the road a mere thirty feet from the closest restaurant."

Both women ignore me as Susannah consoles Olivia. As she sobs uncontrollably, I watch them for a few moments, shaking my head. Olivia is about five-four and blonde. Her golden shoulder-length curls are glistening in the sunlight and her slender arms, a deep brown from all of her beach time, seem to glow. She has the most vivid blue eyes and long, dark eyelashes. She's kind of hot, in a false innocence, batting her eyelashes, annoying kind of way. It still amazes me that Sam had sex with her. I mean, I know she loves straight women and all, but did she have to pick one that was such a pain in the ass? Still, to give her credit, Olivia is good-looking, Sam likes blondes, and maybe she hadn't talked yet before Sam took her home that night.

I grumble to myself as I reach in and put on the parking brake. The ground looks stable enough, so I slip the jack under the car and raise it a bit. Olivia is still crying on Susannah's shoulder. I'm going to cry if I can't get these friggin' lug nuts off.

"...and next thing I knew, there was a loud noise and the wheel started jerking in my hand," I overhear Olivia stuttering to Susannah. I can't handle this. Everyone in the world has had a flat tire. Trying to ignore the women, I finish taking off the old tire and putting on the spare. I throw the old tire into the trunk and turn to my sister and her best friend.

"You're set. Drive over to Hank's and he'll tell you if he can patch the old tire. If he can, it will cost about ten bucks. If he can't, he can sell you some retreads for a decent price." I turn to Susannah. "Take me home."

"No, you can't!" Olivia looks stricken. "I can't go there by myself. They'll eat me alive."

Before I can even open my mouth, Susannah has her arm through Olivia's arm and they're walking toward the Focus together. "I'll ride with Olivia and you can follow us in the jeep."

Fuming, I throw the jeep into drive and head over to Hank's place, not bothering to wait for the women to get themselves situated. For all I know, Olivia has to reapply her eight pounds of lipstick before she goes to see the car dudes.

Pulling into the garage, I raise a hand at the guys and look around for Hank. He spots me first and heads over, wiping his hands on a rag that's covered with oil, grease, and who knows what. He holds his hand out and I shake it.

"You need something? Your sister's jeep got a problem?"

"No, her friend had a flat tire. I put the spare on and she'll need a patch."

The Focus pulls in and I wave at Susannah and point at Hank. She gives me a thumbs up, so I leave her keys in the jeep and head down the road. I figure I'll walk over to The Sands, a high end resort where Sam is the head of maintenance. She can give me a ride home when she gets a break.

A car pulls up next to me and I look in the window. Esmé. Nodding to her, I keep walking. She pulls abreast of me again and sticks her head out the window.

"Where are you going?"

"Not far enough to need a ride."

"Come on." She laughs. "Don't be scared. I don't bite."

"I'm not scared," I mutter. Coming around to the passenger side, I let myself in and slide down in the seat. It's a decent enough car, but small. What is it with these women driving these tiny cars? "You're going to have to be careful on these roads," I say. "The potholes have been known to swallow buffalo whole."

"I didn't realize there were buffalo on the island," she grins.

"There aren't. They were eaten by the potholes."

I direct her to The Sands and fall silent, staring out the window. I can feel her glancing at me from time to time, but I pretend not to notice. Finally, she breaks the silence.

"So, do you want to talk about your dreams?"

"Nope."

"About Fran?"

"Not a chance."

"The price of tea in China? Wow, you would make a fascinating subject for a talk show."

"I'm a fascinating woman," I say, dryly.

She chuckles a bit and stares out the windshield for a couple of minutes. "You know, I loved Fran, too."

"I don't know you." This woman is presuming a lot. "I don't know anything about you. How do I know you even know Fran?"

"I know she used to laugh in her sleep. I know she had a tattoo of a butterfly on her left breast. I know that she thought orange cats were the best animals in the world."

"You could have gotten that from my book," I grumble.

"I know she used to stare at the stars and talk about whether or not her family was ever going to come back for her."

Pausing, I stare out the window. That part wasn't in the book, and as far as I know, no one except me knew that Fran thought she was from another planet. I can feel my ears start to buzz and I'm sure an attack is imminent. Blinking hard, I try to talk myself out of it.

"So, Esmé," I say loudly to combat the buzz. "What made you move to the Caribbean from Chicago?"

"There wasn't anything left for me there. My lover left me for another woman. We'd been together for seven years. I think she was my rebound from Fran."

"How long were you and Fran together?" I ask, though I'm not sure I want the answer.

"Ten years."

I look at her, not sure I can believe that she's old enough to have had at least seventeen years worth of relationships. "How old are you?"

"Thirty-eight."

"So you and Fran were pretty young."

"We were pretty young."

She pulls up in front of The Sands and stops the car. "Are you going in for lunch?"

"No, I'm just going to get a ride home from Sam."

"I can take you home."

"Not in this car, you can't."

Standing outside of the front door of the hotel,

I watch her drive away. She glances back once and I slowly raise my hand. My ears are still buzzing, so I sit down in the lobby and ask the front desk clerk to page Sam. The tunnel comes down over my sight and I can see Esmé and Fran, young and troubled, clinging to each other, both of them with tears in their eyes. I don't know whether it's a vision or my imagination, but I'm drawn to Fran's young face, her light brown eyes and her pale skin. The shock of red hair, curly and full, was just as beautiful in this vision as it was years later when she came into my life. The vision darkens and for a second, all I can see is Esmé. I'm standing on the edge of a cliff, looking back at her. Her face is deathly white and there is a trickle of blood coming out of her mouth. As I slowly become aware that Sam is holding my shoulders and shaking me gently, the tunnel lifts from my sight. Sam's face, full of love and concern is inches from mine.

"Sam," I whisper. "I just can't do it again."

Chapter Three

Sam takes the cap off a bottle of water and hands it to me. With my feet hanging in the pool, and a cool breeze coming in off the sea, I'm feeling refreshed. Leaning back on my hands, I look up at the few clouds in the clear blue sky. Part of me is avoiding Sam's gaze, but the other part is genuinely absorbed by the beauty of the Caribbean. The resort's in-ground pool is on a raised area, so people on the deck can look out over the sea. The water seems to blend seamlessly into the sky and the few sailboats dotted along the horizon just add a bit of color to the vista. Sam is sitting silently next to me. When I look at her, she's gazing at her toes which are wiggling in the water.

"So, I suppose you're wondering why I called you here today." I grin, going for a humorous tone.

Sam isn't buying it. "Let's talk about your episode."

"Let's talk about your incredibly shitty taste in women," I spring back.

"That's a given. I want to talk about this seizure."

"It wasn't a seizure."

"Well, what was it?"

I shrug, staring at the water again. Looking back at her, I open my mouth to speak, but close it again before any sounds can escape. It's crazy, but for a second there, I thought that I was about to cry.

I love my best friend and all, but I definitely don't want to cry in front of her. Hell, I don't even cry in front of myself. As good as a friend as she is, Sam is not particularly sympathetic to tears. The one time I cried in front of her, years ago, a few days after Fran's funeral, she cleared her throat, slapped me on the back, gave me a hard one arm hug, and took off for the kitchen to grab a beer.

Composing myself, I try again. "It was just an episode."

"What's the difference?" she asks.

"Do I look like a doctor?"

Sam shrugs. We both stare off at the water again.

The episodes started on my thirtieth birthday. My mother had died a few months earlier. Susannah was in full melt down mode. Our other sister, Jamie, was in Africa and had not only refused to come back for the funeral, but had continued to refuse to come back long after, despite Susannah's heartfelt pleas across expensive long distance phone calls. Our father, a silent man who made a life out of hiding in his workshop to avoid our mother's constant harassment, had burrowed even deeper into his own silence. I had thought that the death of my mother, a woman who, by her own admission, believed that the only way anyone in the house could be happy was by keeping her happy, would have helped to bring him out of his shell. He would no longer have someone yelling at him if his boots were dirty, or screaming from the upstairs bedroom that he still hadn't fixed that old light fixture. I guess that deep down the old man must have liked having someone control his every move, because once mother was gone, Dad was at a loss. A couple of years after my thirtieth, when

I moved to the Caribbean, Susannah was livid. She felt it was her obligation to stay and take care of Dad, and she wanted me to stick around to help her out. I remain of the opinion that an able-bodied man who is fully functioning and financially independent should be able to take care of himself and I have never had an interest in giving up my own life in order to keep house for the old man.

But on my thirtieth birthday, I was still living in Ohio. I wasn't yet making enough on my writing to do it full-time so my life had become a cycle of working full-time, writing, checking on my father, fielding calls and visits from Susannah, and dealing with Fran. I don't think there's an appreciable way to explain the madness that was Fran except for this - I was in love with her. I was in love with her in a way that I don't think I have ever been with anyone in my life.

I literally loved her from the moment I met her. It was a Hallmark moment. It sounds stupid now, but I did look at her across a crowded room and fall instantly in love. It wasn't even as if she was that gorgeous, at least not at first. Most people didn't think she was even that pretty. I mean, she did have that incredibly cute shock of naturally red hair that curled around her face in soft waves. Her ears were tiny and adorable. To look at her, though, I just don't think you'd say that she was an "across a crowded room" kind of hot. First of all, she was short. Not that I'm that tall, but she was really short. Like five foot two. She was skinny, too. Not that kind of adorable skinny that some women have, but way skinny, with knobby knees and hard pointy hip bones that crushed into me sometimes when we were making love. I always felt that I had to be careful of positioning when I was cuddling with her or I was likely to end up with bruises. Her eyes were just brown. Not a deep brown like mine, but just kind of plain brown. She had sweet lips, but her nose was kind of long. None of her features were offensive in any way, it was just that put together in that way, they looked a little awkward, like they were all meant to belong to different people. Whatever. I don't think it mattered what she looked like. I think the universe determined that we were going to be together and it just happened. We saw each other, our eyes met, we drifted toward each other, while the rest of the room faded into the background and some sappy love song overplayed the whole scene. It might not have happened exactly like that.

On my thirtieth birthday, Fran and I had been together for about four months. Maybe she came into my life right before my mother died. Meeting her and falling in love with her is a whirlwind that's all blurred up in that time frame. It was unlike anything I had ever experienced in my life. Yes, I know all about the big lesbian joke about bringing a U-Haul on the second date, but I had never been that woman. To this day, I am not that woman, though I did move in with Voldemort about six months after our first date. I still don't know why, though I truly think I was still on a rebound from Fran. Somehow, the idea of being with my ex, a woman so radically different from Fran in every way, seemed a good idea at the time. I remember Sam literally begging me not to move in with she-who-shall-not-be-named, but of course, I didn't listen.

Glancing over at Sam, I smile at the memory. Those two hated each other from the beginning, but Sam stuck by me the whole time. Sam catches me staring at her.

"What's up?"

"Nothing. Just thinking about you and Voldemort."

"I can't stand that woman."

Laughing, I punch her on the shoulder. "I know. I was thinking about how you tried so hard to talk me out of moving in with her."

"You know, you met Fran. Your mom died. Fran died. You moved to the island. You met Voldemort. You moved in with her. You didn't give yourself the time you needed to recover from your mom or Fran."

"I was lonely. I thought getting into another relationship would fix me."

"Yeah, perfect fix for a hermit."

"Who knew it would last ten years?"

"I should have clubbed you over the head."

"Probably would have put me in a coma."

Sam grins. "The hospital bills would have been ultimately less expensive."

"Less painful, too."

"Why are you wasting time thinking about her on a beautiful day like this?"

"I was thinking about that whole weird time around my thirtieth."

She nods. "Want to talk about it?"

"I don't think so."

"Fair enough."

She flags down a passing waiter and asks him to go get her a beer. "I'm officially off the clock as of this moment." He looks at her dubiously, but trots off to get it for her.

Part of me does want to talk about it. I've given Sam a glimpse into the strange place that is my head, but I haven't really delved into the details. She read

Annabelle Lies. We've talked a little bit about some of my dreams. I don't know if she really knows what I saw before Fran died.

Fran gave me a kaleidoscope for my thirtieth birthday. She was always doing little things like that. She didn't have a lot of money, and she knew I wasn't into expensive things anyway, but she did like to bring me little gifts. The kaleidoscope was a perfect present. It was a nice one.

I instantly pointed it up at the sky and twisted it around, watching the patterns converging and changing, enjoying the way the colors slid around. Delighted with my interest, Fran was in a joyous mood. She laughed uproariously at my smallest jokes, and flitted around me in a rush of enthusiasm. The cake she had made for me, strangely lopsided and oddly colored, was perfect. I remember her presenting it to me with glee, telling me that it was the best she could do. She said it was Charlie Brown's birthday cake. In a way, I think I was still reeling from the loss of my mother. Bitch that she was, she was still my mother. I thought about her every day. I would wake up in the morning and wonder when the phone would ring. My mother spent hours calling me lazy and stupid, but she spent just as much time lamenting where she had gone wrong with Susannah who had been married and divorced twice already by the age of twenty-five. The only one who had done no wrong was Jamie, and that had to have been because she escaped to college at seventeen and then to the Peace Corps. I think my mother saw her all of twice in ten years and that for only a couple of days. I remember sitting in a restaurant in Germany with Jamie a couple of years before my mother died. I asked her why she never came home. Her response was, "Why have you never left?"

So, though I was in the throes of new and exciting love, I wasn't exactly in a great place. Fran was undeterred in her mission to give me the world's best birthday. After dinner, she cut the cake and sat naked on my lap, feeding it to me. We went to bed and made the kind of love poets write about for years afterward. After, as she was falling asleep on my shoulder, I reached over and picked the kaleidoscope off the bedside table. Squinting against it, I aimed it for the light coming in from the hallway and tried to see the patterns. Within seconds, a buzzing started in my ears and moved into my head. It felt as if something was crushing the sides of my head in on itself. It didn't hurt, but I felt a swelling in my brain, and the buzzing turned to a roar. I tried to speak, but I couldn't make a sound. I was sure I was having a stroke, but I couldn't even move to get Fran's attention. As the roaring in my head increased, a tunnel formed across my vision and it felt as though my brain was being thrown down a long, dark hallway. At the end of the hallway was an image and I moved toward it, determined to see what it was. It was Fran. I called out to her in my head, but she didn't know I was there. She was sitting on the grass in a field I didn't recognize. She was pulling the grass up by its roots and staring at it in her hands. Blood was trickling down her face and I could tell that it had soaked through her clothes and pooled on the ground all around her. Mesmerized, I watched the blood sink down into the earth all around her. A moment later, she looked up at me and mouthed, "Help." In that moment, I was back in my own bed, my arm wrapped around Fran so tightly, she was almost choking. She had poked at me until I came fully awake.

Shaking myself, I realize that Sam has been poking me for several seconds, in the same way Fran had poked me so many years ago.

"Ow," I rub my arm and poke her back, hard.

"Ow, what the fuck?"

"You were hurting me."

Sam punches me on the bicep. "You were out of it. I was about to throw you in the pool, but I was afraid you would drown."

"I know you would save me," I grin.

"Yeah, I might throw you a noodle."

"You're a true friend." I smack her on the head.

"I thought you were having another seiz – uh – episode."

"I was thinking about the first time I had one. It was on my actual birthday."

"So a long, long, long time ago," she jibes.

"Yes. Thank you so much for pointing that out. Your humor is unbearable. I'm laughing on the inside."

"Way deep down on the inside?"

"Exactly."

She pauses. "So, what happened?"

"I was in bed with Fran. She was sleeping. I had a vision of her bleeding from her head."

Sam shakes her head. "How much of the book is true?"

"Basically, all of it."

We stare into the water again, lost in our own thoughts. Trying to smile, I poke Sam on the arm again. "You know, I once went to a psychic. When I walked in, she stood up and pointed at me, screaming. She ran into a back room and refused to come back out. At first, I thought it was some kind of dramatic act, meant to drum up business, but later, I wondered. I mean, it's not as if she got any of my money that day."

Slinging an arm around me, Sam smiles. "I felt like screaming in terror the first time I saw you, too."

"Ass."

"Totally."

Standing up, I reach down for my shoes and hold the other hand out to help my friend to her feet. She grabs my hand and heaves herself up. "Hey, look at that. Graceful as a ballerina and I didn't even spill my beer."

Two women in bikinis walk by as we're gathering our things and Sam automatically flexes her muscles. Laughing again, I punch her on one of her flexed muscles. She grins and suddenly, she looks the same as she did when I met her, so many years ago.

"Everything that happens reminds me of something else. Is that a sign that I'm getting old?"

She reaches up and yanks a gray hair from my head. "Naw, this is a sign that you're getting old."

Laughing and half-punching each other, we make our way out of the resort and into Sam's truck. "Look." She points out the way the leaves along the side of the road are twisting in the wind. "The locals say when the leaves turn upside down on the trees it means a bad hurricane season."

Ignoring her, I stare out the window until we turn on to my road. At the top of the hill, Sam touches my arm before I get out of the car.

"Should I come in for a little while?"

"No, I need to spend some time writing. Come back around seven and I'll cook something for dinner."

"Ah, awesome," she smiles. "I was trying to decide between spam and cereal."

"I'll marinade some shish kebobs and put 'em on the grill tonight."

"You give butches a bad name."

"Your lack of culinary skills are the reason you're still single."

"True. I'm amazing in bed, but I can't cook for shit."

Nodding, I raise my eyebrow at her. "And sadly, my friend, I have just the opposite problem."

Laughing again, she gives me one more punch on the arm. "Now get out of my truck, I have shit to do."

Stepping out of the truck, I wave goodbye and she backs out of my driveway and heads down the dirt road. Staring at my front door, I suddenly feel incredibly vulnerable and very much alone. Well, of course I'm alone. I'm a hermit, after all. I stride into the house, letting the door slam shut behind me. A quick glance in the fridge tells me I have everything I need to make a good dinner for tonight.

I debate for a couple of seconds about whether to sit up on the deck or the living room. Eventually, I decide on my favorite chair in front of the windows where I can see the beauty of the sea and my deck without dealing with the sun glare on my computer. Settling into my chair, I get a creepy feeling up my spine. I look over my shoulder, scanning for something amiss in the apartment. Everything looks normal. The bookshelves are messy and the rest of the house is spotless. There are piles of manuscripts on the floor next to my desk, but the desk itself is shining and free of dust. My only splurge in life is a weekly housekeeper and I love the way she keeps the place sparkling, but I'm a neat person anyway. The creepy feeling persists, though, and I can't shake it enough to focus my mind on my writing. Getting out of my chair with a huff, I turn around in a full circle. Nothing.

I head down the hall and check out my bedroom, the master bath, the spare bedroom, and the guest bath. Still nothing. Coming back into the kitchen, the way I came into the house, I spot an envelope sitting on the counter. I'm a little surprised that I hadn't noticed it before, but not shocked. I do have a lot of paperwork on the island. So, why do I feel so creeped out? Stepping a bit closer, I spy my name on the front and in an instant, I recognize the handwriting. Voldemort. Seriously. What the fuck does she want, anyway? Grabbing the envelope, I consider throwing it into the shredder unopened, but curiosity has the best of me. I tear into it and pull out the letter.

Dear Dana,

Just wanted to let you know that I've decided to quit drinking and turn my life around. Thanks for sticking by me for so long. As part of my twelve steps, I mean to make amends to people I hurt. I know I wasn't as good a partner as I could have been because I didn't help with the housework very much. To make amends, I'll come clean your house on the day of your choosing. Have a great day.

It was signed with her name and the J was swirled and curled with a flourish as if the very act of writing the letter had given her a sense of joy and accomplishment. I crumple it up and throw it at the wall. Seconds later, I'm retrieving it and flattening it out. If nothing else, I'm going to have to show this to Sam. The housework? The housework, really?

Thinking back on all of the hell I went through with that woman, the idea of her apologizing to me for not helping with the housework strikes me as both impossibly maddening and ridiculously funny. And how can she be going through the twelve steps when Sam saw her trashed at the resort's beach side bar just a couple of days ago? Suddenly, I'm struck by a fit of giggles that leaves me struggling for air and nearly choking. Housework. I'm overcome, laughing until tears are streaming down my face. I go back to my favorite chair and ease into a comfortable spot in front of my computer. If nothing else, the years with Voldemort has given me tons of fodder for short stories about horrible girlfriends. Now, apparently, I can branch into comedy. I'm still laughing as I settle in to write.

Chapter Four

I have the grill lit and the coals heating by seven o'clock. Sam shows up right on time and after stowing her beer in my fridge, comes out onto the deck to greet me.

"Hey-o!"

"Dude." I give her a hard, one-arm hug. Sliding onto a stool at the outside bar, she props her feet up and leans back.

"So. How much do you love me?"

Wary, I shake my head. "A lot. Why? What did you do?"

"It's just I saw your sister at the Stop and Save and..."

"You invited her for dinner. Because I just don't see her enough."

Sam is saved from answering by the familiar whine of my sister's transmission making the last stretch of hill to my house. Within minutes, Susannah is trampling through my house with Olivia in tow. Sam looks stricken.

"I swear, Olivia was not with her when I saw her."

That's obvious. If Olivia had been with Susannah, Sam would have sprinted in the other direction. The two women come through the house. Susannah hands Sam a beer and keeps one for herself. Olivia throws herself onto one of my lounge chairs. With one arm draped dramatically over her eyes, she lets out a deep sigh.

Susannah gives me a kiss on the cheek and perches on a bar stool. "Where are the peacocks? Olivia wanted to see them."

"Well, I don't invite them to dinner most days. Then again, I didn't invite you and Olivia, yet here you are."

"I'm your blood. And I'm a terrible cook. It's your obligation to feed me."

Sam studiously ignores the sighing coming from the lounge chair.

"So Susannah."

I chime in. "Or should she say 'Oh Susannah...'"

"Oh, don't you cry for me," Sam sings off-key.

"I've never heard that one before in my life." Susannah gives us both a dirty look and pops open her beer.

"How come you're not out with what's his name tonight?"

Sam perks up. "Who's what's his name?"

Looking up from the grill, I wink at Sam. "He's Susannah's new beau. He's dreamy."

"Oh, McDreamy," Sam grins. She flutters her eyelashes and holds her hands up to her cheek. "Is he a doctor?"

"The important question should be is he married," I add.

Susannah flips me off. "He is not married, his name is Thomas, and he's very sweet."

Sam nods. "Is he a felon?"

"Rex was not a felon." Susannah is irritated. "He had a bit of a run in with the law. It wasn't his fault."

"It never is," I say.

Olivia lets out another dramatic sigh from the lounge chair and Susannah turns to her sympathetically. "Poor Olivia has had a terrible day."

Sam takes a swig of beer so I am forced to respond. "Oh? In what way?"

Olivia sits up, happy for an audience. "Well, of course, first I had the tire blow out. Then it turns out there was a ginormous screw in my tire. They had to patch it and put it back on."

"Wow," Sam mouths at me from behind her beer.

Smirking, I say, "Sounds traumatic. My day was rough, too. Instead of working, which is how I pay my bills and continue to do things such as... oh, I don't know... eat, I had to go change someone's tire out because she didn't know how to do it herself."

Glaring, Olivia tosses her head. "This isn't a game of who had the hardest day," she sniffs.

Sam snorts. "No, we all know who would win every time, Olivia."

"What's that supposed to mean?"

Susannah interrupts. "Come on, everyone. Let's just agree that we're here now, the weather is beautiful, and Dana is cooking an amazing dinner."

"Yes, a free meal at someone else's house is bound to cheer you up, Olivia," Sam grins.

"You're one to talk," she replies.

Grunting, Sam takes another sip of her beer and hooks her feet under the stool.

I can just hear the shrill screeching of a couple of peacocks off on the woods side of the house. Sam lifts her head. "Are they nocturnal or diurnal?"

"As far as I can tell they're all-urnal. I swear to God they wake me up at two a.m. having screaming fights with their reflections in my front windows."

Susannah laughs. "I still think they're beautiful."

"I'm more than half tempted to find out how they taste on the grill."

Olivia purses her lips at me in distaste. I don't know what she's so upset about. She's more annoying than the peacocks and I haven't thrown her on the grill.

After throwing the kebobs on the grill, I send Susannah into the house to get the side dishes, including the bags of potato chips that Sam bought at the quickie mart. Olivia wrinkles her nose as we set out the sides. "I guess we don't have to ask who brought the chips."

"At least I brought something," Sam retorts.

"I didn't even know we were coming here until a few minutes before Susannah picked me up."

I pick up a handful of chips and throw a couple in my mouth. "The single butch dyke always brings the chips."

"You're single and butch," Olivia says. "You seem to know your way around a kitchen."

"How about you, Olivia?" Sam sits up again. "Do you know how to cook?"

"Oh God," she rolls her eyes back. "I was trying to make a quiche for my ex-boyfriend. I took it out of the oven and place it on the stove top. In the meantime, I turned on the front burner to steam some vegetables. Apparently I turned on the wrong burner and next thing I knew, the burner under the glass bakeware was bright red and glowing. I panicked and grabbed my pot holders and lifted the quiche off the burner. When I turned away from the stove, the glass exploded and hot glass and quiche went everywhere. I was burned.

There were scorch marks on the wall. Oh, and there was a huge burn in the kitchen carpet."

"Well, who has carpet in their kitchen?" Sam says.

"It was a terrifying moment, Sam."

"Olivia, you think every moment is terrifying or horrifying or death-defying or something fy-ing."

"Just because I react to life," she spits out, her face red.

Sam waves a hand dismissively. "You OVER-react to life."

Laughing, I join the conversation. "Oh yeah. I remember that time I walked into Susannah's apartment and you were sitting in front of the television, sobbing your head off over the ending of *Pretty Woman*."

"Jesus, Olivia," Sam states. "She's a fucking hooker."

"Or that time your date didn't show and you didn't leave your apartment for three days." I'm on a roll now.

Sam chuckles. "That time your car got scratched in the parking lot of K-mart and you came into the bar bawling your head off. I thought someone had been killed."

"Oh yeah," I say, pointing at Sam. "I remember that. She ordered a shot of whiskey and downed it, still crying."

Susannah is getting pissed. "That's enough."

"What?" I spread my arms innocently. "We're just joking around."

Ignoring me, Susannah turns to Olivia. "I wouldn't take too seriously the opinions of women who belong to a social club called The Love Sucks

Club, membership two."

I feign hurt. "We have three members!"

"We aren't just members," Sam states. "We're the presidents!"

"You two think you're so funny, but you're not. You're assholes." Olivia is blinking back tears and I feel a little bad.

"Okay, I'm sorry. We'll stop."

"Fine, fine," Sam grumbles. "Stop being so damn sensitive. We're just messing around."

"Yeah, really," I add. "I make fun of Sam all of the time and you don't hear her complaining about it."

"Well, there's a lot to make fun of," Susannah says.

We manage to make it through dinner without any more incidents. As we're cleaning up the dishes, Sam says, "Let's get rid of Olivia and Susannah and go to The Grill."

"I'll go down to The Grill, but I doubt you're going to get rid of Olivia and Susannah that easily."

I was right. Susannah and Olivia want to go, as well. They head off in Susannah's jeep and Sam and I get into her truck. "I told you so," I say, as we maneuver down the hill.

"Whatever," she says, shrugging. "I like your sister. It's Olivia I could do without."

"Maybe she wouldn't be so annoying if you hadn't fucked her that time."

"True. I'm so good in bed, they hate me when I stop."

Snorting, I roll my eyes at her. We walk into the restaurant and spy Susannah and Olivia sitting at a table with Esmé. Turning my back on them, I look at the bar. Karen and her husband, Rick, are sitting on bar stools. Rick orders a beer for Sam and an iced tea for me.

"Sam, don't you ever get tired of carting Dana's ass around town?" Karen asks.

Ignoring the hint of nastiness in the question, Sam responds genuinely. "No. I don't. And I never get tired of filling up my truck for free on Dana's credit at the gas station."

"Not that our deal is any of your business," I add.

Changing the subject, Rick interrupts. "So, are you two geared up for our big end of season party?"

"Even the hermit is looking forward to it," Sam answers, gesturing toward me.

To be honest, I am looking forward to it. I like Karen well enough. She's usually pretty nice. As Sam pointed out, she does dress like a lesbian golfer, but she's pretty. She works at the resort with Sam and I know from past conversations that she doesn't have too many close friends on the island. I'm not sure if that's because she has a bit of a loner thing herself, or because she is neither a scuba diver nor a drinker. I've tried to hook her up for play dates with Susannah, but the two of them just didn't click. It's too bad because if Susannah became BFFs with Karen, I wouldn't have to deal with Olivia quite as much. Karen's husband is gorgeous. Sam and I have agreed that if either of us were ever to switch teams, it would be for this guy. He's tall, slender, dark-skinned, and soft-spoken. He mostly seems content to be quiet in groups, but when he does speak, he is well-reasoned and intelligent. I've spent a few evenings at their house talking about everything from women's lib to gay marriage to civil rights with him, and I have yet to find a subject on which he is not well-informed and eloquent. Unlike my ex, who is also extremely intelligent, he doesn't talk down to the rest of us in order to make sure everyone knows it. He's just a smart, humble, and good-looking guy. If he wasn't already married to Karen, I'd be petitioning my sister, Jamie, to come visit so I could set them up. Of course, I don't actually know what kind of guy Jamie is interested in, or if she even dates men, but I just love the idea of Rick being related to me.

Sam interrupts my internal fawning with an elbow in the ribs. "Remember that woman who was hitting on me?"

"Which one?"

"The singer from the east side of the island."

"The big one from Sparky's?" I'm trying to remember who she's talking about.

"Yes."

"I remember." I don't have a great picture of who she's talking about, but I'm pretty sure I remember the woman. Sam and I ventured to the other side of the island one night and ended up in the island's one gay bar. The band was all female and pretty good. Sam kind of flirted a bit with the singer until we realized that her wife was in the audience. After that, she backed off. We stayed for the next set and took off. Pretty unremarkable night, if you ask me.

"She's here," Sam says.

"Yeah? Is her wife here, too?"

"I don't know. But she was at the Sands the other night. I stopped in at the bar to have a couple of beers after work and I swear, she was coming on to me again."

"I don't know." I'm dubious. Sam is pretty slow about women. "She was probably just being friendly."

"She kept rubbing on me."

"You are pretty touchable," I grin.

"Shhh. Here she comes."

We both half-turn as the singer walks up. She's taller than Sam and solidly built. Wearing dark jeans and a tight black muscle shirt that shows off not only her breasts, but her muscles as well. I can't tell if she's butch or just a muscular femme, but either way, she's hot. She puts her arm around Sam. "Hi. Remember me?"

"Of course," Sam says. "And this is my friend, Dana."

"I'm Nan," she says, putting her other arm around me. "It's nice to meet you."

"And you."

She squeezes us both and continues on, in the direction of the bathroom.

"See?" Sam says after she passes.

"See what? You're totally imagining things. Did you see how she put her arm around me?"

"Yeah, and?"

"She's obviously just a touchy-feely kind of person."

"We better go over and sit with your sister for a while."

"I guess."

We gather a couple of beverages and head toward the table. As we're standing there arranging our drinks and chairs, the singer comes out of the bathroom and walks past us to get to her table. As she walks behind Sam, she reaches her arm over Sam's shoulder and puts her hand directly onto Sam's crotch. Sam makes a kind of blerting noise and the singer laughs. Giving Sam one squeeze, she removes her arm and walks on.

We're all quiet for a moment, and then Sam glares at me.

"She's just a touchy-feely kind of person, huh Dana?"

"Sam. Sammie-Sam Sam. You're being paranoid."

She laughs and we turn back to the table.

Esmé is wearing a pale yellow sundress that shows off her slim shoulders and her hazel eyes. Sitting down next to her, I offer a quick hello and turn my attention to the dark beach. The view of the stars from my deck is better. I should have stayed home. Esmé leans in close and puts her mouth next to my ear.

"I had a dream about you last night," she whispers.

Most women would find this a turn-on. Instead, I'm filled with trepidation. "And?"

"You were standing on a cliff, looking down. I was behind you. I kept trying to call your name, but I couldn't open my mouth. When I finally got my mouth open, you were stepping off the cliff. I raced toward you, but the harder I ran, the further away the cliff got. You fell in slow motion."

I'm silent, letting her words absorb.

She pokes me in the ribs. "You're not planning on jumping off any cliffs, are you?" She tries to sound as if she is joking, but I can just discern the concern under the humor. Olivia obviously missed it, because she laughs.

"If you are planning on jumping off a cliff, take Sam with you."

"God, you're hilarious, Olivia," Sam grimaces.

"I don't think that's an appropriate topic for joking around, considering the circumstances,"

Susannah says, pointedly.

"It's fine." I wave my hand, dismissing the whole conversation.

"Sorry, Dana..." Sam starts.

"Sam is so insensitive," Olivia sniffs.

"Wouldn't it be nice if we all had a lovely time for once instead of always bickering?" Susannah is losing patience with Olivia and Sam.

"Actually, we do have a lovely time," Sam replies. "Dana and I are quite adept at lovely times. In fact, we're thinking of starting a business. Lovely Times "R" Us." she lifts her fingers to put imaginary quotes around the "r."

Esmé laughs. "I'd hire you, Sam."

If I'm not interested in this woman, why am I irritated that she's flirting with Sam? Susannah kicks me under the table. "Voldemort," she says without moving her lips.

Sam is facing the door, so she looks up. "Sure enough," she mutters. "Voldemort and Mandy, along with a few other drunk freaks."

"Great." I'm tempted to turn around, but I don't want to give she-who-shall-not-be-named the satisfaction of knowing I turned to look at her. "What's she doing?"

"Looking over here," Susannah says.

Esmé puts her hand on my arm. "Are you all right?"

"Fine," I grin. "I'm just fine."

Sam shakes her head. "In a second, Dana should say something and we'll all laugh."

She looks up at Voldemort and gives me the slightest nod. Turning to look over my shoulder, I make eye contact with my ex across the restaurant and turn back to my friends. I mouth something and the entire table erupts with laughter. It lasts for a few minutes, culminating with Sam picking up a napkin and pretending to wipe away a tear.

"And you say I'm dramatic," Olivia scoffs.

"That was just adding visual interest," Sam replies.

We all laugh again. Esmé squeezes my arm again so I put my arm around her. I'm well aware that I'm doing it to make sure my ex knows that I have a pretty woman with me, but it also feels good to touch her.

"Do you want to leave?" Sam asks me.

"I'm ready." I'm suddenly tired. Having my arm around Esmé suddenly feels uncomfortable. We look into each other's eyes and I feel that she's looking into my mind and seeing all of my hidden skeletons. Needing a break from touching her, I casually remove my arm from her shoulders and stand up. Susannah stands up, too.

"Esmé needs a ride home," she says. "She shouldn't be walking home after dark."

Sam pulls her keys out of her pocket. "No problem. I can drop you off after I take Dana up the hill."

"Good," Esmé says. "I want to see where she lives anyway."

Doubting that my opinion matters, I interject anyway. "I don't suppose I have a say in this."

"None," Sam and Esmé say at the same time.

Bracing myself for the inevitable run-in with Voldemort, I set my face in what I hope is a look of complete nonchalance. The five of us walk toward the door. When we reach my ex, she smiles at me and reaches out her hand.

"Hey, Dana," she says, smiling. "How are you doing?"

"Fine, thank you for asking."

"Did you get my letter?"

"Yep. Just wondering how you got it in my house."

She smiled. "I stopped up there looking for you. Since you weren't there, I just went in and set it on the counter."

Making a note to start locking my doors, I nod. "Well, you aren't invited to just stop at my house."

"Come on, Dana," she says, laughing. "I lived there for five years. I think I can still stop over when I want."

"Guess I'll have to invest in a moat."

Voldemort laughs again. Her girlfriend, Mandy, grabs her hand and glares at me. "Come on. We don't have anything to say to her."

My ex gives me a wink before they turn back to the bar. I have to admit that she still has some kind of sex appeal. She isn't as gorgeous as she was when we got together. The years of drinking and smoking have taken a toll on her skin, giving her a drawn look. The ever-present anger shows in the deep grooves around her eyes and the tight set of her mouth. Still, her eyes are still a pretty shade of blue and her hair which is almost as brown as mine, has only just started to go gray. She's as tall as Sam, but thinner. She used to work out a lot when we first got together, but lately, she has been doing nothing but drinking, so she's getting soft and saggy.

Esmé takes my hand and tugs me along. I notice my ex noticing and fight to keep the smile off my face. She's going to be wondering about this tonight. I give her a big grin and squeeze Esmé's hand. Sam laughs and we all head toward the door. When we reach it, I turn around once more. "Hey, how's that twelve step thing going?"

Mandy looks sharply at the ex, and for just a moment, Voldemort's composure and her smug smile slip. Catching herself, she shrugs and smiles again.

"I'm taking it one day at a time."

"One drink at a time," Sam responds.

In the parking lot, we say goodbye to Susannah and Olivia and pile into Sam's truck. Esmé props herself up on my knee. Her bony butt digs into my thighs and I'm forcibly reminded of Fran. Esmé isn't quite that skinny, but the comparison is there. I stare out the window, ignoring the fact that she is on my lap. Sam, determining that Esmé lives relatively close to the grill, decides to drop her off first. I'm partly grateful. I'm sure she wants to talk to me about the run in with Voldemort. I never did get to tell her about the letter on my counter. On the one hand, I'd like to talk to Sam alone. On the other hand, I'd kind of like to be by myself for a while.

When we reach Esmé's house, she gives me a quick hug before sliding off my lap. She thanks Sam and starts up the sidewalk to her house. We watch her until she's inside the door. Backing down the driveway, Sam is silent for once. Staring out the window, I try to clear my mind, not wanting to think about Voldemort or Mandy or even Esmé. As Sam turns onto my dirt road and starts the long trek up the hill to my house, I'm once again struck with the urge to cry. Blinking furiously, I stare out the window the whole way home.

Chapter Five

The third official meeting of The Love Sucks Club has come to order. We're hunkered down in a back booth at a hole-in-the-wall restaurant on Fifth Street. The Pit is a dirty, ugly place and the service sucks, but the pizza is awesome. Since most of our friends tend to like to sit in places where you can be assured of not sticking to the seat, we are practically guaranteed privacy. Being the founder and the co-president, I rap the table with my gavel and call for order. Since there are only three members, this is, perhaps, not strictly necessary, but I like to do things by the book. Sam calls attendance.

"Dana?"

"Here."

"Roxanne?"

"Here."

"Myself? Here." She makes a check mark in a spiral notebook and looks up at me. "All present and accounted for."

"Excellent, excellent. Do you want to read the minutes from the last meeting?" I nod at Roxanne.

"Sure." Roxanne is a sixty something woman who lives in my neighborhood. We met years ago when she was a co-worker of my ex. For a brief time, I had speculated that they were having an affair, but I eventually came to the conclusion that Roxanne was too classy and smart to get involved with an idiot like my ex. Once my ex got fired from that office and went out to work as a bartender in a string of bars, we didn't see much of Roxanne. After the breakup, she called me and asked if I wanted to start walking with her. We still meet three times a week in the wee hours of the morning and walk several miles. The first time we walked, I'm pretty sure I didn't say more than three words. After a couple of weeks, we were talking about everything from our exes to lesbian invisibility to the issue of Trans people in women-only spaces. Despite the twenty year age difference, Roxanne is vital and strong and fit and she keeps me laughing, even when I feel like shit. She's kept an amazingly positive attitude despite her recent discovery that her long time ex was using her for years. When Sam and I came up with the idea of starting The Love Sucks Club, I instantly thought of Roxanne. Despite her zest for life, she has more reason than anyone to be bitter about love.

She clears her throat and looks down at her notebook. "Notes from the second meeting of The Love Sucks Club. Sam complained about how a cute waitress at the resort told her, 'I wouldn't date you if you were the last dyke on earth.' Dana professed vehemently that she would never date again. Roxanne raised a motion that the purpose of the club should not be to bemoan the suckiness of love, but to find a way to change said suckiness in our own lives. The motion was postponed to be discussed at a later meeting."

Sam smiles. "Roxanne, you don't belong in this club. You're too optimistic."

"If I wasn't in this club, it would just be you two miserable dykes sitting around whining about love. I'm here to provide a positive spin."

"We're not miserable," I protest. "Why does

everyone keep saying that?"

Laughing, Roxanne pats my hand gently. "Okay, you're not miserable. But are you happy?"

"I'm not unhappy."

Sam shrugs. "Neither am I. I have a good life."

Roxanne smiles. "Yet here we all are." She gestures around the bar. I have to admit, it's a far cry from the grill. The few pieces of art are hanging crookedly and covered with dust or grease or other items not worth thinking about. The two employees are an eighty-year-old man who cooks the food and an angry waitress who complains bitterly about her varicose veins whether we ask about her health or not. Most of the tables are in varying states of dilapidation and the chairs are so beat up that Roxanne actually broke one last week. That speaks volumes since she weighs all of about a buck twenty. As I said, this place sucks, but man, their pizza is to die for.

"Well, look." I'm trying to think of a way to defend this stupid idea. "It's just a great way for the three of us to make sure we get together once a week."

"Yes," Roxanne says. "But if we didn't have an actual purpose, we could just have a standing date once a week. Making it a club means we have an ultimate goal."

"Not really." Sam has two beers in front of her. Since we know the waitress won't be back for a long time, we tend to double order. Sam opens one of her beers and grins at Roxanne. "The Italian American club just meets to play Bocci ball and vote on agenda items."

"At least they have agenda items," Roxanne laughs.

"We have agenda items!" I look down at my

notebook. "Item number one – dues."

"That's only going to work when we get more members," Sam says.

"See? It's our ultimate goal," I explain. "We get more members and collect dues. The whole thing takes off. We start franchises in other cities. In no time, we're millionaires."

"I don't want to be a millionaire," Roxanne says. "I just want to be content."

"Maybe the purpose of our club can be to find Roxanne another wife," Sam pipes in.

Shaking her head, Roxanne holds up a hand in Sam's direction. "Not a chance. I'd never trust myself to be a good judge of someone again."

She has a good point there. Roxanne has spent the last decade taking care of her ex-partner, Evelyn. Roxanne has owned the house here on the island for almost thirty years, but when Evelyn moved in, she basically took over. She'd go off for trips with her friends and come home to dump her dirty laundry on Rox. When she was home, she sat on her ass and let Roxanne make all of the meals, do all of the housework, and pay all of the bills. They ended up breaking up because Evelyn was insisting that Roxanne put the house in Evelyn's name. Rox finally put her foot down over that and Evelyn left not long after. A few days after, Roxanne realized that their joint account had been completely drained and with it, all of Roxanne's retirement money. Instead of looking forward to retiring in a few years as she had planned to do, she's working full time to pay the bills with no foreseeable stopping point. It's hard for me to look at someone as positive and loving as Roxanne and understand how she could let someone railroad her like that, but I guess no one really understands what goes on inside another person's relationship. I know most of my friends and family looked at my time with she-who-shall-not-be-named and shook their heads in bewilderment.

"How did that work, anyway?" Sam is curious. "I mean, didn't you know somewhere deep inside that she was using you? Did you know she was cheating on you?"

Roxanne pats Sam's hand. "Don't you know somewhere deep inside that Josie is never going to become a lesbian?"

Stung, Sam pulls back. "I do know that. I'm not counting on her for anything."

"Yet, you're in a holding pattern because you're waiting for her."

"I'm not waiting for her!"

"I still think The Love Sucks Club could be a money maker." Wanting to lighten the mood, I interrupt their exchange. "We could print t-shirts. There could be a picture of a huge mouth sucking on the word love."

"Well, technically that would mean that love is the suckee, not the sucker," Sam points out.

"Fair enough. Maybe love could have a huge mouth and it could be sucking on something."

Roxanne chuckles. "Like what? A giant lollipop?"

"Plus, how do you make love have a mouth?" Sam asks.

"Well, it could be a graphic of a heart with a gaping mouth in the middle of it."

Roxanne shakes her head. "Now you're just getting obscure. I think that's a little too art noveau. Nobody will get it."

"Heartsucker." Sam nods to herself. "That's

what people will think. Heartsucker."

"That doesn't even mean anything," I complain.

"It does to a vampire," Sam answers.

"That would be bloodsucker."

Roxanne is laughing. "Forget the t-shirts. I have a plan." She pauses as our waitress, finally tiring of leaning on the bar swatting at flies, comes over to the table and asks us what we want to eat. We order a veggie supreme pizza to share. The waitress leaves and Sam says, "Well, that gives us another hour until we're interrupted again."

Roxanne continues her previous train of thought. "What if The Love Sucks Club was about learning how to love again?" She holds up a hand to our protests. "I'm not ready to even think about dating again. Dana, I think you feel the same. Sam, you date, but you tend to gravitate toward women you barely like. It's your way of keeping yourself distant."

"And?"

"What if we used the club as a way of reminding each other that love comes in many forms and we just have to be open to it?"

"I'm not following you, Rox." I actually kind of get what she's saying, but I'm not willing to admit it, yet.

She puts her hand on mine. "I'm not saying we should all go out and start a relationship. I'm saying, let's just do a couple of positive things every week that will help to open us up to love. It can be something as simple as having a conversation with someone we find attractive, or going on a date."

Scoffing, Sam opens another beer and gulps it. "Please. The name of the club is The Love Sucks Club, not the Love is just around the corner club."

We all laugh and Roxanne nods. "Yes, you're right. But maybe we can help each other change our attitude."

Sam nods toward the door and I turn around to look. Mandy has come in with some guy I don't recognize. They're both already obviously drunk. Mandy's eyes slide over and past our table without a hint of recognition. Raising her eyebrow, Roxanne catches my eye. "Isn't that you know who's new girlfriend?"

Sam answers for me. "Yeah, Mandy. She used to be married to a guy until she started dating Voldemort. Looks like she might be missing the old ways."

We all watch as the couple takes to the dance floor, wrapping themselves around each other in a way that would be obscene anywhere but here. We're silent for a few moments until the guy slides his hand into Mandy's shirt and starts squeezing her nipple.

"Oh my," Roxanne is flummoxed. "Is that appropriate?"

"This is the Pit, Roxanne," Sam says. "You could walk around naked with safety pins in your nipples and no one would bat an eye unless you knocked over their drink."

It's true. Mandy and her guy aren't the most offensive couple I've seen at the Pit. A few months ago, Sam and I saw a woman flat out going down on a guy in a back corner. Tonight, however, they are the only couple on the dance floor. A local drunk is bobbing around them, weaving and dancing beside them. He accidentally bumps into the couple and Mandy gives him a shove, sending him sprawling across the floor. Oblivious, the drunk keeps dancing on his back, arms and legs waving around in the air.

Roxanne shifts and I put a hand on her arm. "Just leave it be, Rox."

She sniffs and turns her chair a bit so her back is to the dance floor. "I just don't think I have the hang of this place."

Smiling, I give her the once over, taking in her beautiful white hair, usually tied into an elegant bun. Her fingers are long and slender and devoid of jewelry. She's slender and graceful and very fit. She tends to wear long, straight dresses and sandals, even when she's out working in her garden. I once stopped over to her house in the middle of the day and found her hanging laundry in an ankle length denim skirt and an old button front men's shirt that I'm sure belonged to Evelyn. Even in that outfit, with clothespins in her mouth, she looked elegant and classy.

"What are you lookin' at?" Roxanne makes an attempt at a New York accent.

"You're right," I say. "You definitely don't look like the average clientele of the Pit."

"The question," Sam says, "is whether or not we have an obligation to let Voldemort know that her new girlfriend is obviously not interested in a monogamous relationship."

"We don't know that," Roxanne says. "I mean, technically, they're just dancing."

We all look up again in time to see Mandy throw her leg up over the guy's hip and his hand disappear under her tight skirt.

"Okay, maybe a bit more than dancing," Roxanne amends.

"It doesn't matter," I say, making room for the pizza that the waitress has brought over.

Sam gets up and grabs napkins and paper plates

from the other side of the bar. Taking a big bite of pizza, I chew for a couple of minutes. "We don't know anything about their relationship and I certainly don't owe her anything."

Sam nods. "Well, they're putting me off my meal."

We all come around to one side of the table and sit in a line with our backs to the dance floor.

"This is cozy," Roxanne says.

"Better than looking at that," I reply.

We finish our meal and divide the bill. Somehow, we always end up leaving a good tip here, despite the terrible service. Maybe it's a well of sympathy for the waitress who has to watch things like Mandy and some dude having sex on the dance floor. I'd be miserable if I had to see shit like that all of the time. Hell, I'd be sick if I had to see that all of the time.

We leave the bar and walk down the street to where Roxanne is parked. Rox and I came down the hill together tonight. Sam walked over, so Roxanne offers to give her a ride home. As we're standing on the sidewalk discussing it, I see Susannah and Olivia walking out of the quickie mart with a couple of guys. I wave them down. Susannah takes one man's hand and drags him over.

"Dana, this is Thomas," she gushes.

Shaking his hand, I size him up, surprised. He's about my height and kind of muscled. Behind geeky horn-rimmed glasses, his eyes look intelligent and open. He gives me a warm smile as he squeezes my hand. His handshake is firm, but not tight. Touching his hand, I look into his eyes and for an instant, I'm reminded of my father.

"Nice to meet you, Thomas."

"It's a pleasure to meet you, too. I'm a big fan of your work."

"You read lesbian romance novels," I say, raising my eyebrows.

"Since you're a local celebrity, I figured I better see what the fuss is about."

Olivia is clinging to the hand of another man, but since she doesn't make a move to introduce him, I simply nod in their direction and turn back to Susannah. "We're on our way home. What are you up to?"

"Olivia and Gary are going to a movie. Thomas and I would rather get some ice cream and walk on the beach."

Her voice is firm and I wonder if that is really what Thomas would rather do, or if it is what Susannah would rather do.

"Well, be careful to stay on the beaches in front of the restaurants," I caution. "Strange things happen on secluded beaches after dark."

"Don't I know it," the man with Olivia leers. Thomas gives him a dismissive look. I think I like him already.

"Come on, Thomas," Susannah tugs on his hand. "I want ice cream."

She practically drags him away as we say goodbye. Watching them go, I'm suddenly hit by a wave of sadness. As my ears start ringing, I can see Thomas and Susannah, many years in the future. Susannah is berating Thomas for not fixing something. Her face is still pretty, but it has become drawn and sharp. She's simultaneously herself and my mother. I lean against Roxanne's SUV and close my eyes.

"Dana? You all right?" Sam's voice seems to

come from far away.

I drag myself out of the vision and look at my two friends. "I'm fine. I'm fine." I don't know whether I really had a vision, or if I can just see so much of my mother in Susannah that it scares me. Either way, I send up a small prayer that Thomas isn't as much like my father as he seems.

Roxanne puts her arm around me as Sam opens the passenger side door for me. "I really am fine," I insist.

"I'm not saying you're not fine," Roxanne says. "But you looked really gone for a minute."

"Everything changes," I reply, blinking at her. "And yet, everything always seems to stay exactly the same."

"That's life, buddy," Sam says, climbing into the backseat. "That's life."

Roxanne straps herself in to the driver's seat and reaches over to pat my leg again. "Change is the only constant in life, sweetie," she says, smiling gently. "But you can't change anything or anyone but yourself."

We drop Sam off at the resort so she can pick up her car. When we get to my house, Roxanne pulls up in front of the door and turns to look at me. "Are you going to be all right?" she asks me one more time.

Leaning my head back against the seat, I look over at her. Her face, though lined, is still incredibly beautiful. Age has done nothing to diminish the beauty of her blue eyes and her smiling mouth. Aware that I'm feeling lonely and vulnerable, I think about what it would be like to go to bed with Roxanne. She's not a casual sex kind of woman, but then, neither am I. Since neither of us is in the market for a relationship, maybe we could be lovers, just this once. A sort of easing of the loneliness for an evening. I reach out for her hand and she lets me take it.

"Roxanne?"

"Yes, Dana?"

"Do you want to come in?"

She looks at me for a long moment before taking my face in both of her hands. She leans forward and kisses me gently on the mouth.

"Go to bed, Dana," she says softly. "You'll feel better tomorrow."

Sighing, I squeeze her hand and get out of the car. I'll feel better tomorrow. I watch her until I can no longer see her taillights.

Chapter Six

The sun shining through my window is making sleep impossible. I should have closed the curtains last night before I finally fell asleep, but despite a restless night, I don't want to sleep the day away. Lying in bed, I'm debating whether or not to call Roxanne. I wonder if she's upset that I kind of came on to her. Probably not. She's pretty pragmatic. I'm probably more bothered by it than she is. Rolling over to look at the clock, I groan at the creaking and cracking in my back. Frank chirps at me for disturbing his sleep, so I pet his head and get out of bed. He moves into the warm spot I left and plops his head on my pillow. He'll probably wander out into the kitchen in a couple of hours and demand his morning meal. In the meantime, I'm going to make some coffee and get some writing done.

Rummaging around on the floor of my bedroom, I grab a pair of boxers and slip them on. I've never been squeamish about going topless, but even in my own home, walking around fully naked feels strange to me. I just don't relish the idea of putting my bare butt down on certain surfaces.

There's a shimmer hanging at the edge of my vision as I wander around the kitchen, making coffee, cleaning up last night's dishes, and filling Frank's bowls. Over the years, I've come to liken my psychic fits to a panic attack. Sometimes, I can feel it coming on and I'm able to breathe through it, or successfully distract myself in order to ward it off. Sometimes, even though I know it's coming, there's nothing I can do about it, and the best I can manage is to get into a safe space and hope for the best. I don't think of myself as a standard psychic. I can't tell you the winning lottery numbers. I'm certainly not about to have some television show where I convince a studio audience that I can communicate with their dead relatives. *I sense there is someone here who died suddenly.* No shit, really?

When I was five, I had a dream that I died. The next day, my grandfather died. That happened to me a lot when I was younger; I would have dreams that I died and someone I knew would die the next day. It didn't even have to be someone I knew well or even liked. Once, I dreamed that I was hit by a car and the next day, the school crossing guard was hit by a car. It kind of sucked because it would get so that I would have these death dreams and I'd be on edge the next day, waiting to see who was going to kick the bucket.

After I hit puberty, my dreams faded a lot. I could go months or even years without having any dreams or visions. It really wasn't until I met Fran that they started back up in earnest. While we were together, I usually felt like I was on guard. If I wasn't, sometimes the simple act of her reaching over to touch me would send me into a fugue state. Of course, I didn't know what they all meant back then. Hell, I'm not sure I know what they all mean now.

Throwing a muscle shirt on, I head outside. Sipping my coffee on the deck, I try to avoid the eye of my nearest neighbor. We aren't that close, but if he stands in his backyard, he can see onto my deck. His driveway is down some other dirt road that branches off the lead in to mine. Unfortunately, because of the way the land was divided, parts of our properties are just a wee bit close for comfort. If I make eye contact with him, he's likely to come over. It isn't that I don't like the guy; it's just that Sam and I are pretty sure he's a serial killer. He's always walking around looking sweaty and twitchy. I had to borrow his shovel once to dig up some stubborn weeds and for weeks after, Sam would glance over at the shovel, leaning innocuously against the house, and say things like, "Course, now your prints are on it" or "We gotta get that shovel." One time, he was digging something in the yard as Roxanne and I walked by and he about jumped out of his skin when we said hello. Roxanne is convinced that he's just a nervous and unhappy man, but I'm not buying it. Whenever someone turns out to be a murderer, the neighbors always talk about what a quiet and unassuming person he was. Well, Shovel Guy is quiet and unassuming and my prints are on his shovel.

I'm so absorbed in watching Shovel Guy while trying to pretend that I don't see him that it takes me a minute to realize that there's a car coming up my hill. Shovel Guy's driveway is way down the road from my place, before the paved road ends, so this car is definitely coming here. It doesn't sound like the whine of a jeep transmission, but since Susannah is the only person who visits me without calling, I could be wrong. Leaning over the edge of my deck, I can see around to the side of the house and the top of the dirt road. I just have time to note that I don't recognize the beat-up little four wheel drive thing that comes into view before it's out of sight again. Now I'm going to have to go inside to see who's here.

Sighing, I walk into the house and peer out the front window in time to see an extremely familiar woman getting out of the car. Voldemort. Seriously? What the hell is she doing here? This is where the whole thing about being psychic completely breaks down. Why can't my spidey sense tell me that my asshole ex-girlfriend is on her way over? I could have been out the door and into the woods before she even hit the dirt road.

As it is, I open the door and block the entrance with my body. Smiling as she approaches the door, she holds her arms out as if she intends to give me a hug. I lean back and cross my arms tightly against my chest.

"Come on, Dana." She's smiling, but I can see the tightening around her mouth that she gets when she's pissed but trying to hide it.

"Come on, what? What the hell are you doing here?"

"I told you in the letter that I've quit drinking."

"Obviously your girlfriend hasn't."

She laughs. "You can't hold that against me. After all, it wasn't your fault that I was drinking, was it?"

I spit out her name and glare at her. "Honestly, am I supposed to believe that you're suddenly clean?"

"You can believe whatever you want. I'm done drinking. And I'm here for the rest of my stuff."

I can't believe the nerve of this woman. "What stuff? You have nothing left here."

She takes a step forward. "When you kicked me out of here, you gave me shit. I had to come up with deposits for rent and utilities. I had to sleep on friend's couches for weeks."

Straightening my back, I glare up at her. "When you moved into this house, you didn't give me any deposits. You didn't have to hook up utilities. You barely managed to pay me a fair rent or contribute to the groceries."

"That's bullshit. I paid half of the mortgage on this place for five years."

"You paid for nothing. And you have no claim on this house."

"I need some money. I had to quit the bar because of the alcohol. I've got a part-time job at the grocery store, but it won't pay my bills."

"Yeah, well, neither will I."

Grinning, she takes another step forward, getting uncomfortably close to me. I know this game and I refuse to back up. She likes to use her height to try to intimate people. Coupled with the fact that she's a walking time bomb of anger and crazy, it usually works. In the years we were together, she never hit me, but she did hit several walls and in one memorable incident, smashed a television remote to smithereens because it wouldn't change the channel.

We're standing inches apart now and she's talking in that measured way that she talks; like she's talking to a five year old and she needs to enunciate every word so they can understand.

"You gave me nothing. Now I'm about a week away from being kicked out on the street. I either need you to give me a thousand bucks to pay my back rent or I'm going to show up here with my bags and move in again."

"You're insane. I'll call the police."

"Really?" She moves closer, menacing me. I'm half-afraid of what she might do. Just because she's never hit me before doesn't mean it can't happen now. And she has a wild-eyed look on her face. I'm tempted to ask her if she's replaced drinking with crack, but under the circumstances, it might not be the best idea.

Sliding her hand down the side of my face, she leans in close, putting her mouth on my ear. "Maybe you don't realize what you lost, Dana. Maybe you're starting to regret ever letting me go."

I open my mouth to respond, but I'm interrupted by my neighbor. "Oh, hello."

Voldemort takes a quick step back and glances around wildly at the sound. She takes in Shovel Guy, wearing what looks like a pair of expensive men's dress pants that are now completely covered with dirt, ripped in several places, and hanging off his hips, showing equally dirty boxer shorts. The fact that he's not wearing a shirt and appears to have not shaved or showered in a couple of weeks completes the outfit. Glancing down, I confirm my suspicions that he's wearing Crocs, but I'm happy to note that they aren't covered with blood. Making a mental note to tell Sam about this, I smile sincerely at my neighbor.

"Hello...um...friend." Smiling brightly, I raise a hand and wave to avoid the possibility of having to touch him.

He grins widely. "Hi neighbor. I picked these."

Holding out his hand, he shows me a couple of nice size mangoes.

"Hey, awesome...dude. Those are nice looking mangoes."

"Yeah," he says, staring over my left shoulder. "I like mangoes."

Voldemort shuffles her feet. "Well, if that's all..."

Shovel Guy goes on as if he hadn't heard her. "I

have a mango tree in my backyard."

"Do you?" My smile is fixed on my face now.

"But these came from further up in the woods."

"Ah."

"I can get more if you want some."

Voldemort clears her throat several times, but Shovel Guy and I both ignore her.

"Well, thanks, but see, I actually have a mango tree in my yard."

"It's just that these are a different kind than the ones in your yard. I'll leave these with you and you can let me know how you liked them."

"That's nice." Smiling, I reach out for the mangoes.

He holds on to them, pulling them back toward himself. "Maybe you could try one now," he says.

My ex loses her cool. "Oh for Christ's sake, just leave the fucking mangoes and go. We're in the middle of a conversation." She pushes on his arm to prod him along.

"Ahh! Ah! Ah!" The man starts yelling. Dropping the mangoes, he jerks away from my ex and brushes at his arm.

"What the fuck?" she yells.

Turning on her, I grit my teeth and snarl. "Get out of here. Just get the hell out of here."

Shovel guy keeps screaming and jumping around. "She touched me, she touched me!"

Voldemort backs away from him, horrified. She takes off toward her car and I turn back to my neighbor, holding my hands up in a conciliatory manner. He's staring at the ground, breathing heavily through his teeth. I talk calmly to him as I hear my ex get in her car, turn it around and screech down the dirt road. As she passes through the tree line, I turn to watch her go. Turning back around to my neighbor, I'm astonished to see him laughing.

"What the?"

He grabs his sides, laughing hysterically. "Did you see her face?"

It's suddenly dawning on me. "You've got to be fucking kidding me."

Still laughing, he gasps for air. "I couldn't think of what else to do. I knew she could kick my ass if it came to a fight."

Slowly, I get it and the laughter wells up from a deep place. Shovel Guy and I sit down on my front step, laughing until tears stream down our faces. Every time I think I have myself under control, he snorts and I start again.

Finally, we gather ourselves and I apologize. "I don't even know your name."

He smiles. "If it makes you feel better, I don't know yours, either."

"I'm Dana."

"I'm George."

"George, it's nice to meet you. I have a confession to make."

He raises his eyebrow and waits.

"My friend and I call you 'Shovel Guy.'"

He laughs. "Well, I have a confession to make, too."

I deserve it. "Let me have it."

"I secretly call you 'The L Word.'"

Letting out another long peal of laughter, I lean back against my front door. Basking in the sunlight and the release of a hard laugh, my body suddenly feels light. "George, I promise to call you by your rightful name from now on."

He nods and stands. Getting to my feet, I offer him my hand and we shake firmly. "It really is nice to meet you, Dana."

"Likewise. And thank you."

He turns to head back to his yard. At the edge of my lawn, he looks over his shoulder and smiles. "You're going to need to watch out for that one."

"Yeah. She's my ex. She's scary."

"Scarier than you think." On that ominous note, he stalks off toward his house.

His departure is so theatrical, I almost want to laugh. Yet, despite the hot sun, I'm struck with a chill. The swirling vision is creeping back to the sides of my vision, too. Walking back into the house, I lock the front door for the first time in months. A headache starts pounding in my left temple, so I down a glass of water along with a few Excedrin. The roaring is starting in my ears. It sounds as if I'm holding a supercharged shell up to my ear in some surreal game of listen to the ocean.

Frank, curled up on the kitchen table in a patch of sunlight, looks completely oblivious to the machinations in my head. The juxtaposition between the normalcy of the scene and the craziness in my head is making me feel stoned. Carefully placing one foot in front of the other, I pad toward the living room with every intention of curling into my favorite chair and sleeping for a few more hours. When I come around the wall, I stop short, clutching my chest with my hand. My favorite chair is no longer empty. Collapsing back against the wall, I flap my mouth open and shut, trying for sound. Finally, I clear my throat and look at the woman in my chair.

"Hello, Esmé."

Chapter Seven

Swinging her legs around, she stands and walks toward me. "I wanted to talk to you about Fran."

Oh Jesus. Why now? A sweat is breaking out on my forehead. Collapsing onto the nearest chair, I tug at the collar of my shirt, breathing in hard. "I just had a particularly bad run in with my ex and I'd like to be alone."

"I saw it," Esmé says. "I didn't want to interrupt, but if she had gotten violent, I would have nailed her with one of your cast iron pans."

"Well, I'm so glad you have my back. What the fuck are you doing in my house?"

"You said my car wouldn't make it up the hill," she says. "So I walked."

"And got in here without me or my ex or my neighbor noticing."

"Your neighbor noticed, but he just waved at me as I came around to your deck. He was more concerned about..."

She mentions my ex by name and I shake my head. "We call her Voldemort around here. Or she-who-shall-not-be-named."

Esmé laughs.

My head is killing me and this conversation is making it worse. Holding my chest, I breathe in and out several times. Blinking and panting, I try to bring myself out of the darkness. I can't get a deep enough breath. Esmé is staring at me. "Just fall into it."

"What?"

She pulls up a chair and sits knee to knee with me. "Let the vision come. Fighting it is the root of the problem. If you let it come, you'll feel better."

Her voice is vaguely soothing and listening to it feels like riding on a wave. My eyes are closing involuntarily and a deep sense of exhaustion sweeps over my head.

She continues to speak in a soft voice. "Just relax and breathe. Breathe in through your nose and out through your mouth."

Peace settles over me, though my head is still swimming. Esmé's voice is coming from far away. Even with my eyes closed, I can see wavy lines in the sides of my vision. When I try to focus on them, they move away.

"Fran," Esmé whispers. My head recoils at the mention of her name, but my eyes are so heavy, I can't open them. "You're looking at Fran."

The darkness is complete. "I'm in the tunnel," I manage to mutter.

"Walk down it," Esmé commands. "Walk down it and find Fran at the end."

"I can't," I murmur. "It doesn't work that way."

"Breathe in through your nose. Out through your mouth. Let the darkness come down over your eyes. Breathe in, breathe out. Relax into it."

The ringing in my ears has gotten so loud that it seems to be pulsating with my heartbeat. I open my mouth to tell Esmé that I can't take it anymore and suddenly, I'm enclosed in darkness.

I'm walking down a long tunnel. There's a figure at the end of it. She's beckoning toward me. As I get closer, I'm sure it's Fran. She smiles when she sees me and my heart skips a beat. When I reach her, I reach up my hand. She puts her hand up and we stand face to face, one hand up in the air, just touching. I'm marveling at her touch, at the freshness of her face. She smiles at me. I want to talk, but I can't make myself speak. When I move to hold her, I'm swept back down the hall. Being ripped away from Fran feels like I'm having my arms torn off. I'm screaming, but it doesn't help. The blackness comes over my vision and all I can do is scream.

Blinking, I look up to see Roxanne's face hovering over mine. She smiles as I open my eyes. Passing a cold rag over my forehead, she wipes the sweat from my face and neck.

"Don't talk until you're ready," she says.

"Where's Esmé?"

"I'm here," she calls from a chair across the room. "Your friend thought I was killing you or something."

Struggling to sit up, I glare at her across the room. "Well, what the hell were you doing?"

Roxanne presses down on my shoulder, pushing me back down into my chair. She twirls the wet cloth in the air for a few seconds before putting it back on my head. The coolness feels amazing. "You're fine," she says, ignoring the exchange with Esmé. "I came over to bring you the book we talked about yesterday, and I found you having a seizure of some sort. This one was just watching you, doing nothing."

"She wasn't having a seizure," Esmé explained quietly. "She was in a deep meditative trance where she was communicating with my lover."

"My lover," I said.

"She was mine first," Esmé insisted.

"You two broke up."

"Only because she thought her crazy was too much for me to handle," she retorted.

Roxanne held up a hand and cleared her throat. "It doesn't matter now. The young lady is dead. The respectful thing to do would be to let her rest."

Esmé shook her head. "I know Dana had visions of her before she died. I want to talk to her."

"It isn't like that, Esmé. I can't talk to dead people. The Fran I'm seeing is the Fran in my mind."

"Then how do you explain seeing her death?"

"I had a premonition of something that was coming for a live person. I can't explain it, but I know that whatever I see in my visions isn't the real Fran."

We all look up as Sam comes slamming into the room. "Do we need to go to the hospital?"

"What the hell?" I glare at her. "No, we don't need a hospital."

Roxanne shrugs. "I texted her while you were having your fit. I thought she might have an idea of what to do."

"It wasn't a fit." Glaring at Sam, I cut her off as she opens her mouth. "And it wasn't a seizure."

"I vote for the hospital," Roxanne says.

"Forget it." Planting my feet on the ground, I swing myself out of the chair and stalk across the room. "I didn't have a fit. I didn't have a seizure. And I don't need a hospital." Opening the front door with a huge, dramatic sweep, I lean back and narrow my eyes at Esmé. "And I don't talk to dead people!" Storming out the door, I slam it behind me and take off down the hill. I wish I had a car. I could jump into it and gun the gas, throwing gravel and dirt into the windows as I take off. Walking down the hill, the exercise and the fresh air starts to clear my head. I'm starting to feel like kind of an ass. When I hear an engine coming down the hill, I make a game of guessing which one of them got to come after me.

Sam pulls up and motions for me to get in. Climbing into the seat, I pull on my seat belt and we take off. "Where are we going?"

She shrugs. "It's up to you."

"Let's go to Brad's house."

On the way, I fill her in on Voldemort's letter and her subsequent visit. When I finish, she shakes her head. "That's bad news."

"Yeah, I don't know why she's rearing her ugly head now, but it's a hassle I don't need."

"On the other hand," Sam says. "How friggin' funny about shovel guy!"

"I know, right?"

"I love the fake fit thing. I'm going to have to try that sometime."

"Yeah, next time you get bored at work."

She maneuvers around a group of guys who are parked in the middle of the street, drinking beer and having a heated discussion. One of them yells something as she squeezes past but we both ignore him and keep going. Brad lives in the heart of what passes for a city on this island. When we pull up in front of his house, Sam just misses running over a chicken because she is dumbfounded by a large woman with S-E...X-Y written across her chest. The girth of her breasts is warping the letters. I elbow Sam and she grins. "Sorry, it took me a second to figure out the extra letters."

The house is a dilapidated piece of wood construction that looks as if it will fall down at any moment. I don't know how it has managed to hang on through the last couple of hurricanes, but every time we head down to check on him after a storm, it's still here. Sam opens the door and we carefully pick our way around broken weed whackers, three legged chairs, old, yellowed pillows, crumpled up and stained pizza boxes, and stacks of magazines. Brad is sitting in a rocking chair near the window, listening to the neighbors argue.

"Hey," I start, pausing as Brad raises his hand.

We all listen as the neighbors crescendo into a roar. The female voice screams at the male, the male screams back. There are various thuds and yells. I manage to catch a few words, "Whore. Fucker. Bastard. Cheater." They are obviously both pissed, but it's hard to tell which one is the wounded party in this fight. Finally, we hear a gunshot and then silence.

"Holy fuck," Sam says. She digs into her pocket for her cell phone. "I'm calling the cops."

"Don't bother, don't bother." Brad waves his hand dismissively. "This happens all of the time. The cops will show up or they won't."

I've long since stopped fighting against the island madness, so I put the incident out of my mind and motion at Sam to put her cell away. She does so reluctantly.

Bradley sighs. "Are you here for some help? I can see that you are, but I have to tell you that I'm feeling very weak."

I can see why. He's lost weight since we've been here and his dark skin has gotten a kind of yellowish tint to it. His eyes are drooping and red. The dreadlocks, usually clean and gorgeous, are matted and greasy and carrying bits of leaves or possibly garbage. "What's going on, Brad?"

"Too many ghosts. I can't keep up with them all."

Sam rolls her eyes as I whip ten bucks out of my pocket and hand it to him. He barely glances at it before shoving it into the front of his cut off jean shorts.

"Listen, Brad. I've been having some...er... problems. I used to have pretty strong visions, but I got rid of them." Pausing, I think about it for a second. "Well, mostly."

"Ah, they're back now," he said.

"Wow, can't believe you picked up that one," Sam intones. I kick her before turning back to Brad.

"Yes, they've come back with a vengeance."

"There's someone who means you harm. One, maybe two. The spirit is trying to warn you."

Rolling my eyes, I raise my eyebrow at him. "The spirit? God?"

"God. The creator. The universe. Your own mind. Whatever it is, whatever you pray to, it's trying to help you."

"Help me what?"

He shrugs and rolls his eyes. "Dunno. Maybe let go of your past."

"I have let go of my past," I reply, ignoring Sam's skeptical snort.

"Obviously not if the ghosts from your past are trying to talk to you."

Pausing, I stare at the wall for a moment. Brad's apartment is small, dirty, and overloaded with furniture, including the most ridiculous blend of artwork I have ever seen. When his clients can't afford to pay him cash, he will usually take something in trade. By the looks of his art collection, he isn't picky about what he takes, either. Blinking at a velvet clown, I formulate my next question.

"Do you think it's really Fran who is trying to communicate with me?"

Without taking my eyes from the wall, I can feel Brad staring at me. Sam's staring at me, too. Suddenly, I feel like more of a freak than I usually do. Brad hasn't answered, so I clear my throat. "Well?"

Shrugging again, he gives me a half smile. "Her energy never left you."

"It's a curse."

He shakes his head. "Your visions are a gift, not a curse."

"So then what do I do?"

Laughing, he spreads his hands in amazement. "Listen to the voice, of course!"

"Of course," Sam says in the same amazed tone. "Listen to the voice!"

Brad laughs at Sam and pats her hard on the shoulder. "You keep dismissing me, woman, but you will find out someday about these things and you won't be laughing then."

"Food for thought," Sam says, standing up.

The front door slams open and a teenage girl in short shorts and a bra storms into the room. She pushes past Sam and plants herself in front of Brad. "I need to put a hex on someone who's out to get me," she demands.

I dig out another ten and hand it over to Brad who makes it disappear into his shorts again. I shudder at the idea of being handed that same money as change in one of the local shops. Making a mental note to start carrying hand sanitizer, I thank Brad. "We'll leave you to your next client," I say. The girl doesn't even look up as we depart.

Sam is chuckling before we make it to the car. "Are you serious?" she says as we drive out of the city. "You're taking advice from a man who keeps his money in his crotch?"

"Maybe I should get hypnosis."

"Maybe you need therapy."

Shrugging, I look out the window. "I'm not saying that's not a distinct possibility."

Susannah and Thomas are sitting at a table outside of Seth's coffee shop, so Sam pulls over to the curb. Thomas jumps up and leans in the window. "Can I buy you ladies a coffee?"

"I have to get back to work," Sam says. "Do you want me to drop you off here or at home?"

Envisioning Roxanne and Esmé drinking tea and comparing notes about my sanity, I decide that home is probably not my best bet at this point. Slugging Sam on the shoulder, I thank her and jump out of the car. Susannah stands to give me a hug and Thomas goes in to buy me a coffee.

"I heard Voldemort showed up at your house this morning," she says.

"How the fuck is that even possible?"

"I just ran into Esmé at the gas station."

Island grapevine. At least I know she's not hanging out at my house waiting for me to come home. Thomas returns with my coffee and sits next to Susannah, touching her arm gently as he sits. She smiles at him. They look happy.

"Well," Susannah prods. "What about it?"

"What about what?" Thomas looks from one to the other.

"Yes, my ex showed up at my house today. Shovel guy saved me. His name is George, by the way."

"George." Susannah tries it on. "George. Weird that it never occurred to me that he might have a name."

"Everyone has a name," Thomas says.

Susannah sips her coffee. "Thomas and I were at the gallery. Did you know that Esmé is an artist?"

"I didn't." Thanking Thomas for the coffee, I stand up and walk toward the art gallery. Two streets over, I see Voldemort leaving one of the corner bars and I duck down an alley to avoid her. Two men step out from the shadows with intent on their faces, but I raise my hand and lower my voice. "Don't even fucking think about it," I enunciate as I stalk past them. My face must be something else, because they both slink back into the shadows as I pass. I make the street and I turn toward the gallery. I'm nearly running as I get to the door. Why the hell wouldn't she mention being an artist? Certainly having a showing at the only gallery in town would be cause for at least a casual mention in conversation.

Slamming through the door, I startle a couple of tourists who are looking at trinkets in the front of the shop. The woman drops whatever it is that she's holding. Ignoring her gasp, I push past them into the main showroom. The room is filled with paintings, but I recognize Esmé's immediately. They're daytime forest scenes, but they are all somehow terrifying. The trees are twisted and warped. The shadows seem to meld into almost recognizable shapes on the ground and on the other trees. The sky, though blue, barely makes an impression through the intertwined branches of the trees. In each one, a woman is standing. It's a series, so in the first one, she's too far away to see. She moves progressively closer in the point of view of the artist until, in the last one, she is near the front of the painting, and she stands, smiling awkwardly, but happily, like a lonely teenager who has been asked on her first date, but isn't quite sure if it really happened or not. The woman is Fran. Reeling, I make it back to the sidewalk before I pass out.

Chapter Eight

This is getting familiar. I blink into the sunlight and wait to see whose face is going to appear in my line of vision. It would almost be funny if it wasn't such a pain in the ass.

"Well, look who's awake." a strangely familiar voice says.

Voldemort. My eyes fly open and I blink them furiously to clear the clouds. I'm in the front seat of her car. She's sitting in the driver's seat, smiling. "It's good to see you alive."

"I'm out of here." I grab the door handle as she grabs my wrist and pulls me back.

"I saved you," she grins. "The least you can do is hear me out."

Her grip on my wrist is strong and I know from past experience that if she decides I'm not going anywhere, it's going to take a lot of effort to change her mind. I don't know if I have the strength for that right now.

"What do you want?"

She releases my wrist. "I came on a little too strong earlier. I need your help."

Sighing, I lean back against the car door. She-who-shall-not-be-named could sound so sincere sometimes. I wasn't as stupid as I used to be, but it was still hard to disbelieve her when she had that look on her face. Part of the problem is that she believes herself when she's talking like this. A part of her truly believes that the world is against her and she is just doing her best to be a good person in a bad world. If I hadn't caught her in so many lies, I'd be a lot more likely to believe her now. "Well?"

"I'm about to be kicked out of my apartment. I need some money to cover the rent."

"And I was your first thought as a benevolent benefactor?"

"I know you've got some stashed away."

"It's what I live on when the royalties aren't enough."

"Your house is paid for. You don't drink. You don't have any credit card bills. If you loan me, say, five thousand dollars, I can pay you back at five hundred a month. That's more than enough to cover expenses and you'll be paid off within the year."

"And have you given a thought to how you're going to shell out an additional five hundred a month when you can't make your expenses right now?"

"I've stopped going to the bar. That's more than five hundred a month right there."

Laughing, I look at her incredulously. "I just saw you coming out of a bar."

Pursing her lips, she shakes her head. "I went in to drop something off. I wasn't there drinking."

"Whatever. And even if you're not lying, how long will that last?" I spit her name out in disgust, practically choking on the words. "Seriously. When we were together, I had to fight with you every day to keep you out of the bars because you were draining my bank account. Every time I turned around, you were buying shots for the bar. Fuck. If I had been counting on you to actually pay the rent that we agreed on, I'd have lost my house."

Her fingers are gripping the steering wheel and the wrinkles around her mouth are getting more pronounced. When she speaks, she measures out each word in an attempt to sound as though she's not losing her cool. "If we're going to start making a laundry list of our past transgressions, give me a second to compile yours."

"It would take more than a second, I'm sure." Trying to diffuse the situation, I resort to joking, as usual.

She allows a fleeting smile to cross her mouth. "Well, we both know you're perfect."

"Perfectly awesome," I grin. "It's hard to be me sometimes."

"Indeed."

"So, are you going to loan me the money?"

Slipping my hand into the door handle, I am halfway out of the car before she reaches out to grab me. I manage to yank my hand out of her reach. "No, I'm not. I don't have the kind of income that allows me to just throw money away. Giving money to you would be dumb. Giving money to you and expecting repayment would be beyond stupidity."

She makes another grab for my hand, but misses again. "Dammit, Dana. I'm in a lot of trouble here. I'm going to end up homeless."

"Oh come on. I'm sure you have enough friends that you can find a couch to sleep on."

"Mandy won't be anxious to share someone's couch."

"Oh, I'm sure Mandy will not have any trouble finding a place to live if you get kicked out of your apartment."

"What's that supposed to mean?"

I glance back into the car and for a brief second, I'm tempted to tell her what I saw on the dance floor. It's really none of my business and I don't owe her anything. Slamming the door without answering, I take a few quick steps toward the sidewalk, listening for her car door. I don't want to look back and give her the satisfaction of knowing that she's rattled me. Walking down the street, I hear her engine directly behind me. There's no traffic, so she can keep pace with me as long as she wants. Yet again, I almost wish I had a car. She's staying out of my peripheral vision, but I can hear the vehicle. I can cut across to the busier market street, but to do so, I have to cross in front of her. If I take a turn up one of the next alleys, I'll end up in a more secluded and seedier section of town. My ex revs the engine a bit, just in case I didn't know she was there. I'm trying to present a nonchalant stance because I don't want to let her know that she's getting to me. This is her M.O., pushing and pushing until she gets her way. I'm not afraid of her, but her intimidation tactics can be a little unnerving. I don't know who would win in a fair fight, but I'm not willing to try to figure it out. I'm a lover, not a fighter and she's got all of that suppressed rage on her side. Continuing to walk at a brisk, but not rushed pace, I weigh my options. I could duck into one of these businesses in the hope that she would get bored and leave. If I did that, she would know that she's freaked me out. If she decided to wait me out, I'd be stuck in the store. I'm saved from making the decision by the ring of my cell phone. Fumbling it out of my pocket, I'm relieved to see Sam on the display.

"Dude."

"What's up?"

"I'm walking down Magnolia being somewhat slowly chased by my ex-girlfriend."

"Near what?"

"That scary bar where the prostitutes hang out on Saturdays."

"I'm on Steel. See you in less than ten minutes." She hangs up and I toss the phone back into my pocket. Sam will be coming from the other direction, so I need to get across the street. Voldemort is still pacing me. Some panicked voice inside of me is telling me that she wants to kill me. This is ridiculous. It's broad daylight. Yet, every time I think about crossing the street, I see a vision of myself flipping over her hood. I'd be worried she was going to kidnap me and break my legs in the fashion of "Misery," but since she's about to be evicted, I can't imagine where she'd keep me. Still, I can see her standing over my bed with a hammer. I'm starting to freak myself out.

Assessing my situation, I notice a couple of guys hanging out in front of the bar across the street. They look pretty shady, but I'm willing to bet that even my ex wouldn't run me over in front of a couple of witnesses. Checking the street lets me know that there is no one coming from the opposite direction. I can't hear any engine noise but hers, so I'm pretty sure there is no one else behind me. It's time to make a break for it. Without warning, I make a quick dart into the street. Running for the space between two parked cars that will come out directly in front of the dudes in front of the bar, I chance a glance back over my shoulder. Voldemort is staring at me with her mouth hanging open, though whether she's amused or

surprised, I can't say. Tensing to make the small jump
onto the curb, a chicken wanders out from under the
parked car. I have just enough time to realize that
I can't miss it before my foot slams into the stupid
bird. Squawking, the chicken goes flying toward the
men and I go flying face down toward the pavement.
My hands spring out automatically and I land hard
on both hands and one knee. The chicken slams into
the leg of one guy, who swears and kicks at it. It goes
screaming away, scolding me in a high pitch screech
the whole way. The other guy stands over me.

"You okay?"

He reaches a hand down and I grab it, letting
him haul me up. I can hear my ex laughing wildly from
her car. Without looking back, I lift my arm in the air
behind me and flip her off. Stupid cow. She peels off
and I thank the man who helped me up. Limping a few
steps tells me that nothing is broken. Stupid island.
Why the hell are there farm animals everywhere? The
two men are staring at my back. I can feel their eyes on
me. A couple of cars pass as I'm pacing. Finally, Sam
pulls up.

She skips the formalities and goes straight for
the scoop. "What the hell?"

"She-who-shall-not-be-named apparently found
me in the street during one of my fits."

"Dude, it's time to get you to a doctor."

"I don't think a doctor can help me."

"Seriously, what happened?"

Mimicking her tone, I parrot back to her.
"Seriously, why aren't you back at work?"

She shakes her head and glares at me. "Captain
sent me out to get some primer."

"I was lucky you were so close."

Instead of answering, she stares out the windshield, concentrating on the road. Lost in thought, it takes me a while to realize that we are nowhere near my house.

"Look, I just want to go home."

Still silent, she turns onto the dirt road that leads to one of our favorite hikes. Resigned, I stare out the window at the view from the bottom of the mountain. A few minutes later, Sam parks the truck on the side of the road near the bushes. Grabbing a few bottles of water from the back, we take off into the woods and hit the trail. It's a steep uphill climb and for a while, we just focus on walking and breathing. Sam has a harder time than I do because she is an on-again off-again smoker. By the time we reach the top of the trail, we are both sweating like crazy and Sam is doubled over with her hands on her knees, trying to catch her breath. Finding a nice boulder, I plop down and take a sip from a bottle of water. Sam finally straightens up and sits down beside me.

"I suppose you're wondering why I brought you here today," she says, grinning.

"I'm actually wondering how you don't get fired from your job."

"I'm the only one who knows how to do any of the things I do. So, it takes me two hours to go get a bucket of primer every once in a while. That's better than having to hire ten guys to do my one job."

I open my mouth to call her on her arrogance, but I know she's right. Stalling, I take another sip of water. Sam waits patiently.

Finally, I look at her. "Okay. What do you want to know?"

"I want to know why the seizures have suddenly

come back with a vengeance."

"They're not seizures!"

"Fine. Fits. Whatever you want to call them."

"You've know about my visions for years."

"Yes."

"And you know my visions are accompanied by some physical issues."

"They seem to be getting worse."

"They are getting worse. Or at least, more frequent. I don't know what's going on. I had almost gotten rid of them altogether for a long time there. And then I woke up one morning feeling like I was having a heart attack. Since then, the attacks have been coming more and more frequently."

"Well, what can we do about them?"

"According to Brad, I need to focus on them and listen to the voice."

Sam's sniff is all the answer I get to that.

"Actually," I continue, "Esmé feels the same way."

"She's new agey," Sam protests. "Of course she wants you to move into your visions or whatever the hell it is."

Laughing, I put my arm around her shoulders. "What do you think I should do?"

"I think you should go to the doctor and have them check you out. If this started with heart attack symptoms, you should already be in the hospital."

"It wasn't a heart attack. It was a panic attack."

"You can't know that for sure."

I debate about how much to tell her. I know that Sam's belief only goes so far. She trusts me and she knows that I wouldn't lie to her. So, she wrestles with her skepticism about things beyond the "norm" of the world and the fact that her best friend has dealings with the spirit world.

"The panic attacks and the visions are connected. I think the panic attacks are my body's reaction to the visions. Either that or the vibrations coming through are too intense for me to handle so I react physically, either with the panic attack or passing out."

Trying not to look at Sam, I stare over the side of the mountain at the sea. As far as geographic cures go, this was a pretty smart move. Still, I'm starting to wonder if I got far enough away. Maybe my sister had the right idea in escaping to the other side of the world.

We pause at a thumping noise coming through the woods. It sounds like a herd of goats. Scanning the woods, I listen to the sound of hooves getting louder. They sound heavy, but then, goats can sound like elephants when they are crashing through the woods. Sam is grinning. She's probably remembering Susannah's retelling of my last goat encounter. Finally, the animals push out of the tree line and I realize it isn't goats. It's three men on horseback. Sam tenses beside me, but her face remains perfectly calm. The men pull up short when they see us. Horses are pretty popular around here, but they aren't well cared for. These three look skinny and dull. It's hard not to judge people by the condition of their animals. Sam's shoulder muscles are tight and I can tell she's worried. The men are ignoring us, circling around to the other side of the clearing. Dismounting, they tie their horses to a tree and wander in our direction. Sam's hand goes into her pocket. I'm not worried. They look innocuous enough.

The shortest one, a college looking guy with

glasses and longish hair, steps forward. "Hey, ladies. What's going on?"

At least he pegged us both as women. Sam has been called "Sir" more times than I can count, and while I have long hair, I have occasionally been subjected to the gender police in women's bathrooms.

Sam nods and I smile. "What's up with you?"

"Well, we were just wondering if you wanted to smoke a joint with us."

Sam relaxes her muscles as I chuckle. "Thanks boys, but we're fine."

"Aw, come on," one of them wheedles. "We love hanging out with lesbians."

"Oh yeah," the third one says. He's the only one who looks a little seedy, but he doesn't scare me. He looks more like that guy who gets trashed in the bar and spends an inordinate amount of time trying to convince you that he really is a lesbian trapped in a man's body.

The first guy, the college looking one, shrugs. "Well, y'all are missing out."

The third guy steps forward a little and reaches out like he intends to touch my shoulder or something. Sam grabs his hand and whips out her knife. "I don't want to hurt anyone," she says. "But I will if I have to."

Seedy guy snatches his hand away. Whining, he says, "I didn't mean anything. I was just going to pat her shoulder."

"She isn't a puppy."

The other two guys are grabbing seedy guy and coaxing him to leave it alone. He turns away and then turns back around. "You're just a man hating dyke," he spits out.

Sam holds up the knife again. "I may not be able

to win a fight against all three of you, but I guarantee you that I will take your balls off before you can kill me."

The other two yank on his arms and they go back to their horses. As they are riding away, the jerk raises his middle finger and holds it up until they disappear back into the woods. When they're completely gone, I whip around to glare at Sam who is laughing hysterically.

"Oh what?" She blinks innocently. "Come on. That was funny!"

"Yeah, it'll be really funny when you get us killed one of these days."

"That guy was going to grab you."

"He was harmless. He was doing that creepy shoulder pat thing. Yeah, it's gross, but he wasn't going to hurt me."

"All men are potential rapists."

"Well, all women are potential psychopaths."

"The ones who want to date me are."

"Could you at least pretend to be a functioning member of society?"

Standing up, she wipes off her pants and grabs the water. "That's pretty rich coming from you."

She has a good point. I'm not sure what my problem is, but I know I'm not right in the head. Wrestling between the part of me that wants to see Fran and the part of me that wants the visions to stop is exhausting. Lost in thought on our way down the hill, we walk in silence. Sam hasn't asked any more questions, but whether that's because she's thinking about my problem or thinking about what happened up there on the hill, I can't say. Glancing at her profile, I smile at her features that are so similar to mine. My soul sister.

She feels me looking at her. "What?"

"You're gorgeous."

Laughing, she reaches over and smacks me on the head. "And you're blind."

"Obviously."

"Come on," she says. "Let me drive your ass home yet again."

"You must be prince charming. You're always coming to my rescue."

"That's me." Sam blows on her fingers and rubs them on her shirt.

"What the hell does that gesture even mean?"

"It means you're posh."

"Yeah, but why?"

Shaking her head, she pushes me into the passenger door and walks around to the driver's side. "The thing is," she says as she starts the truck, "what if you do have something seriously wrong with you and you didn't get it checked out because you were convinced it was some sort of message from beyond?"

"Sam, there is nothing wrong with me physically."

"I'm just saying you don't know."

Refusing to answer, I stare out the window as we drive back to the other side of the island toward my house. Sam's jaw is clenched which means she's either worried or pissed. I don't want to upset her, but I don't know what to do to make her understand. Wanting to break the silence, but not sure what to say, I finally just poke her in the arm. "Hey."

She looks over at me and I can see the concern in her face. "Hey what?"

"What if I agree to give Dr. B a call tomorrow?"

"For real?"

"Totally."

She nods and smiles. "I think that would be a fantastic idea."

"Okay, I'll do it." I stare out the window for a few moments before turning back to her. "If I turn out to have a brain tumor, you're taking Frank."

"I can live with that. Me and Frank...we have an understanding."

Grinning, I look back out the window. Maybe going to the doctor isn't a bad idea. I mean, I'm pretty sure there is nothing wrong with me, but it wouldn't hurt to rule a few things out. After all, I am becoming a "woman of a certain age" as an ex of mine used to put it. Besides, if I do have a brain tumor, I can act as crazy as I want and no one will bother me about it. Smiling, I look back at Sam to catch her glancing from the road to me. We grin at each other and for a second, I am so overcome with my love for her that my heart literally feels as if it is swelling. She reaches over and takes my hand and I lean my head back against the seat, closing my eyes. When the truck makes the turn onto my dirt road, I open my eyes and look out the window as we head up the hill. I smile as we pass Shovel Guy's driveway. "George," I remind myself. At home, Sam pulls up next to my door and offers to come in to make sure there's no one staked out at my house. "No, I'm good. I'm sure Voldemort is done with me for the day."

Sam shrugs and releases my hand. Out of the car, I lean back in the door for a moment. "Hey, Sam, don't tell anyone I'm going to the doctor, okay?"

"No problem," she says, nodding. "Don't tell anyone I held your hand. They might think I'm queer."

Laughing, I slam the door. Sam drives away,

waving as she disappears around the bend in the road. At the front door, I suddenly get a knot of anxiety. I never used to be afraid to come home, dammit. This is starting to piss me off. I'm a hermit for shit's sake. Resting my forehead against the front door, I try to clear my mind. It's hard to tell if I'm having premonition anxiety or just general anxiety. Maybe I'm depressed or maybe I'm just feeling the general malaise of humankind. The smooth wood of the door isn't telling me anything.

I'm half tempted to just turn around and walk back down the hill, but where would I go? I suppose I could walk over to Roxanne's house. If she's home, I can sit and have tea with her. I wouldn't even have to tell her that I was freaking out. I need to apologize for running out on her today anyway. This is why this gift, as Brad calls it, really pisses me off. If I'm a psychic, I should be able to see things like my ex showing up and going psycho on me. At the very least, I should be able to tell if someone is in my house, and if so, if they are friend or foe. While I'm at it, I should be able to pick out the winning lottery numbers, too. And I want a pony. Sighing, I decide to take my chances. Turning the handle on the front door, I find it unlocked. When the ladies left today, they must have left it open. Sticking my head in, I glance around the foyer. The coast is clear so I wander into the kitchen. Frank is sprawled on the kitchen counter with his tail in the sink. That's no indication. There could be an entire militia in here wandering through with hand trucks taking everything I own and Frank's only question would be whether or not they had any beef jerky with them. I tickle the top of his head with my fingertips and he lets out a tiny "blert." Still no sign of any intruders as I look from the kitchen into the front room. Wandering through the house, I touch my things, trying to judge by feel if someone else has been touching them. Here and there, I lay a finger on the back of a chair, on a side table, or on a framed picture. Everything looks strange to me somehow, as if I don't really belong here. Staring at the wall, I try to make sense of the family in those pictures. Do they know me? Do I know them? I touch the picture of my mother and suddenly, I'm near tears again. My mother was such a bitch but I loved her so much. I love my dad, too, but I don't know him. I doubt he knows me at all. My sisters love me and I love them, but looking at their faces, I realize that I don't know much about them at all. I know that Susannah loves ice cream, but I don't know what scares her. I don't know if she has any dreams or if she's satisfied with her life. Jamie is a completely mystery to me. All I really know about her is that she never stops moving and that sometimes, she forgets to leave me her newest address and I don't even know that she's moved until a letter I've sent comes back to me. One of these days, she's going to forget to call me at all and I will have lost her forever.

Touching Jamie's face in a photograph, it occurs to me that if she died today, I don't know how I would find out about it. The floor creaking interrupts my thoughts and I look up, resigned to whatever is happening next. Esmé is walking into the room, holding a copy of *Annabelle Lies*. Shaking my head slowly, I sink slowly onto a chair. Her feet come into my line of vision and a hand rests on my shoulder.

"Esmé," I whisper. "I just don't have the strength to do this right now."

She drops to her knees in front of me and puts

her hand on my chin. "Come on, Dana," she says, quietly. "Let's see if we can make contact."

"You have the wrong idea about me."

"I've read the book. I know you and Fran had a telepathic connection."

"That was me and Fran. And it was most likely facilitated by Fran."

"We can find out."

I'm too tired to argue. The logical part of my brain is trying to break clear of the fog and demand to know why she thinks she has a right to just barge into my house. The other part of my brain is too tired to fight. Maybe Esmé is right. Maybe I should try to go deeper and find out what Fran is trying to tell me. If Brad is right, she has a message for me from beyond. If Sam is right, there's something physically wrong with me and all of this is just a manifestation of some sort of brain problem. Esmé puts her hand against my forehead.

"Just relax," she says in a soothing voice.

Her voice is low and lovely and her hand is so strong. I can feel myself leaning forward, but she's strong enough to hold me up. She continues to talk in a soothing voice and I can feel it turning into a murmur. My head feels so heavy. I can't hold it up any longer. All I want to do is fall asleep to the sound of her beautiful voice.

Fran and I are in my car, driving home from a friend's house. We've both had too much to drink but she's way drunker than I am. That's why I'm driving. I have to keep us safe. Fran is drawing little hearts in the condensation on her window and singing along with the radio. Reaching over, I rest my hand on her thigh and she lays her hand on top of mine. I'm smiling. I feel great. Fran was a hit with my friends and that makes me happy. She didn't exhibit any particularly weird behaviors tonight. At one point, I did overhear her talking to one of my buddies about aliens, but someone else started in on me, and I missed the conversation. We had a good time. Happy and grinning, I tap my other hand on the steering wheel with the beat of the music. Fran's voice is slurred but sweet and I ask her to sing louder. Laughing, she smacks at me. It's a perfect moment until she suddenly stops singing and presses both hands to her chest. I look over at her and her face is stricken. "It's me," she tells me. "I'm the one." Grabbing for one of her hands, I swerve over the yellow line and correct back to my lane too fast, knocking her against the door. She lets out a small moan and I grab for her hand again. "I can see it in your mind. You know my people are coming for me." Shaking my head, I try to keep my eye on the road, but the vision of her, the one that I've had before, is coming in fast. I know that in a second, I won't be able to see anything but the inside of my own mind. Slamming on the brakes, I reach blindly for Fran. The vision consumes me for a minute or so, and when I come to, Fran is pale and shaking. I reach for her and she collapses into me, crying and mumbling. Holding her, it takes me a second to realize that there are headlights in my back window. Big, bright headlights. I have only a second to wonder what it means before they slam into the back of my car.

Blinking in the bright light, it takes me a minute to realize where I am. Banging my head back against the chair, I shake both fists in the air. "Come on. I'm sick of this shit." Esmé is still sitting on the floor in front of me.

"I saw it, too," she says.

"That wasn't a vision, it was a memory." Shrugging her off, I walk into the kitchen and hold my head under the faucet to drink some water. If that was just a meditation-induced memory, than why does my body hurt so much?

Esmé has followed me into the kitchen."She didn't die in that crash, though." It isn't a question. She knows how Fran died.

Without looking at her, I shake my head.

"What else happened?"

"We were taken to the hospital."

"And?"

"And I decided I didn't want a car anymore."

"The crash really wasn't your fault."

"I was stopped in the middle of the road," I snarl at her.

"What else?"

Whirling around, I glare at her. "None of your fucking business. This has nothing to do with you. I want you to leave my house and I don't want you to come back."

Standing her ground, she points her finger in my face. "It has everything to do with me. Fran left me because she thought she was a danger to me. If she thought she was a danger to you, why didn't she leave you, too?"

"She did," I said, deflated. "She did leave me."

She backs against the kitchen wall and stares at the floor. Silent, we ignore each other for a few moments. Finally, I brush past her on my way to my bedroom. "Get out," I say flatly, without looking at her. "Get out of my fucking house."

I slam into my bedroom without waiting to see if she complies.

Chapter Nine

Dr. Brawley's receptionist sounds entirely too cheerful when she answers the phone. I ask to speak to the doctor, but she's with a patient.

"Okay, fine. I need to make an appointment then."

"We have a cancellation at three o'clock today. Can you make it then?"

"Sure, just let me check my calendar." I stare at the wall for a few moments. I figure, they make me wait when I'm there, I might as well take the advantage while I have it. "Three will be fine."

"Thank you, Ms. McComb. See you this afternoon," she chirps.

I'm half-tempted to just stay in bed until this afternoon, but I drag myself out of bed and head to the kitchen to feed Frank. A text to Sam confirms that she can take me to the doctor. Another text gets me a walking date with Roxanne. She shows up at my house in a light jacket and matching yoga pants. She looks fit and trim and for a second, I can see why I was hitting on her the other night.

We walk down the hill a bit to a path we created through the woods. It winds around until we crest the other side of the hill and look out over the sea. With scenery like this, it's sometimes hard to imagine how I can still have stress in my life. Roxanne is easy company, perhaps picking up my contemplative mood. Walking in silence, enjoying the woods and the view of the water is helping to clear my mind. On an incline, we pick up the pace to add some cardio to the walk. Roxanne pushes us until we're breathing heavily. I'm the one who finally slows us down.

Panting, I lift the bottom of my tank top and use it to wipe my face. "Are you trying to kill me?"

Roxanne laughs. "I'm twenty years older than you. You should be ashamed that I am in better shape."

"It must be all of the hookers and blow. I just can't sustain that rock star lifestyle and still keep up with you."

We reach our favorite stopping point, but Roxanne keeps going. Mopping my face, I struggle to keep up with her. I'm calculating the return walk in my head already. Smiling, Roxanne glances at me over her shoulder. "Come on," she laughs. "We're doing an extra mile today."

"We've already gone at least an extra half mile. By the time we get back, that will be an extra mile."

"Stop complaining. I have another half mile after we get to your house."

"I'll drive you home."

She laughs again. "Dana, it isn't like you to be so anti-exercise."

She's right. I usually love a good hike. I've got to get my mind right. Being all wrapped up in my anxiety is bad for my body. Taking a few deep breaths to clear my head, I catch up to Roxanne and keep pace with her until she turns around. On the way back to my house, we keep up a pace that precludes conversation. At my front door, Rox gives me a quick hug and starts to leave.

"Wait, Roxanne."

Turning back, she gives me a sympathetic look. "Yes?"

"About the other night..."

"It's fine. You were in a bad place. I get that way, too."

"Lonely?"

"Yep."

"Depressed, anxious, and wracked with terrifying nightmares?"

She laughs. "Maybe not that bad."

"I think I'm a wreck."

"You're not a wreck. You just need to readjust your mindset."

"That's one of those platitudes that's easy enough to say."

"That attitude is what I'm talking about," she says.

We walk into my kitchen and I pour us both a glass of water. Wandering into the front room, I plop onto the couch and gaze out across the sea. Roxanne lowers herself gracefully beside me, waiting for an answer.

Finally, I sigh. "I don't think I have an attitude. I think I have some genuinely shitty stuff going on in my life right now."

"I'm not saying that you don't. I'm sure I don't know the half of it. What I do know is that spending all of your time worrying about what's going on does nothing but make it worse. Instead of just dealing with problems when they happen, you're anticipating them. So, you get to be upset about the same situation over and over again. And if nothing comes of it? You've still made yourself sick and anxious worrying over something that may not come to pass."

Sipping my water, I let her words sink in. I'm well aware that I'm pouting and I'm also aware that Rox knows it. Playing around with a response, I realize that everything I want to say just adds to her belief that I'm choosing to feel this way. Finally, I put my water glass down on the table and turn to face her. "There is a part of me that thinks all of this shit is just karma for what I did to Fran?"

She places her hand on my shoulder. "What did you do to Fran?"

The words I've been swallowing are sitting in my chest like a rock. Blinking back tears, I look at Roxanne. "I killed her."

She puts her arms around me and cradles me while I cry. For a few minutes, I'm trying to gather myself. Butches don't cry. Scolding myself doesn't help. All I can think about is the way Roxanne's arms feel around me and how much I need this.

It was a beautiful, sunny day. In my memory, I always want it to be a dark and stormy night. In my book, it was. It had a whole "Hemingway to die alone in the rain" kind of feel. In real life, however, it was about seventy-five degrees and sunny. There was a nice cool breeze. The day probably started with a rainbow. It was as if Mother Nature herself was conspiring to make me think that life was perfect. That bitch. Fran had been acting weird for several days. Well, in Fran's case, I should say, weirder than usual. She was always a little strange and that was one of the things I loved about her. This was different, though. She kept starting and stopping sentences. She'd sit down in front of me and tell me that she wanted to try a new communication technique that her therapist had mentioned. I like to think that I was always open to trying whatever she wanted, but in the back of my mind, I have to admit that I thought most of it was ridiculous. Still, I wanted her happy. A happy Fran was a wondrous thing. She floated around me in a golden haze, dropping magic on my head. She changed me in those moments. She made me believe in a fairy tale world where I could live happily ever after.

That day, though, Fran was not happy. She bounced around the house, starting the dishes, moving to the bedroom, she got out some furniture polish and started taking books off the shelves, and when that failed to keep her interest, she announced that my baseboards were shockingly filthy and plopped down on her hands and knees to wash them with vinegar and water. I had a deadline for the article I was writing and I didn't have time to cajole her out of a mood. I just sat there at my computer getting annoyed as she knocked around from room to room, slamming things around and muttering to herself. When her frenzied activity became too disturbing, I finally told her she had to go. I couldn't write with her bouncing around like that. She stood silently and looked at me for the longest time. I could feel her eyes on my back, but I didn't turn around to engage. I knew if my eyes left my article, I would be sucked into whatever was going on with her. Finally, she whispered something to me. It didn't register what she had said and I didn't ask her to repeat it. I told her I would call her the next day. When she left, I actually breathed a sigh of relief. As much as I loved her, I found her bad moments exhausting and dealing with her while she pinballed around the world left me feeling drained. With her gone, I instantly switched my mind back to my work and for a few hours, she didn't even exist. Later, much later, I missed her and regretted sending her away, but at the time, I was relieved.

Roxanne is stroking my hair and I'm aware that my tears have subsided. She pushes some hair out of my face and I sit up, embarrassed by my outburst. Sensing my mood, she's quiet. She hands me a box of tissues and I blow my nose loudly. We both laugh a little when it makes a big honking noise and for a second, the tension is broken. Roxanne weaves her fingers through mine and I look up at her. She's looking at me affectionately and I realize I have no reason to be ashamed. The soft lines around her bright eyes only add to her gentle beauty. Reaching out to tuck a strand of hair behind her ear, our eyes meet and I lean forward to kiss her on the mouth. Her lips part slightly and I move in closer, wrapping my arms around her slender frame. Leaning into me, she shifts slightly to allow our bodies more contact. She feels firm under my hands and the heat starts in the base of my spine. It's been far too long since I've had sex with anyone and even longer since I've had good sex. After Voldemort and her own particular brand of me me me lovemaking, I think I went into a shut down. Sex with Roxanne would be different. She's kind and loving and I can imagine it being good – really good. Trying to shut my brain off is useless, but at least in this case, my brain and my body appear to have reached an agreement. Pulling Roxanne closer, I deepen the kiss, letting my hands slide down her back, shifting myself again to get even closer. As I move one hand around to her throat, she lets out a little whispered moan. Desire clenches around my gut and I groan, pulling her onto my lap. She lets me, but once she's on my lap, she pulls back from my mouth, and grabs both of my hands, effectively stopping their exploring.

"What?"

Smiling, she lets go of one of my hands, and kisses it. "You're in a very vulnerable place right now."

"I'm in a very aroused place right now."

She laughs, throwing her head back and I'm tempted to put my lips to her throat. Before I can decide, she lowers her head to look at me again. "I'm not denying the temptation. I just think that now would be a bad time to give into it."

"Who was it that said something about the only way to resist temptation?"

"We're not giving into it. I care about you. You're a dear friend and I'm here for you when you need me. I'm just not doing this."

"Sometimes lovemaking is a beautiful expression of affection between two people who care about each other. It doesn't have to be anything more than that."

"I agree. Trust me. At my age, I've had my share of intimate encounters with dear friends that were never meant to be anything other than a beautiful night of lovemaking. I just don't think you're in the right place for that."

"Well, where the hell am I?"

Unfazed, she smiles again. "You need to figure that out on your own."

"Some help you are," I pout, though I'm smiling.

"Listen Dana. You told me that you killed Fran. Since we both know that isn't true, you need to work on why you still have so much guilt over something that happened so many years ago. You need to figure out what Esmé wants. And you might want to work out what's going on with your ex before she does something drastic like kill you."

"Well, that sounds easy enough. I'll make a list

and start checking things off."

"In the meantime, it might not be a bad idea for you to think about seeing someone."

Affronted, I try to make a joke of it. "I thought I might start seeing you."

"Our age difference alone would be a problem. Our attitude difference would cement the doom."

"Well, you sound as pessimistic and bitter as I do."

She laughs. "You're a good woman, Dana. You just need to do a little soul cleaning."

"Maybe I should join a commune."

Standing, she leans down to kiss me on the forehead. "Maybe that's a good idea."

I stand to give her a hug and she wraps her arms tightly around my waist. Holding her, it occurs to me that this hug feels more intimate than anything that happened in the last several years with my ex. Roxanne's thin arms feel solid around my waist and her face fits perfectly against my neck. Breathing against the top of her head, I'm tempted again to try to take her to bed. It wouldn't be a bad fit to be with Rox. I mean, yes, she is a lot older than I am, but she's vibrant and active. She's happy and optimistic and she keeps an incredible garden. Between her organic gardening and my incredible cooking, we'd be set for food. We could live here overlooking the water and rent out her little house. She could retire for real and spend her days with the garden and her creative tasks. She loves Frank, so there's another bonus. The entirety of our life together rushes through my mind and in a heartbeat, I almost ask her to marry me. Reality stops me before I make a fool of myself. One kiss doesn't make a relationship. I swear, I'm starting to sound like a stereotypical lesbian. "No U-Haul," I mutter under my breath.

Leaning back to look at me, Roxanne smiles, her eyes crinkling up at the corners. "Never. I'm so past that point in my life."

"Besides which, a U-Haul would never make it up this road."

Laughing, she gives me another squeeze. "I'm going home. Walk me to the door and get some work done. You'll feel better."

"Tell me what to do about everything," I implore.

She takes my hand and walks me to the front door. "I don't know what to tell you, Dana. I think you should get back into meditating, but I'm worried about the visions."

"Me too. It seems that whenever I let my guard down, they creep back in."

"Maybe you should go to a meditation group. Get help from a professional guide."

"Maybe," I answer flatly.

"Call me later," she says, stretching up to kiss me once more on the tip of my nose.

Touching her cheek, I smile at her, happy that she's in my life. "I will."

I open the door to let her out and we both stop, staring at the enormous tent that is erected in my front yard. Gaping at the monstrosity, I'm trying to wrap my mind around it. Turning to look at Roxanne, I manage to ask, "Is there a giant purple tent in my yard?"

Before she can answer, Voldemort pops her head out of the flap. She's wearing cargo shorts and a t-back and she has a mesh bag in her hand.

"Hi," she says, smiling. "I was hoping I could use your shower."

.

Chapter Ten

Police in the States have a motto- To Protect and Serve. The Island police have a motto as well- Protect and Serve Yourself. After several failed attempts to get through to a live voice at the emergency number, I finally got someone to answer and my cell signal dropped the call. "I hate this fucking island," I yell at the kitchen wall.

Roxanne smiles sympathetically over her shoulder. She's decided that a pot of coffee is the best response to this situation. Standing on one foot with my neck craned toward the window, I redial the police and listen to the recording. "Jesus. I mean, what if I was being murdered?"

Shrugging, Roxanne finishes setting up the coffee and switches it on. "You'd be dead already? Your final gargled words would live in infamy on the Island police voice mail?"

"You are so funny."

Roxanne looks up at a persistent knock on the door. Walking over to the window, she glances out, and then opens the door to admit Sam, relocking the door behind her.

Sam gestures over her shoulder back to the door. "I'm guessing you already know this, but your ex-girlfriend is brewing coffee on a camp stove in your front yard."

"I'm aware."

She grins. "There are so many ways to go with this. I'm not sure how to begin."

Roxanne hands her a cup of coffee. "Well, since we're all here, we could call this a meeting of The Love Sucks Club. Agenda item number one – Dana's ex-girlfriend has decided to camp out in her yard for the foreseeable future. Action item ideas? Anyone?"

They both laugh and I raise my middle finger in their general direction. "I'm so glad that my miserable life is giving the two of you such pleasure."

Sam grins and pops open a beer. "What the hell is she doing here anyway?"

"Last time I talked to her, which let me remind you was when she kidnapped me and threatened me, she was in danger of getting kicked out of her apartment. She wanted me to give her a loan so she could pay the rent."

"You didn't give her the money," Roxanne says.

"Obviously. Why she can't camp somewhere else is completely beyond me."

Perched on my counter, Sam shrugs. "Well, it's a relatively safe location. On the beach she'd have to worry about getting killed or robbed. This way, she can leave her stuff and it will be fine when she gets back."

"It won't be fine" I growl. "I'm going to pitch it all as soon as she leaves."

Roxanne looks pained. "It's just..."

"What, Roxanne?" I snap.

"She is so desperate that she has resorted to pitching a tent in her ex-girlfriend's yard. Obviously something is really wrong."

"Yeah, and whatever it is doesn't involve me."

Sam nods. "I agree. Dana doesn't owe her

anything."

Listening to the police recording for the fifteenth time, I nod toward Sam. "Quite the opposite, in fact."

"I just think we should try to find out what's wrong. Maybe we can help in ways that don't involve giving her money."

"Rox, listen to me. She spent our entire relationship taking everything she could get from me. And I let her because I thought I deserved to be treated like that."

"And now you know that you deserve better?"

"Now I don't know what I deserve, but I don't want to live with someone who treats me like shit. Not ever again."

Sam stands up. "Want me to get rid of her?"

Holding up my hand, I motion her to wait. A live human being is finally talking to me on the phone. "Yes, police, thank you. I need a squad car sent to my house."

"What's the nature of your emergency?"

"A woman has set up her tent in my yard."

I can hear the woman's gum snapping in the long pause that follows my statement. "A woman has set up a tent in your yard?"

"Without my permission."

"I see."

"You probably don't. She's my ex-girlfriend and she threatened me earlier. Now she's camping in my yard."

"And she has threatened you?"

"Well, she wouldn't let me out of her car earlier?"

"She forced you into her car?"

"Not exactly. I fainted and she put me in her car."

Another long pause for the woman on the other end of the phone to chew her gum and digest what I'm telling her. "So she helped you into her car."

"None of this has anything to do with the fact that she is now trespassing on my property."

"In a tent."

"Yes."

"Have you asked her why she's there?"

"I know why she's here."

"Ma'am, give me your address and I'll send a squad car."

"Today?"

"Your address, ma'am."

Sighing, I give her my address and hang up. Sam is already laughing before I hang up the phone. "How long do you think it will take for the cops to get here?"

"Considering we called them when the Grill was being held up at gunpoint and they didn't show up until six hours later, I'm guessing never."

Roxanne shakes her head. "I called once when I overhead my neighbors having a violent argument. I was put on hold and then promised a squad car. No one ever showed up. I called the next day to ask about it and the lady on the phone said she had no record of me calling."

"Of course not," Sam scoffed. "If it doesn't directly involve their friends or family, they don't bother. And why would they? It's not like there's ever any recourse."

"So what do I do?"

Roxanne pats my shoulder. "I think we should talk to her."

Sam claps her hands together and jumps off the counter. "Yeah, so do I."

"Sam." Roxanne gives her a warning look. "Let's agree to be civil."

"I'm always civil."

"Please." Roxanne rolls her eyes, but gives Sam a one armed hug. "Let's just hear her out if nothing else."

I don't know if I want to do this, but if I can't do it with Roxanne and Sam around me, I can't ever do it. I'm pretty sure Sam could take my ex in a fair fight, if it comes to that. I just don't want it to come to that. I want her to be out of my life without any hassle. Maybe in the end that's all I want out of life. I just want to be left alone. Nodding to my friends, I unlock the door and step out into the sunshine. The beauty of the day again belies the surreal events taking place in my life. If Fran were here, I think she'd be laughing her ass off. Then again, if Fran had never died, I would never have started dating Voldemort. Speaking of which, she's no longer outside of my house. The tent is still there, but everything is neatly packed and her vehicle is gone.

Sam peeks into the tent and glances around. "Her clothes are here." She glances up at the tarp strung up above the tent. "She has a good setup here. It's a good tent and the tarp should help protect her from a moderate rain."

"How joyous," I intone. "I'd hate for her to be inconvenienced."

Roxanne puts her arm around my shoulders. "I think either Sam or myself should stay here at all times until she's gone."

Sam flexes her biceps. "No offense, Roxy, but this is going to take a butch."

Rolling her eyes again, Roxanne grins at Sam. "And I think it's going to take a diplomacy that you both lack."

We all pause at the sound of an engine coming up the driveway. Sam raises her eyebrow and steps slightly in front of me. When the vehicle crests the hills and comes into sight from the tree line, we all breathe a sigh of relief.

"I should have recognized that jeep whine," I grin as Susannah pulls up to the door. She looks at the tent as she gets out of her jeep.

"Are you having a camp out?"

"It's a long story," Sam says. "Let's go back inside and we'll fill you in."

Roxanne nods. "We can leave the door open and we'll hear her engine when she comes back."

"When who comes back?" Susannah looks from one face to the next.

I usher her inside and we all perch around the kitchen again. Roxanne pours coffee and hands Sam a beer.

Sam and Roxanne fill Susannah in on the latest happenings while I pace around my kitchen, irritated. I will not be held prisoner in my own home. If the cops don't show up to take care of my trespasser, I'm going to have to take care of her myself.

Roxanne gets to the part where my ex asked for a shower and Susannah laughs. "Man, she is nothing if not ballsy."

"Oh, yes, she's certainly that." Glaring at my sister, I stalk into my bedroom and rummage in the closet until I find a baseball bat. Roxanne intercepts me as I come back into the kitchen and head for the door.

"Dana, come on. What are you going to do? Beat her tent to death?"

Aware that I'm losing it, and unable to stop myself, I raise my voice. "I don't know what I'm going to do! I really have no fucking idea what I'm going to do. I'm trying to figure it out and it isn't easy with the three of you sitting here gossiping about my life like a bunch of bitches at a tea party."

Sam grins. "I've never been to a tea party in my life."

Deflating, I punch her on the shoulder and drop the bat on the counter. "I don't know what I'm doing. I just know that I want her gone."

"Well, let's start by taking her tent down," Susannah offers. "I mean, it's not like we're doing anything wrong. We're just cleaning up your yard."

We all traipse outside and start pulling stuff out of tent. She has several boxes and a few duffle bags in here. I'm not sure where the rest of her stuff is unless she sold it all. We finally clear out the tent and Sam starts pulling off the rain flap. Roxanne and Susannah set about stacking all of my ex's stuff off to one side. Sam and I get all of the stakes pulled out and flatten the tent to the ground. Susannah pulls a tent bag from the rest of the stuff and brings it over. Sam and I fold the whole tent into a small rectangle and manage to get all of the poles and clips into the case along with the tent and the rain flap. Standing as a group surveying the pile, I'm struck by a wave of pity for the woman. She really must have nothing and no one in her life if she's up here trying to camp in my yard. On the other hand, she basically kidnapped me in town yesterday. Roxanne puts her arm around me and smiles. "Compassion is our greatest gift to ourselves and others."

Sam rolls her eyes. "Compassion for those who

would treat you shittily?"

"Shittily? Is that even a word?" Susannah is laughing.

Roxanne is unperturbed. "Sam, what's that old saying about holding on to anger being the same as drinking poison and expecting the other person to die?"

Shrugging, Sam smiles. "Better to just poison the other person and move on with your life."

"Yes," Roxanne replies. "But allowing for the idea that we can't just kill everyone who hurts us or pisses us off, then forgiveness is the best gift we can give to ourselves."

"Fine," I interject, ending the debate. "I forgive Voldemort for everything she did to me before this. That said, I can't forgive her for something she is actively doing to me. So, we need to get her out of my yard and out of my life, and then I'll forgive her for this shit, too."

"Wow," Susannah says flatly. "You really have that anger thing under control."

Back in the house, we take our positions around the table, keeping our ears open for the sounds of an engine. Susannah goes out on to the porch to call Thomas. When she comes back in, she gives me a kiss. "It looks like you ladies have this all under control. I'm going down the hill to meet Thomas."

Sam waves her off. "Don't worry about it," she mutters. "We're just dealing with a psychopath who wants to pull a Single White Female on your sister. I'm sure it'll be fine."

Laughing, Susannah raps on Sam's head. "I have faith in you to protect my sister from her evil ex-girlfriend."

When she's gone, Roxanne dials the police again on my cell phone while I cook lunch for the three of us.

"It's been a long day already," Sam says, stretching. "I didn't expect to be over here doing manual labor."

"I didn't expect to have a circus tent pitched on my front lawn."

"How did she get here, get all of her gear unloaded and set up without you hearing her?"

"Rox and I were on the front side of the house. We wouldn't have heard the vehicle."

"Susannah was right about one thing; it was pretty ballsy."

Roxanne holds the phone away from her mouth. "Not really. I don't think she much cared if Dana came out while she was setting up. She's acting like a very desperate woman."

"Desperately psychotic," Sam quips.

Laying food out on plates, I drop one in front of Sam and another in front of Roxanne. Eating directly from the pot, I shovel stir fry into my mouth. Roxanne eats with one hand, holding the phone with the other.

"Don't waste your time, Roxy," Sam says around a mouthful of food. "Even if you get them, they aren't coming."

"It's an effort in hope," she says.

"It's an effort in futility."

"Speaking of futility," I say. "I need to go pretty soon." Giving Sam a pointed look, I look up at the clock on the microwave.

"Yeah, we better head out."

"Where are you going?"

I decide to level with her. "I'm going to the

doctor to find out if my head problem is physical."

She nods. "Probably a good idea to rule it out. Though, I don't think your visions are the symptoms of an illness."

"Sam does."

"I just said that they might be!" Sam is indignant.

"At any rate, we need to go. Rox, we'll drop you off at your place first."

"You go on. I'll stay here and talk to Ja..."

"No!" Sam and I both yell.

"She-who-shall-not-be-named!" I continue.

Sam falls back against her chair, gripping her head. "My ears! My ears!"

"Oh for Pete's sake," Roxanne scoffs. "Am I dealing with teenagers here?"

"Totally," Sam grins.

"And I don't want you to stay here and talk to her," I add. "She's dangerous."

"Fine." Roxanne hangs up my phone and tosses it to me. After checking to make sure that all of my doors and windows are locked, we all pile into Sam's truck and ride the short distance over to Roxanne's.

"Call me as soon as you're done," she says, getting out of the truck. "I don't want you dealing with all of this on your own."

"What am I?" Sam says. "Chopped liver?"

"More like spam," I reply.

Roxanne shakes her head. "We need to stick together over this. Besides, someone has to be the voice of reason for you two."

Sam nods. "Good point."

We wait until Roxanne gets into her house before taking off. When Sam backs out of Roxanne's driveway, I direct her back to my house.

"Let's get her shit and go drop it off at her work."

Back at my house, we quickly gather the packed gear and toss it into the back of Sam's truck. When we get to the store where my ex said she was working, I scan the parking lot for her odd vehicle.

"There it is," I call.

Sam pulls up behind it. The vehicle is a strange kind of Jeep/SUV hybrid and it looks as if the back window has been broken out of it. Lifting the plastic that is glued around the back opening, I motion to Sam to start passing me the stuff. When the back is full, we both put our hands on the pile and give it a huge shove. Some of it crushes into the front seat, leaving us room to wedge in the last few bits. We high-five each other and jump back into the truck. After laughing for several minutes over our brilliance, Sam falls quiet. Fiddling with the radio, I let her stew in silence for a while. When we pull into the parking lot of Dr. B's, I turn to her. "What's wrong?"

"I guess I'm just worried about what the doc is going to say."

"She's going to say that I'm a nutcase and I should be locked up for life."

"Well, that part is obvious."

Laughing, she slaps my arm. "You're fine." She looks out the window at a woman walking into the doctor's office. "You're totally fine."

"Are you trying to convince me or yourself?"

"Come on, let's go spend a couple of hours sitting around a waiting room."

"Dr. B is pretty good, from what I've heard."

"Whatever. They're all the same."

We walk into the waiting room and Sam plops down into a chair. The woman at the front desk gives me a sheaf of papers about the size of a manuscript and tells me to fill everything out.

"Jesus," Sam says when I sit down next to her. "Do they want your life story?"

"I guess. It's medical history."

"I thought you'd been here before."

"No. I just know Dr. B socially."

"Me too," Sam says with a wink. "If you know what I mean."

"No, I definitely don't know what you mean."

She laughs. "Okay, not really. But she was totally flirting with me last time she was at the resort."

"I'm sure."

She takes out her phone and starts checking Facebook while I fill out the forms. The woman sitting to the left of me is fidgeting. The heel of her shoe strikes the wood of the chair leg every time she jiggles her foot. The noise is sending little jabs into my brain and the longer the noise goes on, the more irritated I become. The woman next to me, staring into space, is oblivious to my irritation. Glancing around, I notice that a couple of the other patients are glaring at the woman as well. Ignoring all of us, she continues to slam her heel against the wood.

Trying to put it out of my mind, I return to my papers. Flipping through the pages, I can feel the muscles in my neck getting tighter with every slap of heel against wood. Every time I read a question, the heel strikes again. Finishing the papers, I sign my name with a flourish and jump up to turn them into the woman behind the desk. With my back to the room, I miss what happens next, but a man's voice makes me jump.

"God dammit, shut up!"

Turning around, I see the whole room staring at a red-faced elderly man with a cane. Struggling to his feet, he points the cane at the woman with the high heels. "Shut up!"

"Fuck you," she responds, snapping her gum and returning her gaze to the wall.

"Fuck me? Fuck me?" The old man rocks back on his feet, his face turning a deep shade of purple. I step quickly over to him and put my hands on his shoulders.

"Hey, buddy," I say in a soft voice. "It's bothering me, too."

A nurse steps into the waiting room from the office area. "Mr. James," she says, soothingly. "It's time for you to come in."

Mr. James takes a deep breath and starts to walk toward the door to the office. The nurse guides him into the back with one hand on his arm.

When I return to my seat, Sam is laughing quietly. "I thought he was going to beat her with that cane," she whispers.

"I wish she had gone back instead. I'm about ready to beat her with her own shoe." The woman has resumed her foot tapping and without paperwork to distract me, I'm aware that I won't last long before I have to say something to her.

Another woman beats me to it. "Hey, lady."

The shoe-tapper looks up. "What?"

"Stop tapping your foot. It's pissing me off."

The tapper stands up. "Oh yeah. Well, your ugly face is pissing me off."

The other woman stands, as well. Sam grins. "Chick fight. Yeah."

Sighing, I stand up as well. "Ladies, seriously."

The tapper barely glances my way. "Fuck you."

The nurse steps out of the office again. "Ms. Lowry? You're next."

The tapper stalks toward the nurse and I breathe a sigh of relief. The other woman goes back to her seat. Sam is shaking her head and laughing. "The locals say when two women have a fist fight in the waiting room it's going to be a bad hurricane season."

"Oh, very droll."

With the tapper out of the way, the tension has gone out of the room. I still feel on edge, though. Picking up a magazine, I flip through it until the nurse comes for me.

After weighing me and taking my blood pressure, she leaves me in an examination room. I barely have time to get impatient before Dr. B taps on the door. She comes in, smiling.

"Dana, how are you?"

"I'm fine."

"If you're fine, then why are you here?"

I look at her face for a few moments, wondering how much to tell her. Dr. B has a genuine smile and a warm, open face. When I first met her, I guessed her in her forties, but up close, I'd say she is probably in her fifties. The lines around her eyes and mouth suggest a lot of laughing and smiling. Her hair is a lovely shade of light brown and today, it is pulled back in a professional looking bun. She sits patiently through my assessment. After a few moments, I decide to tell her everything.

"There once was a little girl who used to have dreams about death."

Dr. B smiles. "And?"

I launch into the whole story. This is going to

take forever and I know she has other patients, but once I start talking, I can't seem to stop. "And then Fran came into my life and the visions came back."

"Tell me more about the visions. Does your vision change before they occur? Do you see spots? Headaches?"

"They feel like the beginning of a panic attack. It's worth noting that I have those as well, but whether they are caused by the visions or something entirely different, I don't know."

She nods and I continue. Telling her about the arrival of Esmé on the island and how things have gotten worse since then. I even tell her about Voldemort's tent in my yard and tripping over a chicken. I feel as if I'm half out of myself, watching me tell the story from a distance. I'm disconnected from this entire scene.

Dr. Brawley listens quietly until I have talked myself hoarse. When I finish, she says, "I think I'd like to order some tests to rule out any physical ailments. I can schedule an MRI and..."

"Wait. I honestly don't think there's something physically wrong with me. I only came here because Sam was going to have a breakdown if I didn't."

"Still, it wouldn't hurt to rule out the possibility of neurological disorders or epilepsy."

"Or schizophrenia?"

"I think we should start with sending you to a neurologist."

Shaking my head, I lean back on the table and close my eyes. "Modern science always assumes those who fall outside of the laws of physics are psychotic."

"Dana, I don't think you're psychotic. I just want to make sure you aren't in danger. Brain trauma can be very serious. I don't want you to die of something

I could have prevented if only I convinced you to get some tests."

"Are you even willing to entertain the idea that there isn't something wrong with me?"

She smiles. "Absolutely. Like Agent Mulder, I want to believe. I have an open mind. I am well aware that there are things out there in the universe that I can't possibly explain. Just let me rule out the ones I can explain and we'll work on the other options."

"But if I've been having visions since I was a kid..."

"You've only been getting dizzy and passing out over the past couple of weeks. That's what has me worried."

After poking and prodding me and asking more questions, Dr. B pronounces me free to go.

"Did you find anything out by fondling me or did you just want to make it look like you did something?"

Laughing, she opens the door and waves my file folder at me. "I'll drop this off at the front desk and they'll help you schedule your other appointments and tests. We'll do a follow up when you're done with all of that."

"Thanks for listening, Dr. B."

"Anytime, Dana."

She leaves the room and I sit for a minute, staring at the wall. I have to admit that I probably should go see the neurologist and get these other tests. It's just that I don't think there is anything wrong with me. Long ago, when I had my first panic attack, I went to the emergency room. I was convinced I was having a heart attack. After countless expensive tests, they determined that there was nothing wrong with me. Nothing. Apparently, I was just having massive chest pain that radiated up my left arm, irregular heartbeats, and an inability to breathe for no reason. It was only through my own research that I chalked it up to panic attacks and since I've diagnosed myself, I've been able to control them pretty well. It's only been since the arrival of Esmé that things have gotten so much worse. The dreams of Fran, the fainting spells, the nightmares, and the panic attacks. There has to be a connection.

At the front desk, I tell the receptionist that I have to check my calendar and then I'll call to schedule my other appointments. Sam stands when I enter the waiting area and we walk out to the car.

Sliding into the driver's seat, she glances at me. "Well?"

"Dr. Brawley says I am in perfect health and everyone should stop worrying."

"Are you lying to me?"

"Totally."

"So what comes next?"

Grinning, I point out a couple of wild pigs rolling in the mud in front of the business complex.

Sam laughs. "Gotta love the island. It's the perfect juxtaposition between feral and industrial."

"With beautiful beaches."

"Great food."

"Gun violence."

"Drugs."

"Roaming wildlife."

We pass the pigs and I call out a hello to them as we drive past. "It would only have been better if they were rolling in the mud outside of the police station."

"Hey. Some of my best friends are cops."

"Not island cops."

"Good point."

"Anyway, speaking of pigs, my next stop is my house where I will see if my ex has come back."

"And then?"

"Then I need to talk to Esmé."

Concentrating on the road, she doesn't answer for a few minutes. I take the time to stare out the window and try to gather my thoughts. Things got worse for me when Esmé came to town, even before I knew she was here. Why is that? Sam is staring out the windshield, singing along with some country tune on the radio. I wish my life was as simple as hers. Then again, I guess her life isn't easy, either. Maybe I'd be better off being like Susannah, who always seems to get her way in everything. She never seems unhappy, either. I wonder if she really is happy, though.

"Hey Sam," I say, punching her in the arm.

"No hitting the driver." She punches me hard on the thigh.

"Ow, fucker."

"You had something to say?"

"Do you feel like we ever really know anyone?"

"Maybe not all of their inner workings.... but I feel like I know you very well."

"I feel as if I haven't made an effort to get to know my loved ones as well as I should."

"It isn't too late."

Pausing, I look at her out of the corner of my eye. "For some."

"Maybe it's a lesson to start paying attention to those who are still in your life."

"Maybe. Sam. What do you dream about?"

"A bacon double cheeseburger. Want to hit the Grill before I take you home?"

"Totally. I need sustenance to deal with she-who-shall-not-be-named."

Reaching over, I turn up the radio and lose myself in some song about heartache and tractors as we drive to the Grill.

Chapter Eleven

Karen and Rick are at their usual places at the bar, so we detour over to say hello to them. Rick stands as we approach and offers his chair. Sam perches on it and I stand behind her. Slinging an arm around Rick, I ask how everything has been going for them.

"Just gearing up for the big party," he says.

"Need any help with anything?"

"Well, I'd be happy if you would be willing to bring a cooler full of ice. We always seem to run out."

Sam nods. "I've got a couple of big coolers. We'll get several bags on our way."

"Thank you," he replies. "I think we've got everything else under control."

Karen hasn't said a word, so I pat her on the shoulder and ask how she's doing.

"Fine. Thanks for asking."

"I'm looking forward to the party. Call me if you can think of anything else you need."

"I will. Do you know if Roxanne is coming?"

Sam grins. "Absolutely. The entirety of The Love Sucks Club will be in attendance."

Laughing, Rick waves at the waitress to bring a round of drinks over. He shakes his head. "Are you still doing that? How old are you? Twelve?"

Feigning hurt, Sam puts her hand over her heart. "Twelve? Come on. This club offers an important public service to those who have been wronged by love. We gather together in solidarity and console each other on the suckiness of love."

He laughs again. "Isn't it kind of a self-fulfilling prophecy? You call yourselves The Love Sucks Club and you wonder why love sucks."

Karen sniffs. "You're all lesbians. Imagine how much more your love lives would suck if you had to be with men."

With my arm around Rick, I can feel his muscles tighten when she speaks. Speaking slowly, he replies, "Not all men are villains."

Karen ignores him and orders another drink. Sam raises an eyebrow at Rick in question, but just gets a shrug in response.

"Well, at any rate," Sam says in an overly cheerful voice. "We're going to get some food and head back to Dana's place. Her ex is camped out in her yard right now and we need to figure out how to get her to leave."

"Call the police," Karen says.

"Yeah, right," Rick and I both say at the same time. The three of us laugh hysterically while Karen purses her lips and turns away from us. She's giving us the cold back of death. I would know – I've experienced it a million times in my life. Saying goodbye to the two of them, Sam and I sit down at a table and order some food. We're just settling in to eat when Susannah and Thomas come in, trailed by Olivia.

"Aw shit," Sam mutters. She immediately starts shoveling food into her mouth as fast as she can.

"What the hell, dude? You're going to choke."

"Just hurry up and eat so we can get out of here."

"Stop it. We're going to have to suck it up."

The ladies and Thomas arrive at our table and

pull up chairs without waiting for an invitation. Olivia dips her fingers into my basket and steals several fries.

"I don't know where your hands have been," I snap.

"I'm sure they're cleaner than anything else you've touched today."

Sam is still jamming food into her mouth at an alarming rate. Susannah gives her the once over, but refrains from commenting. Thomas smiles at me. "How are you feeling, Dana?"

"Fine, thank you. How are you feeling today?"

He's not oblivious to the sarcasm in my voice. "I just heard you had a hard time after we saw you in town the other day."

"I'm fine. I'm perfectly fine. There's nothing wrong with me. Life is wonderful. Life is grand. In fact, I'm feeling so great, that I think I'll order some ice cream to celebrate."

"Wow," Olivia intones. "Bitter much?"

"I'm not bitter. I just don't want to have to keep talking about my brain damage."

Susannah laughs. "Yeah, that's an old subject."

"Anyway," Thomas continues. "We were up at your house to see if you needed help evicting your unwanted tenant. She wasn't there and all of her stuff is gone, too."

"Well, I know where her stuff is." I grin.

Sam laughs out loud, spraying bits of chewed food out of her mouth.

"Since she didn't come back, maybe she got the hint."

"Good," I say, still grinning. "Maybe she decided to harass someone else."

Thomas nods. "We'll still go home with you, if

you want. Better safe than sorry."

"No, it's fine. Sam and I can handle her on our own."

Sam mumbles what I take to be acquiescence around a huge mouthful of food. A chunk of burger falls out of her mouth as she speaks. She picks it up off her plate and puts it back into her mouth.

"Gross, Sam!" Olivia squeals.

Forcing a swallow, Sam grins at Olivia. "Glad to be of service."

"You're a pig."

"A proud pig." Sam says.

"Pig in a poke," I add.

"Porky pokey pig," Sam responds.

"Pork chop," I answer.

"Enough," Susannah cuts us off as Sam opens her mouth. "You two really are mental teenagers."

"At least we're improving," I say. "We were called twelve a few minutes ago."

Sam has crammed the rest of her food in her mouth and signaled for the check.

"Are you in a hurry?" Olivia asks.

"I have to get back to work for a while after I take Dana home."

"Well, we can take Dana home," Susannah says.

"No, it's fine. Sam and I need to stop at the store before we head up the hill," I say, waving in the general direction of my house.

Thomas squares his shoulders. "I still think we should come back up with you, just in case she comes back around."

"Don't worry about it. We crammed her stuff into her car. I'm sure she won't be back."

I hand Sam some money and she goes up to the

bar to pay our bill while I suck down the rest of my food. Susannah gives me a hug as I stand up and offers to come up tomorrow morning for breakfast. I decline politely, insisting that I haven't had a moment to write in what seems like weeks.

"Good idea. How else can you keep your refrigerator stocked for me if you aren't bringing in any royalties?"

"Exactly."

I shake hands with Thomas and say goodbye to Olivia. Sam is waiting for me by the exit. Olivia sniffs. "Apparently she isn't going to come back to say goodbye."

"She's thinking it," I say, grinning.

Jumping into the truck, Sam smiles at me across the seat. "That went well."

"You have ketchup on your chin."

She pulls down the rear view mirror and scrubs at her chin with a finger. "Still, it was worth it to get out of there without having to talk to Olivia." Backing out of the parking space, she winds around the beach front road before turning off into the woods toward my hill.

"You're kind of a jerk to her."

Throwing her head back against the seat, she clutches at her heart with one hand. "I'm sorry. Who the hell are you?"

"Come on. She's annoying, but she's Susannah's friend. Maybe she just needs some compassion."

"Who are you and what have you done with my friend?"

"Hey," I counter, affronted. "I've always been a compassionate person."

"Not to Olivia."

"Well, she does kind of irritate me. But I've started to wonder lately if maybe there's a story there that we just don't know."

Sam looks doubtful. "Maybe."

When we get to the top of the hill, I scour the yard, but it doesn't look as if she's moved back in. Sam puts the truck in gear and looks at me.

"Want me to come in with you just in case?"

"Forget it. Her car isn't here. Her stuff isn't here. Her ugly mug isn't here. I think I'm safe."

"Okay. Thanks for letting me take you to the doctor."

"Thanks for taking me." I reach over to give her a half hug before getting out of the car. "Want to have a club meeting tomorrow?"

"Yeah, four o'clock at the Pit?"

"Sounds good. I'll text Roxanne and make sure she's available."

She waves as she turns around. I unlock my front door and walk inside. There's no dramatic tension, so I'm relatively sure that I'm alone–at least as far as human beings go. Frank gives a blert to me from his exalted position on my counter. Scratching between his ears, I lean down and give him a kiss right on his big brown and beige face. He scrunches his nose up at my kiss, but he tolerates it because somewhere deep down in his kitty heart, he does love me. Tossing down a couple of kitty treats, I wander into the front room to check my email.

I know I need to get some writing done today. I've been such a wastoid lately. I pull my cell out of my pocket and text Roxanne to let her know about the meeting tomorrow. She writes back almost instantly to ask if I need company. It would be nice to have her here and there's a good chance that we will make love if I invite her over for the evening. I could use a little intimacy right now. On the other hand, bringing another woman into my life right now is probably not the best idea in the world. Roxanne is a lot older than I am, too. Maybe at forty and sixty that doesn't matter, but it will at fifty and seventy. She's in great shape, though. Maybe better shape than I am. She's a great friend. It just doesn't make sense for us to be a couple. I text her back that my ex is gone and the place is secure. Let her know that I'll see her tomorrow at The Pit. It's the right decision, but I still feel like shit. I want her to be here with me. I'm feeling so lonely all of a sudden.

Stretching out on the couch, I decide just to close my eyes for five minutes. It's been a long day and I'm tired. A power nap will give me enough energy to face the evening.

I'm coming out of a dream in which I'm trapped in some kind of caul and trying to break through it to make it back into this world. Tearing at the caul, I wrestle my way out of it and back into consciousness. My heart is pounding, my head is pounding, and someone is pounding on my door. "God dammit!"

Struggling off the couch, I stomp my way into the kitchen and stalk over to the door. With every intention of fucking up whoever is on the other side, I throw open the door, scaring the crap out of my ex. Advancing on her, I poke my finger into her chest.

"I'm done with this. I do not want you here. I don't owe you anything. I am not going to give you money. You are not going to stay at my house. You need to get your ass out of my life. I don't want to see your face ever again." My voice is going up in volume as I continue to jab her repeatedly with my finger. The shock on her face almost makes me laugh, but I shake it off as I continue my tirade. "You will not come to my house. You will not speak to me in public. If you see me at a bar or a restaurant or a store, you will pretend that you don't see me and look the other way. Are we totally fucking clear?"

Stepping back, she looks at me. Coming down from my tirade, I realize that she looks neither pissed off nor scared. Just sad. She shakes her head at me for a moment and looks down at the ground.

"I get it. I understand. I'm sorry. I guess I was counting on the fact that we once loved each other. I thought the fact that I'm in trouble might have stirred your compassion. I won't bother you again."

"That's all I want. I just want to be left alone."

She nods. "You will be. All alone. And someday, you may regret it."

Walking back to her vehicle, she pauses once to look back at me. She opens her mouth to speak and then thinks better of it. I watch her get drive away and suddenly, I think I'm going to cry. Back in my kitchen, I perch on a stool and rest my head on Frank's tremendous girth. He chirps once as I lay my head down. I can feel his purr rumbling through his rib cage against the side of my face. I think I could be happy like this for the rest of my life. Just me and Frank and a few million cans of tuna. I think if we ever have a zombie apocalypse, Frank and I will be set. We'll just hole up here and pick 'em off one by one, tossing the bodies over the porch and down the hill. Frank shifts and turns, going back to sleep. I wish I could come back as a cossetted house cat. Closing my eyes, I turn off my thoughts and go back to sleep.

Chapter Twelve

S am is already at the Pit when Roxanne and I walk in. She has one of those looks on her face that automatically puts me on guard.

"What?"

She nods in the direction of the bar. Olivia is sitting there with a guy in cut off jean shorts and a deplorable tank top. To be fair, I've worn that same outfit before, but if they are on a date, he is seriously lacking in the style department. The dude's hair is longish and curly and he has a plethora of body hair that's visible across his back and everywhere else.

"He looks like Ron Jeremy," I say.

"Who's that?" Roxanne asks.

"A porn star."

Sam laughs. "More than a porn star. He's the world's ugliest man with the world's largest penis."

Roxanne glances back as we sit. "Olivia is sweet. Should we invite them over?"

Coughing, Sam puts her hand up in a stop gesture. "A. No. And B. No."

"Roxanne thinks everyone is sweet," I say.

"Maybe it has something to do with my attitude in life," she replies. "I believe in the best in people, so people show me their best."

"Yeah, yeah," Sam says, taking a chug of her beer.

The waitress drags over to our table and

mumbles, "What ya want?"

We order a pizza and a round of drinks. The waitress shuffles off without acknowledging anything we said.

Sam looks after her. "Think she got that?"

"Not a chance. We'll end up with a meat lover's pizza instead of a Greek."

"And I'll get a whiskey sour instead of a rum and coke," Roxanne adds.

"As long as we get something edible and something drinkable, we'll be ahead of the game," Sam laughs.

Olivia and her companions appear to be deep in conversation at the bar. I catch Sam checking them out and raise an eyebrow.

"I'm just making sure she's involved enough in her date to ignore us."

"It's looks as if she's having a much easier time ignoring you than you are her," Roxanne replies.

Over on the other side of the bar, one of the local drunks is swaying precariously at the jukebox. Michael Jackson blasts from the speakers and Sam immediately lifts her arms in the Thriller dance. Roxanne hums along. Leaning back in my chair, I can just make out a group of drinkers in a corner table doing shots. It's a pretty dull crowd for The Pit, but then, it is quite early.

It's time for me to get this party started. "So, The Love Sucks Club comes to order yet again."

"Wait. I have to interrupt." Roxanne looks serious.

"What's going on?"

"I'm going to have to leave the club," she says, completely straight-faced.

"What?" Sam looks shocked. "You can't. If you leave, it will just be Dana and I sitting here complaining to ourselves."

Laughing, Roxanne leans out of the way as our waitress brings our drinks. "Sam, come on. That's all we do anyway. We get together and complain about love."

"Well, Roxanne." I'm using a voice one might use to explain the color of the sky to a four year old. "We are called The Love Sucks Club. It rather makes sense that our main topic of conversation would be the suckiness of love."

"That's my point," she replies. "We're setting ourselves up to fail at having a positive attitude. Okay, the name is cute and all. I just don't want to be part of something that indicates that anything sucks. Anything at all. Yes, there is suckiness in the world and in our own lives. We don't have to go looking for it."

Sighing, I slam a big gulp of water and slam my glass down on the table. "Oh Roxanne. I just can't believe you're breaking up with us."

"I'm not breaking up with you. I'll still hang out with you two. Just not under this premise."

"So let me get this gay," Sam interjects. "If we change our name to something like the We Have Hope Club or the Let's All Believe in a Better World Club, you'll still be part of it?"

"I don't know that the name of the club is truly the point."

"I guess I see the point," I add. "We're all a little too old to have a club."

"Exactly," Roxanne says. "If we want to get together and go do things or collect money for charities or take SCUBA lessons or anything like that, I would love to do it. This sitting around in a bar talking about love sucking is depressing."

"Still, it's not like it's doing anyone any harm."

"I think it is doing harm to all of us."

Sam shifts some of our drinks to make room for the pizza which appears to have the correct toppings. "All right. Here's my counter offer."

Roxanne snorts. "Okay, let's hear it."

"We will table the motion of changing the name of the club until next week."

"And then what," Roxanne says, grinning. "We take a vote? We cast an anonymous ballot?"

"Well, it will give me a week to think of a winning argument that will keep you in our club without changing the name of it."

Glass breaking across the bar catches our attention. I look up to see Olivia standing next to her bar stool, mopping at her skirt with a napkin.

"Looks like someone couldn't hold her liquor," Sam whispers.

"Literally," I reply.

Roxanne stands and sweeps off toward Olivia.

"Ah Jesus. You know, she really doesn't belong in the Love Sucks Club," Sam says.

"I know. She's too good for the likes of us."

"You like her, though. I mean, really like her."

"There's a connection. I just don't see how it would work. When I'm her age, she'll be eighty. That's a big difference."

Roxanne has her arm around Olivia and is talking to her while the porn star continues to slouch on his stool.

"She just better not bring her over here," Sam

states. "I...aw...shit."

"Your wish is her command," I laugh, as Roxanne walks Olivia over to our table.

"I'm joining your stupid club," Olivia says, slamming into a chair.

"Hell no," Sam says. "It's for homos only."

"Sam!" Roxanne is affronted. "No it isn't. Of course Olivia can join."

"Two minutes ago, you wanted to disband us."

Taking advantage of the quarrel to grab the last piece of pizza, I lean back in my chair and watch the fireworks. I can tell from long experience that Sam is seriously annoyed.

"Well, now that we have another member, we are more like a club and less like three losers sitting around in a bar."

"First thing," Olivia says. "We should change the meeting location to The Grill. It's nicer and at least there's a sea view. We'd be out in the fresh air. This place stinks."

Sam throws her hand up in the air. "First thing, you don't get to make changes. And second thing, why were you here with Ron Jeremy if you hate it so much?"

"Who's Ron Jeremy?"

"Never fucking mind." Sam takes another gulp of her beer, scowling.

"My date's name is Cal," Olivia sniffs. "But I'm sick of men. I'm going to become a lesbian."

"You can't become a lesbian," I reason. "You either are or you aren't."

"Well, considering I've had sex with a woman, obviously I can become one."

"No, I'm just that good," Sam responds.

Pointedly ignoring her, Olivia continues. "Men are just big, smelly pigs and I'm tired of them."

"Some women are pigs, too," I say to the background noise of Sam making grunting pig noises. "Becoming a lesbian doesn't make your chances in love any better than they do as a straight woman."

"Well, maybe. I still want to join your club. What do you do? Try to find ways to alleviate the loneliness? Encourage each other to emotional growth? Analyze your past relationship mistakes so that you can do better in the next one?"

Looking at her blankly, I stutter for a second. "Uh, kind of like that. Except that we mostly just sit around here and talk about our sucky love lives."

"Well you and Sam do that anyway. I would have thought that having Roxanne here would class the group up a bit."

Olivia's date ambles up to the table. "I paid the damn bill," he says in a nasally voice.

"Good for you," Olivia replies. "It's the least you can do after spilling your drink on me."

"We thought you spilled it on yourself," I say.

"I'm not a complete buffoon," she says.

"Well, come on, then," porn star guy says. "I'll drive you home."

"She's fine," Roxanne says, putting her arm protectively around Olivia. "We'll make sure she gets home safely."

"Whatever. I'm sure you'll have an awesome night with two dykes and an old lady."

Standing, Sam flexes her muscles. She stands about three inches taller than the guy and he turns around without another word. As he slams the door on his way out, Sam looks at Olivia incredulously.

"How the hell did he even get a date with you?"

"In case you haven't noticed, there is a dearth of eligible men on this island. I'm running out of choices."

"According to Susannah, all of the good ones are married or gay," I say.

Sam nods. "She's dated her fair share of married men and convicts."

"She didn't know he was married," Olivia snaps.

"All right. We've agreed to table the changing of the club's name to next week," Roxanne says. "But tonight, we are welcoming our new member, Olivia."

Disgusted, Sam takes another sip of her beer.

"Another motion has been made to move the meetings to The Grill instead of here," Roxanne says. "Shall we take a vote?"

Sam pokes me and we both look at the dance floor. Our favorite local drunk guy is moving around the dance floor by himself. It looks as if he is trying to do a cross between the robot and some kind of disco move. As we watch, he jumps up and down, screaming the lyrics of the song. Everyone in the bar turns to watch as his movements get wilder and wilder until finally, on a particularly exuberant jump, he spins around in the air and slams right into a bar table, knocking it to the ground and falling over it. The drinkers at the next table start applauding. Sam and I look at each other.

"We're staying here," we say together.

Rolling her eyes, Olivia signals to the waitress who pretends not to see her. "The service really sucks here. And the clientele is kind of trashy."

"Well, we're kind of trashy," Sam replies.

"It wouldn't kill us to go somewhere else," Roxanne says. "It doesn't have to be The Grill. We could go to that little park off of Forest Road. No one is ever there and they have picnic tables and everything."

"That sounds absolutely lovely," Sam chimes, clasping her hands together. "We can have a little picnic and I'll make tea cakes and finger sandwiches."

"Excellent," Roxanne says, firmly. "So it's agreed."

Olivia stands up. "I have to go to the girl's room. One bad thing about the park is there's no bathroom."

"There's the ocean," Sam counters.

"You're a pig," she says.

"Never said I wasn't."

She strides off to the bathroom. Roxanne looks around the table. "I think it will be good for her to join us. I think it will be good for us, too."

Sam shakes her head. "I can't see any way in which letting Debbie Downer into our club could be beneficial."

"Maybe we'll all learn something," Roxanne says.

"Come on, Sam," I say. "It might not suck as bad as we think."

"Fine, I give," Sam says. "But I'm collecting dues from her."

Chapter Thirteen

My head is aching so much, I might as well have a hangover. Dragging my butt out of bed takes an act of supreme will. I debate a quick walk up the hill and decide against it. Sam and I are doing the island tourist thing today and that should be enough exercise for anyone.

Frank sits in the bathroom with me as I shower and follows me through the house chirping and meowing as I get dressed. When I'm dry and clothed, I scoop him up and hold him upside down, cradled in my arms like a newborn baby. Kissing his big face, I coo, "Aw, isn't hims precious? Isn't hims the sweetest widdle thing?" He glares at me for about thirty seconds of this torture before sinking his teeth into my arm. I give him one more kiss on the nose and set him on the counter for some wet food. Susannah hates that I feed Frank on the counter. She swears that I'll get cat food or hair or germs or something mixed into human food and we'll all die. All I know is that Frank and I are equals in so far as we can be and though he may have to suffer the indignity of pooping into a box, I do my very best to treat him as a friend and a valued companion.

At any rate, this is mine and Frank's house and we make the rules so if Susannah doesn't like sharing counter space with Frank, she can go eat at her own place.

I can hear Sam's truck pulling up outside, so I open the door and usher her in. Her tourist for the day outfit consists of white board shorts with gigantic blue flowers and an orange and yellow color themed Hawaiian shirt. She refills her travel mug from my coffee pot while I gather a couple of bottles of water and some snacks.

"I have to say that I am mightily disappointed in your wardrobe choice for our big day," Sam says.

Looking down at myself, I shrug my shoulders. "What? I look great." I'm wearing my standard baggy cargo shorts and a tank top, but in concession to the tourist day, I've added a bright teal, red, and purple hibiscus covered Hawaiian shirt.

Sam shakes her head. "You could have at least added a visor or something."

"I think my shirt is gorgeously clashy enough to stand alone."

"Whatever." She leans down to kiss Frank on the top of his head. Frank responds by flattening his ears and looking grumpy. "He's mad because I didn't bring him any beef jerky."

We take the beachfront road all the way to the other side of the island. It would be a lot faster to take an inland road, but if we're going to be tourists, we have to do it right. It's important to remind ourselves of why we live in the Caribbean and sometimes, just taking a drive along the shore is enough. The water is gorgeous today. The blues are all clear and bright and it looks as if we could go out forever and still see down to the bottom. Whenever you talk to a sea captain or a dive instructor here, they will inevitably tell a tale of a tourist who came to visit and asked for a vial or a bottle so they could take some of the blue water home with them. It's an old wives tale, which doesn't stop just about everyone I know from telling it to tourists and locals alike as if it had truly happened to them.

Our first stop is the pier at East Beach. Sam and I live on the working class side of the island. Most of the people there have jobs and many are struggling to get by. There is quite a bit of poverty, but it is also rich in local culture. The east side of the island has all of the multi-million dollar homes and the huge, fancy resorts. This is where you can find the specialty food shops, the expensive jewelry stores, the trinket shops and the boutique clothing stores. We don't tend to spend a lot of time over here, but it is nice to drive over every once in a while, mainly because this side of the island hosts the cruise ships. There is no better place for people watching than in a crowd of cruise ship passengers. Parking the truck, we slip into the crowd of cruise shippers and move with the flow of people. Sam points out a man wearing a black mesh see-through shirt. "1980s gay dance club fashion," she whispers.

There are enough men wearing black dress socks with shorts and sandals that I stop pointing them out. We wander into a souvenir shop and Sam picks up a t-shirt that has two giant roosters with surfboards. The caption says, "Cocks on vacation."

"No, absolutely not."

"Come on," she wheedles. "We can get matching ones. It'll be perfect."

"Oh what the hell."

The saleslady barely looks at us as we approach the counter with the shirts. Sam clears her throat until the woman looks up. "We'd like to buy these please."

The clerk, who looks barely eighteen, sighs

deeply and drags herself over to the cash register. She rings up our shirts without smiling. Handing over the money, Sam says, "You may not like cruise ship passengers, but they're the reason you have a job."

"Yeah," the clerk replies. "Well, they leave trash everywhere. This island was beautiful before the cruise ships started coming."

"Cruise ships have been coming to this island since 1980. What year were you born?"

The young woman slams the change down on the counter and turns away from us. Sam calls after her, "I don't think it's cruise ship passengers throwing old refrigerators and used tires back in the bush."

"Come on." I pulled at her sleeve and we leave the store. "Why do you have to do that?"

Pulling off her Hawaiian shirt, she slips her new cock shirt on instead. Following suit, I do the same. Now we not only look like tourists, we look like idiot tourists. We wander back into the crowd and head for the main boardwalk. Sam is still fuming.

"Seriously, dude. What is wrong with you?"

She grimaces. "I just hate that bitchy attitude. If you work in customer service, you better damn well act as if you care about customers."

"Well, she's a teenager. They don't care about anything."

"I just hate that snootiness. Like she's doing us a favor to take care of our purchase. I don't get why cruise ship passengers ever come back here after getting that kind of attitude."

"They probably don't."

She opens her mouth to answer me, but is interrupted by a large hairy man in a "Cocks on vacation" shirt. He slings an arm around her and leans in close, whispering, "Hey, we have the same shirt. Great minds, right?"

"Uh huh," she responds. "Great."

Maneuvering out from under his arm, she rolls her eyes at me. Laughing, I show him my shirt. "It looks like we're all soul mates."

"Oh yeah," he yells. "Totally!"

He turns his head and yells back over his shoulder. "Hey, Bob! I found us our double dates."

"You've got to be kidding me," Sam mutters to me. "Only us."

"How drunk does a man have to be to hit on us?" I ask, laughing again.

"Well, I mean, we are sexy bitches."

"That part is a given. But we do look like dykes."

Bob has reached us and is grinning like an idiot. He's wearing tiny jogging shorts and a nylon tank top worthy of Richard Simmons. Trying to be subtle, I glance down at his feet and press my lips together to keep from laughing out loud at the obligatory black socks and sandals. He holds out his hand and I shake it.

"I'm Bob," he says. "Who are you?"

"I'm Dana, this is Sam, and we're leaving."

"Aw, come on," says the original guy. "We want to hang out with you."

"I mean, it's kind of fate," Bob says.

"Because of our shirts?" Sam is trying to look annoyed but I can tell she's having a good time.

"Yes. So come hang with us. It'll be fun."

"Look, guys," Sam says, grinning. "We're not interested. We're lesbians."

"Please, girlfriend," says the original guy, waving

a beefy hand around. "Do you think I can't recognize a couple of dykes when I see them? We're the gays."

Snickering, I take a second look at them. "Sorry, guys. I would never have guessed you as gay in a million years."

Bob puts his hand on his hip and cocks is chest forward. "Why is that?"

"Because you're dressed like slobs," Sam says.

"I'm dressed like Richard Simmons, for Liza's sake," Bob declares. "How could that not clue you in?"

"Anyway," the other man says, "we're on vacation. We can look as slobby as we want."

The big guy, whose name turns out to be Manny is excited to find out that we're locals and insists that we take them to a local gay place.

"There really aren't any particularly gay places around here," Sam says. "I mean, there is one gay bar on the island, but we'd have to leave the boardwalk to go to it."

"There won't be anything going on there at ten o'clock in the morning anyway."

"Well, where do homos hang out for fun?" Manny is dumbfounded.

"Manny, where are you from?" I ask.

"Santa Cruz, California?"

"So, civilization, basically."

He and Bob laugh and we decide to continue walking along the boardwalk instead of going to the bar. None of the stores catch their attention until we see a colorful sign advertising an adult novelty store a couple of streets off the boardwalk. Of course the guys want to go into it.

"Oh come on," Bob insists. "You wouldn't take us to the gay bar. The least you can do is let us look at

Caribbean theme dildos."

"It's a great idea," Sam says. "If I went in there with Dana, it would look as if we were shopping for something together. This way, it's just a group of friends going into a sex shop together."

"A healthy all American activity," I say, flatly.

"Come on," Bob grabs my hand and pulls me into the shop. Sam and Manny are already in there, giggling over penis shaped ice cube molds.

"I actually love these," Sam says. "I could make a bunch of them and bring them to Rick and Karen's party next week."

"Oh, straight people love penis shaped ice cubes," Manny squeals.

The shop is surprisingly full of tourists. I wouldn't imagine that sex toys would be high on the list of vacation souvenirs, but perhaps vulva shaped cookies and naked lady playing cards are popular amongst the cruising crowd. Approaching the front desk, I smile at the woman behind the counter. A slender black woman with a soft smile, and pretty eyes, she looks to be in her seventies. Her mostly gray hair is cropped close in what could almost be a buzz cut. She notices my discomfort.

"First time in here?"

"Yes," I reply. "If I were to purchase a sex toy, it would have to be through the anonymity of the internet."

"There is no anonymity on the internet," she counters. "The government knows everything you do...or buy."

"I don't disagree that they could find out anything about me that they want to know," I say. "That's supposing they actually want to know anything about me."

"True enough," she laughs. "You'd have to be pretty important for the government to care about whether or not you had ever bought a vibrator."

"I don't think I'm that important," I say, laughing.

"Oh, I don't know," she says, slyly. "The famous island writer. There are some who would be very interested in your sex toy purchases."

Given pause, I lean back a bit, studying her. It always throws me a bit when someone recognizes me in public. I don't generally put my pictures on my books and I rarely give interviews, so unless someone knows me in real life, they don't usually equate me with my books.

"My name is Nadia," she says, holding out her hand. "My daughter is a big fan of your books. One of my friends pointed you out in the crowd at the animal shelter donation drive last month."

"Well, that's cool. Now you can say that you saw one of her favorite authors at your sex shop."

She laughs. "My sister and I opened the store together many years ago. My former husband, may he rest in peace, was tolerant of the idea. He thought it was funny, though he refused to let me come to the store by myself after dark for many years."

"Have you been successful?"

"You'd be amazed by how much money we make, despite the religious majority on this island. Of course, having a sign on the boardwalk to direct tourists over was one of the smartest things we ever did."

We both look over at a particularly loud screech of laughter from the corner. Manny is waving a huge plastic vagina at Sam and she is doubled over laughing. Bob pretends to be fanning himself in front of a display of purple dildos. Looking back at Nadia, I wonder how a classy woman like her even thought to open a store like this.

"You're wondering why my sister and I didn't just open a sewing store or something," she grins.

"Not exactly, but it does seem a little unusual."

"My sister read something in a magazine about how stores like these were coming out of the closet, to use one of your people's terms."

Raising my eyebrow, I give her a piercing look. "My people?"

She laughs and continues. "We thought it would be a money maker. We decided it would be decorated nicely and beautifully lit with comfy chairs and classy window displays. We had to do a lot of fighting to get our permits, but eventually Sheba, my sister, had an affair with a guy in the city council and he pulled some strings."

I find other people's lives fascinating. I'm half-tempted to ask Nadia out for lunch so I can get her entire life story. "Is your sister still alive?"

"Oh yes," she answers. "She just had her eightieth birthday."

"Does she still work in the store?"

"Of course. She works a couple days a week. We're winding down now. Neither of us is as young as we were."

"Your daughter doesn't want to take over the store?"

"No, not in the least. She lives in the States now. I have a son who might consider coming back after he retires, but that's another fifteen years from now, and I somehow don't see myself selling plastic penises at eighty-five."

Sam approaches the counter with the men in tow as several more people enter the store. It's time for me to stop taking up her time. Sam slams an armload of penis and vulva shaped ice trays on the counter and pulls her wallet out of her shorts.

"Sam, you have got to be kidding me."

"Come on, it'll be funny."

"I want no part of this."

"Don't be such a spoilsport. I'm going to store them all in your freezer until the party."

"Nadia, it was such a pleasure to meet you," I say, holding out my hand to shake with her once more. She smiles warmly and tells me to come back anytime.

I introduce Nadia and Sam. When the men make it to the counter, I excuse myself to wait outside so I am not tempted to look at the basketful of merchandise that they have picked out. There are some things a person doesn't need to know.

Standing on the sidewalk, I lean back against the building, waiting for the group to finish so we can move on. Maybe I should buy the sex shop and run it for the rest of my life. I'd meet a lot of interesting people. People shuffle by and many give me a second glance. Whether that's because they recognize me or because I'm standing outside of an adult store wearing a cock t-shirt is hard to tell. I decide to make a game out of trying to make eye contact and smile at everyone who looks at me. Some of them smile back. Most cast their eyes away as soon as they know that I know they're looking. I probably should have majored in sociology or psychology. I could have gotten a grant to study the social habits of humans within a small, closed in ecosystem. Minus the addition of several thousand tourists every day, the population is pretty small here. On the west end, it is pretty common for me to run into a handful of people I know whenever I go out. On this side of the island, it isn't as likely. That said, there's my ex-girlfriend sauntering along the sidewalk in front of me. She hasn't seen me yet and I'm trying to decide if I should duck back into the shop or not. As I'm debating with myself, Sam and Manny come out of the shop and I turn toward them so my back is to my ex.

"Where's Bob?"

Manny rolls his eyes. "He decided at the last minute to get three more pairs of undies because they were on sale. We left him debating on the colors."

Sam holds up her bag. "I got all of the ice trays."

"Don't look, but she-who-shall-not-be-named is across the street."

Of course Sam immediately looks. "Well, she's not looking this way. She's talking to someone in the doorway of that store."

Half-turning, I move my head just enough to see her out of the corner of my eye. She isn't looking in this direction at all. She's engrossed in conversation with a long-haired woman in a flowing purple dress. The store is one I've been in a few times. It's a new age type place. They sell crystals and tarot cards and the woman in the purple dress gives readings. Another woman offers reiki out of the same store. I can't remember the purple dress lady's name, but I remember she once sold me a book on lucid dreaming. She's seems pretty legit, but I just can't buy into a lot of the hokey stuff she sells.

"They seem to be pretty involved," Manny says, as Bob comes out of the store, carrying two bags.

"Who seems involved?" Bob asks.

"My ex-girlfriend and that woman over there," I answer.

"They're involved?" Bob looks fascinated. "Oh, I love lesbian drama."

"Not like that. I just think we can get away while they're talking."

"Without a doubt," Manny says. He moves to the other side of me and his bulk almost completely obscures my ex from view. We all move as one in the direction of the boardwalk. When we are ready to turn the corner, I can't resist looking back over my shoulder. She-who-shall-not-be-named is looking straight at me. I can feel the ice in her glare all the way over here. I swear several minutes pass as we stare at each other and in that span of time, I can feel a hand gripping my chest, pulling the air out of my lungs. Sam puts her hand on my arm and the spell is broken.

"Are you all right, Dana?"

"I'm fine," I reply. "Let's go get some lunch."

Manny claps a hand across my shoulder. "Now that is a stellar idea."

Glancing back one more time, I see that my ex is still staring and now the woman with the purple dress is looking at me, too.

We get around the corner and I shake my head, trying to forget about it.

"Are you sure you're okay?" Sam whispers, putting her arm around me.

"I just hate the way she was looking at me."

"How?"

Shaking my head, I move on, pretending not to hear the question. I didn't want to talk about it to Sam, but for a second there, I was pretty sure that my ex wanted to kill me.

Chapter Fourteen

Standing in my sister's apartment, surrounded by tarps, tape, cans of paint, and facemasks, I ask myself yet again why I agreed to do this.

"Seriously, Susannah. Between playing tourist with Sam, rescuing Olivia, getting kidnapped by my ex, avoiding crazy dream lady, and doing your household chores, I barely have time for myself. How am I going to keep buying clothes for you to steal if I don't have time to work?"

Ignoring me, she continues doing the cut work along the ceiling. "So then what happened?"

"Then the guys bought us lunch and we walked back to the cruise ship pier."

"So how did you end up on the news?"

"Sam and the guys had several of the free rum samples meant for cruise ship passengers. When one of the ships started moving, she went running down the sidewalk with her shopping bags in hand yelling, "Wait for me, wait for me.""

Susannah bursts out laughing. "That's so like her."

"At any rate, she ended up slamming into a garbage can, flipped completely over it, and fell into the guy who plays the steel pan drum outside of Sandy's on the Strand."

Giving up the pretense of working, Susannah leans against the ladder and laughs. "I wish I had been there to see it."

"While she extricated herself from the man's drums, and Manny and Bob laughed their asses off, I talked the drummer out of calling the cops."

"So where did the news come in?"

"Channel eight was doing a piece on crime against cruise ship passengers and the reporter asked if we wanted to be interviewed. Before I could say no, Sam agreed. So there we were on channel eight in our matching cock shirts."

"Can I have that shirt?"

"Yeah, but I've already cut off the sleeves and the neck."

"Of course you did."

We paint together in silence for a while. I really do like my sister and I enjoy her company. She just knows how to push my buttons. That's what comes from being raised together, I guess. No one else in the world can ever really understand what it was like to have our exact formative experience, but a sister comes closer than anyone else. It pains me to see her becoming more and more like my mother, though. Thomas stopped over on his way to work to bring her doughnuts and coffee and she barely even thanked him. When I questioned her on it, she said it was the least he could do since he wasn't going to be here to help her paint. I started trying to explain to her that people want to feel appreciated, but then I decided it wasn't worth it. Besides, with my track record, I'm not really in a position to give dating advice to anyone. Sometimes I wonder if Voldemort and I would have worked out if I hadn't still been so fucked up over Fran. No, she has a host of other personality problems that really have nothing to do with me. Still, time was what I needed. I should never have considered getting involved with someone else so soon after Fran's death. I don't know what I thought would happen. I know my ex never got over the story in Annabelle Lies, though I feel I had given her enough background that she shouldn't have been overly shocked. It really was a work of fiction, after all. I explained that while it was based on my own life, I was writing it as fiction and as such, there was a lot in there that simply wasn't true. I don't know how much she believed. To be fair, I don't think I ever really treated her very well. Not that I want to get back together. I just think if I had been honest with her and with myself, I would have cut ties long before I did.

"Earth to Dana," Susannah says.

"Sorry, I was lost in thought."

"Obviously. What's on your mind?"

"I'm wondering if I ruined Jackie's life."

Shocked, Susannah rocks back, holding on to the ladder for balance. "Whoa, you said her name. Should I notify the papers?"

"Well, even Voldemort had a name in the books."

"Whatever will Sam say?"

"She'll cry."

Moving over with my roller, I make it to the last wall. Susannah has actually done a great job with the cut work. I have to give her credit, she had most of it done by the time I got here. Still. "You owe me one, you know."

"Yep. Let me know when you decide to decorate your house and I'll give you some fashion advice."

"I don't need fashion advice. I like my house the way it is."

"There's barely anything in it."

"That's the way I like it. Besides, Frank doesn't like flashy fabrics."

"Of course he doesn't."

There's a tap on the door and Susannah yells, "Enter."

Olivia pops her blonde head in the door and smiles.

"Oh, good, you're almost done."

Raising my voice an octave to match hers, I squeal back at her. "Oh good, you're here to finish up."

"Shut up, Dana," Susannah says before Olivia can open her mouth. "Olivia is going to take us out to dinner."

"Lovely. Where are we going?"

"There's this new sushi place on seventh. Thomas took me there last week and it was delicious."

"Sam hates sushi."

"Sam isn't invited," Olivia sniffs.

"Au contraire, my friend. I told her I'd get dinner with her when I was done painting. I'm done. I'm going to get dinner with my best friend. If I am also to get dinner with you, you're going to have to put up with her."

Putting away the paint and wrapping my roller, I turn my back on her. I don't really hate Olivia. I don't even really dislike her. She just doesn't have a great deal of bearing on my world.

"Fine," she snaps. "You can bring along your jerk best friend."

Gritting my teeth, I count to ten in my head. "Sam isn't a jerk."

"Why do you always defend her? She's a total asshole."

I whirl around, making her jump. "You know,

she wouldn't be so mean to you if you didn't complain all of the time. We all have problems. We're all trying to get by. It's just you seem to have this need to play some kind of pity me game, being so overly dramatic about everything that happens to you. People get flat tires. People sprain their ankles. A lot of people have it a lot worse than you do and they don't complain nearly as much."

Spinning back around, I knock into Susannah's ladder with my knee, and take a stumble onto the floor in front of it. The paint tray on her ladder shelf tips and burps a huge splash of paint onto my neck and back.

I breathe deeply for a three count. "Of course. Of course this happened."

Olivia and Susannah are pointedly looking anywhere except at me as I stand up and grab a roll of paper towels. "Of course. Of fucking course." Toweling myself off furiously, I walk into the bathroom and look into the mirror. I have smears of sea blue paint all over my neck and coming around to the front. There are dots of paint on my ear and in my hair. One side of my ponytail is completely blue. Shaking my head, I walk back into the kitchen and look at my sister. She meets my eyes and we both lose it, laughing until we're crying.

Finally, Susannah wipes her eyes and gets herself under control. "Well, at least it's a pretty color."

"Text Sam and ask her to meet us at the restaurant. I'm going to take a quick shower."

I jump out of the shower and vacate the bathroom so Susannah can get in there. Clean and naked, I stand in front of Susannah closet looking for something to wear. What kind of idiot shows up to paint without bringing clean clothes. I guess I could have had Sam meet me here and bring me something to wear, but it's too late. Listening to make sure the shower water is still running, I rummage through her drawers until I find a pair of men's khakis that look as if they'll fit. Checking another drawer, I find several shirts that used to belong to me. I throw one on and check myself in the mirror. Slicking my hair back into a ponytail, I nod and flex at my reflection. Not bad looking for a middle-aged woman. Might need to lose a couple of pounds around the middle. I've been noticing a bit of a paunch lately. Susannah walks in wrapped in a towel as I'm sucking in my stomach and flexing my biceps. Embarrassed, I lower my arms and pooch out my gut.

"What?" I grunt, pretending to scratch myself.

"You're the picture of class," she says, dryly. "When you're finished admiring yourself, can you get the hell out of my room so I can get dressed?"

Saluting sharply, I turn on my heel and stalk out of the room.

Olivia is standing in the hallway applying makeup in the mirror.

"Jesus, Olivia. It's eighty-eight degrees. How long do you think that makeup is going to stay on your face?"

"Mind your style, Dana, such as it is, and I'll mind mine."

"Whatever."

Stomping out to the living room, I gather up my keys, wallet, and cell phone and wander outside to wait next to the jeep. My cell rings as I close the door behind me.

"Hello?"

"Dana?"

"This is she."

"It's Esmé."

Sighing, I consider pretending that I have a bad signal. "How are you?"

"I'd like to see you."

"Well, I've got plans."

"It doesn't have to be today."

"I have plans tomorrow too."

I hear her sigh at the other end. "Look, Dana. I don't mean you harm. I'm just looking for some answers."

"And I've told you that I don't have any answers for you."

"Then let's agree that we can just get together and talk about Fran. Maybe we can help each other.'"

"I don't need help!"

Aware that Susannah and Olivia have come out of the house, I hold up a finger to let them know I need a minute.

"Look, I've got to go. I've got a thing."

"So when can I see you?"

"I'll see you at Rick and Karen's party next week."

"That's not what I mean."

"That's what you get."

I hang up and launch myself into the back of the jeep. Susannah deftly swings the jeep around while Olivia complains that the top being down will ruin her hair. She pulls a bandanna out of her purse and wraps it around her head. Leaning against the back seat, I stretch my legs over the center console and cross my hands behind my head. The sun is shining, the wind is blowing my hair around, and I'm on my way to have dinner with my sister and my best friend. Life could be worse. Closing my eyes, I relax my neck and try to clear my mind.

I'm sitting on a blanket with Fran. She's playing the ukulele, badly. If it was anyone else, I'd beg them to stop, but I love everything that Fran does. Her attention never stays in one place long enough to get particularly good at a thing. I found it for her at a flea market and couldn't resist picking it up. Fran loved music and she wanted to know how to play everything. She could just make out recognizable noises on the uke after six months of practice. I had offered to buy her formal lessons, but she said she couldn't possibly stand the discipline of having to show up to a regular appointment and have set practice pieces. There's an ant crawling on her leg, so I reach over to scoop it off and set it to the side of the blanket. She smiles at me and my heart explodes. I've never felt like this before. When she smiles, I feel a warm wave of pressure move up from my stomach to my heart and my chest swells with an emotion that I can only describe as love, inadequate though the word seems. She looks at me as her fingers strum out the little tune. As I reach up to touch her face, she shifts slightly, and the glare of the sun from behind her head makes it difficult to see her face. Peering into the light, I'm convinced that all I can see is a skull – a Fran shaped skull sitting on top of her skinny shoulders. A shudder runs through my body and though the thought of touching her is suddenly repulsive, I reach out anyway. She shifts again and her face is back. I stroke it gratefully, blinking back tears. "Dana," she says. "Am I going to die?" I tell her that we're all going to die and she shakes her head, either to refute me or to show disdain for my petty answer. She says that she knows I've seen it happen, she can sense it. Trying to shield my emotions from her is useless. Somehow, she always seems to read me. "Dana," she insists. *"I want to know if you've seen me die."*

"Dana. Hey, Dana." Susannah's voice yanks me out of my dream or whatever it was. She's standing next to the jeep, staring at my face. Olivia is applying fresh lipstick in the rear view mirror. The color of it has me fixated. It reminds me of something, but I can't pull it into my head. "Dana," Susannah calls again. "Wake up. We're here."

Forcing myself to come fully back, I sit up straight and pull myself over the wheel well of the jeep. "I must have fallen asleep."

"Well, wake up. It's time for dinner."

"Hey, by the time Olivia finishes putting on her lipstick, we'll be through the second course."

"Ha ha, Dana," Olivia says, slamming her lipstick into her purse and sliding out of the jeep. "You really crack me up."

"You and everyone else, baby," I say, taking her arm. Linking my other arm through Susannah's, I guide them both to the restaurant door.

"Oh, Dana," Olivia drawls as I hold the door open for her. "You're almost a gentleman."

"A gentlewoman," I correct.

"A gentle butch," Susannah adds.

"Ah hell, she's not a butch," Sam says from the other side of the waiting area.

We give each other one arm hugs. She greets the ladies and gestures toward the seating area. "I have a table already."

Olivia takes Sam's arm forcefully and marches her through the restaurant. Sam looks back at me in question, but all I can do is shrug. Susannah smiles.

"Olivia likes to make a scene and if she can't show up with a man on her arm, then she's going to show up with a woman."

"Sam's a good-looking dyke," I agree. "She's certainly a better catch than the porn star Olivia was dating the other night."

"Oh God," Susannah rolls her eyes. "Don't even mention him."

We reach the table and I hold a chair out for my sister. Olivia is already seated.

"All we ever do is eat," she complains. "There's nothing to do on this island but go out to eat or drink."

"Make your own fun," I answer. "Take a hike. Start a volleyball game. Go snorkeling. Learn to play the harmonica."

Flopping back in her chair, Sam rolls her eyes. "Please do not counsel her to learn the harmonica. I can picture her whipping it out at every bonfire and blasting all of our ears."

"Why are you such an asshole?" Olivia asks.

"Why do you take everything so personally?"

"It's hard not to take it personally when you're talking specifically about me."

"She's got a point there," Susannah says, picking up her menu.

"Okay, okay. I'm sorry for hurting your overly sensitive feelings," Sam says.

Interrupting before Olivia can respond, I ask my sister what we should order. She points out her favorite items on the menu and we make a plan. Sam flips to the back where they have food for non-sushi eaters and scans the page. "Here we go. Cheeseburger. It better be good."

"You're so worldly, Sam," Olivia says.

"I like meat, potatoes, football, and belching," Sam replies. "I'm an all-American butch."

"All-American redneck is more like it," Olivia sniffs.

"Give me a break. I saw that Country's Best Hits compilation in your car."

"So? You don't have to be a redneck to listen to country!"

"No, but it helps," I add.

The waiter brings our drinks and takes our food order. As he's leaving the table, I notice Mandy sitting across the room from us with a woman I vaguely recognize from The Sands. Elbowing Sam, I nod in their direction. "Who's that?"

"That's...ah...what's her name."

"Thank you. That's incredibly helpful."

"She used to date the woman who runs the chiro office on the east side.

I snap my fingers and nod my head. "Yeah, yeah, yeah. Oh God, what's her name?"

Olivia glances across the room. "That's Vickie Jane Lowry."

"How do you know?" Sam looks incredulous.

"I don't live under a rock. I know people."

"How do you know her?" Sam wants to know.

"She came on to me one night at The Loon. We talked for a couple of hours. She's a very nice woman."

"She's not at all nice," Sam replies. "She's a snooty realtor type. Why the hell was she hitting on you?"

"Wow, Sam. Jealous much?" Olivia asks.

Affronted, Sam snorts, but doesn't reply.

The waiter starts laying our food out on the table and Susannah grabs her chopsticks. She takes a

California roll, lays out a sliver of fresh ginger on top of it, dips it into the slightest bit of wasabi and holds it out to Sam. "Just try it," she cajoles.

"Forget it," Sam says, shaking her head. She takes a huge bite of her burger and pronounces it perfect.

Pretending to be enjoying my meal, I keep taking sidelong glances at Mandy and Vicki. I wonder if they're dating each other now. As I watch, Mandy takes a piece of food from her own plate and feeds it to Vicki. Her fingers linger on the other woman's lips. I wonder if my ex knows that Mandy is whoring around. Then again, why should I care? I guess I don't like her that much, but we do have a history. I don't want to see her get fucked over.

"It's probably none of my business," I mutter.

"What isn't?" Susannah asks with her mouth full.

"This is an expensive meal," I tell her. "Shouldn't you be savoring it instead of stuffing it in your mouth?"

She picks up a slimy-looking piece of fish and waves it around in front of me.

"You're disgusting," I say.

Sam swings her head in the direction of the women across the restaurant. "Are you bothered by that?"

"A little. I don't know why, though. I guess it's just that all of her other faults aside, Jackie was never a cheater."

"Oh my God!" Sam holds her fingers up in the shape of a cross. "You said her name!"

"Oh grow up, Sam!" Olivia glances across at the women again. "It's about time Dana stopped calling her Voldemort. I mean, what are you? Twelve?"

Sam shakes her head. "Why does everyone keep

saying that about us?"

Susannah pops another piece of sushi in her mouth and sighs. "God, this is delicious."

I force myself to eat several more bites before allowing myself to look back at the women. Mandy is falling out of her shirt. I swear we are about to witness a wardrobe malfunction in the middle of the restaurant. Catching my eye, Sam grins and looks back to the women. Vicki has one arm around Mandy. With her other hand, she is running her fingers over and into Mandy's extensive cleavage.

"Oh my!" Olivia is shocked. "That hardly seems appropriate."

"Well, Mandy is used to going to the Pit on her dates," Sam says. "This kind of behavior is not only tolerated, but welcomed there."

Popping the last piece of sushi into her mouth, Susannah laughs. "I once saw a guy shaving his dog at The Pit."

Reeling back, Sam almost chokes on her last French fry. "Is that a euphemism?"

"No. I mean, he was literally shaving his dog. He had clippers plugged into the wall and he was using them to shave his dog."

"Dogs aren't allowed in public restaurants," Olivia exclaims.

"The fact that there was a dog in the place is probably the least offensive part of the whole thing," I laugh.

"In his defense, he was cleaning up the hair as he went," Susannah adds.

I can't quite wrap my mind around the entire situation. "That's something, I suppose."

"Well, I think the Pit is awesome," Sam grins.

"And obviously Olivia doesn't have a problem with it since she was there with her hot date the other night."

Sam and I both laugh. Olivia kicks Sam under the table. "Fuck you, Sam."

"Aw, come on, Olivia. Seriously. You make fun of me all of the time. I can't say one thing about you going out with Ron Jeremy?"

"Why do you have to pick on me so much"

"You make it so easy," Sam says.

"You're just such an asshole about it."

"You're an asshole to me. You just take everything so personally. It's like you have to be so fucking dramatic all of the time. If you broke a nail, you'd go wailing to Susannah and demand bandages and some codeine. You're a drama queen and you want everyone to know it."

Olivia stands up, glaring. "Have you ever considered that what you call drama, I call feeling? Yes, I feel things? Yes, I cry over things." Her eyes start tearing up and Sam looks uncomfortable. "I'm sensitive. I'm afraid. And I don't want to have to face these things on my own. Should I know how to change my own tire? Yes. Does it make everything better to know that I have a friend who will come and stand by me when something unexpected like that happens? Yes." She's full on crying now. Sam stands up, too, and puts her hand awkwardly on Olivia's shoulder.

"Look, I'm so..."

Olivia interrupts her. "You're so sure of yourself and your place in this world. You know how to do stuff and you aren't afraid of anything. It's easy to take things lightly when you aren't afraid. Well, I've been beat up and assaulted and stepped on and laughed at and treated like a little girl who can't do anything for herself and if I'm going to be treated like shit, I'm going to get something out of it!"

She stalks out of the restaurant. The people at the next table are glaring over at us. "Mind your own business," Sam tells them. The woman mutters something to the man and they both shake their heads.

Standing up, Susannah throws her napkin down on the table. "Thanks a lot, you two. Really. I hope you feel really great about yourselves."

She starts for the door. "And you can pay the damn bill," she tosses over her shoulder.

Leaning back in her chair, Sam crosses her hands behind her head and closes her eyes. "I really do have a way with women, don't I?"

"To be fair, I didn't think you were that bad."

"I hurt her feelings. I kind of feel bad."

"And now we have to pay the bill. Thanks a lot."

"And by we, I think you mean you. I don't have any money until I get paid tomorrow."

Sighing, I reach for my wallet. "Of course you don't."

I signal for the bill and hand over my credit card to the waiter. He brings it back and I leave an overly generous tip to make up for the drama. Looking across the room as we stand to leave, I see Mandy slide over onto Vicki's lap. She's full on grinding against her. We have to walk past them to leave. As we get close to their table, Sam stops mid-step and stares at them with her mouth hanging open. The manager of the restaurant tears over to their table and taps Mandy on the shoulder. "This is not appropriate behavior."

"Oh please," Mandy says. "You're just saying that because we're women. If we were a hetero couple, you wouldn't have a problem with this."

"I have a problem with inappropriate behavior in my restaurant. I don't care who you are."

Vicki starts trying to release herself from Mandy. "Look, I'm sorry. I got a little tipsy."

"Just pay your bill and leave," he says.

Mandy rears back and glares at him without releasing her grip on Vicki. "I could sue you for discrimination."

Sam laughs loud enough that everyone involved in the strange situation turns to stare at her. Mandy narrows her eyes as she catches sight of us. "You two should be involved in this," she says, extricating herself from Vicki's lap. Standing up in a huff, she yanks down her skirt which has gotten bunched up around her hips. "This man is discriminating against our people."

"Mandy, we are so not your people," Sam snorts. "*Your* people are at The Pit having a contest to see who can fit the most peanuts into their mouths at one time."

"One of them will choke to death and his last words will have been, 'Hey honey, watch this.'" I add.

"God, you're so funny," she screeches.

Pulling herself to her feet, Vicki stands in front of me. She towers over me by about four inches and outweighs me by about eighty pounds. She looks like my old middle school gym teacher. She turns her back on me and motions to the manager of the restaurant. As she fumbles for her wallet to pay the bill, Sam and I make a quick departure.

"Hey," I hear her call from behind us, "I want to talk to you."

Ignoring her, I drag Sam by the arm. When we get to the truck, we jump in and Sam takes off.

"Never let it be said that we run away from a fight," Sam gasps, laughing.

"We didn't run away. We walked away quickly."

"Yes, I was practicing for the speed-walkers race at the mall."

Laughing again, I reach over and smack her on the arm. "We've managed to piss off four women this evening. Is that a new record?"'

"Not for me," she says, shaking her head.

"I think you should probably apologize to Olivia."

"Yeah, I'll call her after I drop you off." She fiddles with the radio until she finds a country song that she likes. "I really don't hate Olivia, you know."

"Yeah, I know."

She pulls up in front of my house and I pat her on the shoulder. "Call me tomorrow and let me know if you've made up with Olivia."

"And let me know if you make up with Susannah," she says.

"Please. She's my sister. We fight all the time and it's forgotten by the next time we talk."

"I wish all women were like that."

"No you don't."

She pulls off and leaves me alone in my yard. Staring across the yard toward the sea, I'm struck again by how beautiful it is. Even in the dark, I can see the whitecaps on the waves and I can almost hear them from all the way up here. Tempted by the starlight reflecting on the water, I wander up toward the front of the house and climb the outside stairs to the deck. Plopping down into a porch chair, I lean back and prop up my feet. Lost in the waves, I try to clear my mind of everything that has been going on in my life. Jackie's face appears and I turn it into a puff of smoke and watch it drift away. The same thing happens with Esmé and Susannah and Brad and Dr. B and the small fear that I might be wearing a tumor on my brain. They all turn to smoke and dissipate. The fog comes over me again and this time I let it.

Chapter Fifteen

For a few minutes, I can't make any sense of where I am. Then slowly, it comes to me that I must have fallen asleep on the deck. The plastic cover of the footstool has pressed a noticeable groove into the backs of my calves and they feel tender. Stretching each leg one by one, I bring myself into more of a sitting position. It's full dark and the moon has gone behind the clouds. I'll have to go back down the stairs and around the house to get inside, since I'm sure I didn't leave the sliding glass door unlocked.

Blinking up at the sky, I try to remember what I was thinking about before I fell asleep last night. I vaguely remember meditating myself into a peaceful state. After that, it's all a blank. My back is screaming as I drag myself to my feet. Actively forcing myself not to grunt and groan as I stand takes a force of will. My body feels so much older than I really am some days. Shuffling along the deck, yawning and stretching, I make my way to the stairs and around to the front door. Frank is patiently waiting on the counter next to his food bowl. Though it isn't empty, I give him a refill and change his water. I hop up onto the counter and sit there swinging my feet while he eats. His fur feels soft under my hands, and he purrs around mouthfuls of food as I stroke his back. Sometimes, I wish my life was as easy as Frank's seems to be. He has a pretty smooth life here. On the other hand, I did leave him alone all day and most of the night. I wonder if he was afraid of being alone or if he thought I wasn't coming back. We've reached a comfortable level of commitment in our relationship. I feed him, water him, pet him, and give him treats. In return, he gives me constant companionship and occasionally pukes on the one rug in my house. It's never that easy with women. Maybe I should just stay single and have cats for the rest of my life.

As long as I'm awake, I might as well be productive. Stripping off the khakis I borrowed from Susannah, I take a quick shower and put on clean boxers and a tank top. Back to the kitchen for a cup of tea and a snack. With cup and plate in hand, I wander into the front room and situate myself on the couch with my computer on my lap. Frank follows me in and sits on the other end of the couch. Two old grumps hanging out in the middle of the night. I have a deadline approaching on two articles for a magazine, so I knock those out first. They were mostly done anyway. I just had to put the finishing touches on them and get them in the proper format. Procrastination is my middle name. I've been working on the same novel for six months and I swear I only have it half finished. Admittedly, it took me two years to write *Annabelle Lies*, but I usually whip out these romance novels in a few months. Rereading what I have written to date isn't helping. None if it is interesting to me.

I must be the world's biggest hypocrite. I write all of these amazing love stories with super happy endings and in real life, I am the president of The Love Sucks Club. And it isn't just a joke, though we treat it like it is. I really do believe that love sucks. Even when I was with Fran, for whom I would gladly have died, I didn't find love to be some rosy and beautiful spiritual experience. It was tough and messy and painful. Fran was always going off into her own brand of craziness and I was always chasing after her to bring her back to the real world. So, I guess it is fair to say that I've never really been happy in love. I did love Fran. That's not in question. I loved her the way some people love a tornado. It's dangerous and unpredictable and if you get too close, you're going to get hurt. Doesn't stop people from chasing them. I think I even loved she-who-shall-not-be-named. Okay, okay, Jackie. I mean, I know I felt something for her, especially in the beginning. We had a good time together and even though I had quit drinking by then, we still seemed to have enough in common to make it work. We both loved the same authors and we could spend hours talking about our favorite books. In the beginning, when we were still new enough to not have that wall of resentment between us, we used to play Scrabble almost every night. Flipping over to a solitaire game from my latest manuscript, I move the mouse mindlessly, putting one card on top of another. Jackie wasn't a complete nutcase when we got together. She seemed kind of solid and ordinary and after the whirlwind with Fran, I thought it would be a welcome change to have a relationship that was kind of boring. Back to my manuscript. I erase about six sentences, write one, erase that one and five more. Back to the kitchen for more tea and I'm ready to work. Frank makes his blerting noise and comes over to my side of the couch. Scratching his head, I stare at the screen, reading over what I wrote the last time I sat here. I pound out a few more sentences. Slamming my computer shut startles Frank. "Sorry, old pal," I whisper, petting him on the head again.

Leaning back on the couch, I cross my hands behind my head and stare at the ceiling. It isn't writer's block. It's life block. And it all started when Esmé came on the island. Aw shit, to be fair, it all started with Fran. Let's go back even further then and say it all started when I was a child. Suddenly, I'm so tired I can't even face the short walk back to my bedroom. My computer goes on the floor under the couch so I don't step on it when I wake up in the morning. Pulling a thin blanket over myself, I stretch out on the couch, carefully lifting and rearranging Frank so as not to upset him. He walks around on my stomach for a few moments before settling back into a comfortable position. It's a muggy night and I wish I had thought to flip the ceiling fan on before stretching out. It's too late now, though. Even if I had the energy to get up, Frank wouldn't like it.

I'm kind of in that weird twilight area where my thoughts start to get a little stranger than usual and a kind of filter falls over my mind. I know I'm not sleeping, but I'm not completely coherent. Esmé is standing over me, telling me to go deeper into my subconscious. For a second, I'm sure I can feel my soul hovering over my body and I almost believe that I'm having an out of body experience.

"Open your eyes," I mutter to myself, but it's too late.

I'm on a cliff, looking over the side. Esmé is standing beside me, shouting something in my ear. The wind is whipping around us so hard that I can't hear what she's saying. Strands of her hair whip around so furiously that some of them hit my face with the force of a slap. Looking down, I can see the billowing shape of a red dress, floating down on the wind. *"You let her go,"* Esmé says. *"You let her go."*

"I know," I agree. *"I killed her."*

"She should never have been with you."

"I know that, too."

Swinging around to face me, she puts her hands on my face and tries to force me to look at her. Fighting, I shove her hands off. I can't take my eyes off the dress. It's still floating down and part of me knows that it's Fran, but I can't figure out why it's taking so long for her to fall. Esmé scratches at my face, trying to get my attention. "You killed her," she screams. "You did this!"

"I know," I whisper, knowing full well she can't hear me over the wind. *"I know I did."*

Dropping to my knees, I bow my head over the cliff, looking at the dress. "Fran," I yell. "Fran!" Suddenly, I'm in a panic and I'm screaming her name over and over, but it doesn't help because the only thing left of Fran is a red dress blowing in the wind at the bottom of the cliff.

Awake, I sit up, knocking Frank to the back of the couch. He grunts a mild protest, rights himself, and stalks down to the empty cushion beyond my feet. I'm sweating and my heart is pounding and for a few minutes, I know I'm on the edge of a panic attack. Grabbing my cell, I send a text message to Esmé asking if she's awake. She responds immediately by calling me.

"Of course I'm awake," she says instead of hello.

"I think we need to talk," I answer.

"I agree. Do you want to meet for breakfast?"

"No, let's meet for dinner. Can you come over here? I'll cook."

She pauses. "Is this a date?"

"Don't flatter yourself. I need to talk about Fran."

"What time?"

"Six."

Hanging up the phone, I reach down to grab Frank and cuddle him to my face. I ask him what the hell is wrong with me, but he doesn't have any answers. Neither do I. Looking out the window, I see that it's close enough to sunrise that I can get up and make some coffee. Every day is a new chance to change your life. That's what Fran used to say to me. As I stumble into the kitchen, weary to the bone, I don't know if I find that comforting or terrifying.

Chapter Sixteen

For some reason, making the date with Esmé has cleared my mind a bit. I don't know why, but I just have a feeling that she might be able to help me through this if I will just let her in. Feeling better than I have in days, I bust out a full chapter of my book before taking a break. Brewing another pot of coffee, I look at the clock and decide it's late enough in the morning to call Sam. Before I can dial her, she's calling me.

"Hello?"

She sounds cheerful. "Dude, what's up?"

"Sam, I was just about to call you."

"And I called you instead. What are you doing today?

"I was going to call and ask if you want to go hike to the lighthouse."

"That's exactly what I was planning."

"Sounds awesome. Want to pick me up?"

"Yep. I'll be there in half an hour."

Hanging up, I pull on some cargo shorts and lace up my hiking boots. My walking stick is in the back of Sam's truck, so all I have to do is fill up a water bottle.

"I'm going out, Frank."

He looks up at me from his spot on the counter and chirps.

"I will have a good time. Thank you."

He chirps again.

"Really? Then what happened?"

Bored, he lifts his leg and commences licking himself. So much for that conversation. I'm ready to go when Sam pulls in. When I open the door for her, she gives me a half hug and heads for the coffee pot. "Got any brewed?"

"Yep, help yourself."

She takes one of my travel mugs from the cupboard and fills it up. Watching her stop to talk to Frank, I wish for not the first time that there was any kind of chemistry between the two of us. Logically, I think we would make a perfect couple. Yes, we're both on the butch end of the scale, but we get along so well. We respect each other, we laugh at each other's jokes. She can't cook for shit, but I can. Besides, other than changing a tire, I'm basically lost on any kind of car repair, whereas she's a genius at fixing anything. We'd complement each other well. Still, there is that complete lack of desire on either side. That's what proves to me that we were sisters in a past life. She's still my sister. And I guess it's better to have a lifelong friend than yet another girlfriend. She's too normal, anyway. I'd never be able to be involved with someone who wasn't psychotic in some way.

Sam notices that I'm staring at her. "Are you checking me out again?"

"In your wet dreams."

"Oh baby."

"I feel as if I've had this same conversation with myself a million times."

"Which one?"

"The one in which I chastise myself for not being attracted to you."

She flexes her biceps. "Yeah, I don't get that

either. I mean, I'm hot."

"Put it away stud. Your bulk does nothing for me." We wave goodbye to Frank and I lock the door behind us.

Sam smacks me on the shoulder. "Let's go. I don't want to keep the girls waiting."

Suspicious, I look at her. "What girls?"

We walk out to her truck and get in. "Uh, Olivia and Susannah."

It takes a minute for my mind to wrap around what she has just said. "Olivia and Susannah are going hiking with us."

"It's kind of a long story," she says, backing out of my yard and turning around on the road.

"You have ten minutes."

"A funny thing happened on my way to... Aw, fuck. I just called Olivia to apologize for being such an asshole and one thing led to another and I asked if she and Susannah wanted to go hike with us."

"And if I hadn't been available?"

"You always want to go to the lighthouse."

She has a point there. It's a long, uphill climb, steeper than our other regular hike, but shorter. I like it because I'm breathing like a freight train by the time we get to the top, but once we're there, we're looking at one of the most beautiful views on the island. The lighthouse is rusted and falling apart, but I can still climb the staircase inside, as long as I skip a few steps and am willing to live with the possibility of falling to my death. Sam likes it because we can take pictures from up there that truly show off how far we've come. She likes to send them to her sort-of girlfriend back in the States.

We drive along in silence for a few minutes.

Finally, Sam taps my arm. "Hey, are you mad?"

"Huh? No, not at all. I actually do enjoy spending time with my sister. I think it will be fun. I'm just surprised."

"I was surprised, too. She was just complaining again about how there's nothing to do on the island and I told her that she obviously had never been to the lighthouse. She hadn't, so there ya are."

"Well, it should be interesting, if nothing else," I laugh. "My sister hates to get sweaty."

"I figure we'll set a brisk pace and wear Olivia out. By the time we get to the top, she'll be too out of breath to annoy me."

Susannah and Olivia are waiting for us in the clearing where we usually park. From here, we'll walk through the woods until we find the path up to the lighthouse. The first part of the hike is pretty easy, but it has a gradual incline which warms us up for the big climb.

As we exit the car, Sam says, "Olivia, what the hell are you wearing?"

After hugging my sister, I turn to look at Olivia. It looks as if she raided L.L.Bean. She has cuffed khaki shorts with a perfect crease, a bright pink polo shirt, white socks with a bright pink band that folds down perfectly to show right above the top of what look to be brand new hiking boots. Sam is bending over to look at the top of Olivia's socks. "Are those little hearts?" she asks incredulously.

Ignoring her, Olivia turns to me. "The only thing new about my outfit is my boots. I didn't have any appropriate footwear for this occasion."

"What about tennis shoes?" I say.

"The guy at the sporting goods store said they

wouldn't have enough traction for the steep climb," she answers, staring at all of our sneaker-clad feet.

"Well, I hope you don't get blisters from wearing new boots," Sam says.

"Way to have a positive attitude, negative Nelly," Olivia laughs.

"Me?" Grabbing our walking sticks from the back, Sam grins across the truck bed at Olivia. "That's a change of pace."

"Maybe I'm turning over a new leaf. I'll become a Pollyanna."

Sam rolls her eyes. "I only have one extra walking stick." She hands the extra to Susannah and gives hers to Olivia.

"Want to use mine?" I offer.

"No, I'll find one on the path."

Starting up the first part of the path, we all spend a few minutes finding our rhythm. Despite her threats, Sam sets a decent pace. We're going fast enough to gradually raise our heart rates, but not fast enough to have someone passing out in five minutes.

Sam takes the lead, with Susannah and Olivia right behind her. If someone needs a break or stumbles, I won't have to worry about losing sight of them. Susannah is already breathing heavily by the time we get up the slight incline onto the wooded path. Sam pauses for a second to look back at all of us.

"You okay, Susannah?"

"Fine," she says, shortly. "I just have loud breath."

Laughing, I wink at Sam over her head before she turns around to continue on.

The incline changes and I can feel my breath starting to pick up. Olivia picks up her pace and comes abreast of Sam. Scanning the woods, Sam finally sees a suitable branch for her walking stick. She grabs one from the ground and peels off the side branches. "This is perfect," she says.

"I don't know," Olivia answers. "It doesn't look as sturdy as these."

She's right. Our regular walking sticks are strong and sturdy. Sam and I picked the sticks carefully, sanded them, and coated them with several layers of polyurethane. Then Sam drilled small holes in the top to string through with leather straps.

"Whatever," Sam says. "What do you know about walking sticks?"

"Nothing, I guess."

Susannah is flagging, so I motion for her to stop and pull out my water bottle. She takes a gulp. "Sorry, Dana. This is just not my thing."

"You should consider making it your thing," I say. "You may be young and skinny now, but soon enough, you'll be an old woman like me and you'll need all of the help you can get."

"Ha. You're only four years older than me. And I'm in perfectly great shape."

"You were about to pass out there."

"Hardly. And this is a tough climb."

"It hasn't even started to get tough yet."

"Great." She takes another chug of water. Handing it back to me, she stomps off. Looking after her, I see that Sam and Olivia are waiting for us at the top of this hill. Sam is leaning on her stick and Olivia is laughing. Maybe being told that she's a drama queen was good for her. Perhaps she'll start trying to change her attitude. At any rate, she's being a lot less annoying than she usually is and I'm surprised to realize that I'm not even upset that she's here.

When Susannah and I finally make the top of the hill, Sam high fives me and puts her arm around Susannah. "Are you going to make it, buttercup?"

"I doubt it. Can you carry me?"

"Probably," says Sam, laughing. "But we'll both regret it at the top."

"You'll be fine," I add. "The next hill is longer, but it's nowhere near as steep. Then there's a sharp turn and one incredibly steep hill."

"Steeper than this?" Susannah looks dubious.

"Yes," Sam says. "But not as long."

Dancing around a bit, Olivia looks anxious to go. "Well, let's move on then."

"Jesus, Olivia, settle down." Sam sounds as cranky as ever, but she's smiling and Olivia laughs instead of getting pissed.

Bending at the waist, Susannah struggles to catch her breath. "Look, Su, if you need to stop, I'll stay with you," I say.

"No, I'm good. I just can't believe how much better shape the rest of you are. Especially Sam."

"Why me?"

"Because you drink beer like it's water," she says.

Grinning Sam wags her finger at Susannah. "Ah ha. But I also drink plenty of water and get a lot of cardio. There's the difference."

"You eat spam and beef jerky," Susannah retorts.

"Only when your sister isn't cooking for me."

"Maybe you and Dana should get married," Olivia says, starting to move on.

We all follow her.

"No, that would be queer," Sam says.

"Why?" Olivia is laughing, but she looks honestly

interested.

"Butches don't date butches," Sam replies.

"Not true," I counter. "My ex was a butch. I knew a lot of butches in the States who date butches."

"Are you saying you want me, Dana? Because I'm not sure how I feel about that at this late date in our friendship," Sam grins.

Rolling my eyes, I snort my answer. Susannah is panting beside me, but she seems to be okay, so I decide not to call a halt for a break.

Olivia keeps prodding. "So some butches date butches and some date femmes?"

"Yes," I say. "But don't simplify it. Some lesbians consider themselves femmes who will strictly only date butches and vice versa. Some femmes will only date other femmes. Some butches will absolutely only date other butches. Some don't care whether their partner is butch or femme and tend to get together with either, depending on other factors. And some lesbians don't label themselves as either butch or femme."

"Don't forget the varying degrees of butch and femme," Sam continues. "I mean, I am definitely way butcher than Dana."

Raising my eyebrow at Olivia, I tilt my head toward Sam. "And then there are the butches who are so insecure in their butchness that they have to put themselves higher on some imaginary butch scale."

"Hardy har," Sam says.

"My ex was like that," I say. "She didn't like other butches and she was constantly putting down women who didn't live up to her grunting and oil-changing brand of butchness."

"But you consider yourself butch?"

Nodding, I think about it for a second. "I guess

I fall close to the butch side of the scale than not. It isn't a label that makes a big difference to me, though. I mean, I don't wear it like a badge of honor or a point of pride like some butches. I just am what I am."

"Well, I think it sounds totally confusing. Like, if two butches get together or two femmes, who is supposed to lead on the dance floor?"

"Oh Olivia," Sam says, as we round the corner to the last hill. "You couldn't possibly hope to understand. You may be wearing a polo shirt, but you're no dyke."

"Whatever, Sam!" Affronted, she pulls ahead of Sam and starts stalking up the last hill, pounding her walking stick into the ground in front of her. "I'm down with the lesbians," she calls over her shoulder. "I've read Curious Wine. I listen to Crys Matthews!"

"Who's Crys Matthews?" I ask.

"What's Curious Wine?" Sam responds.

Sighing, Susannah glares at both of us. "You two are so ignorant of lesbian culture."

"You're just cranky because you're tired," I say, patting her shoulder. "You'll feel better at the top."

"Yeah," Sam says, turning back to the path. "This is the hardest one, but it will be over soon."

She looks up the hill. "Olivia," she calls. "You should stay with us. This part is steep and you might need help." She slams her walking stick down on the ground in front of her and it shatters as she's making her first step. Before I can react, she tumbles to the ground and lands face first in the dirt. Olivia hears the commotion and comes running back to see if she's okay. It's a good thing she does, because I am laughing too hard to be of any help. Holding on to the side of a tree, I lean over, laughing until I can't breathe as Sam pulls herself off the ground and kicks at the broken pieces of her makeshift walking stick.

She turns to glare at me for a second before she starts laughing as well. Olivia hands Sam's walking stick to her. "Take this," she says. "I honestly don't need it and you obviously do."

Sam takes it begrudgingly and we all start off again. This section really is terribly steep and I find myself leaning on my walking stick more often than not. Olivia is in the lead now and she's just traipsing lightly up the hill without pausing to catch her breath.

"Let her go ahead," Sam huffs. "It's safe enough for her to wait for us at the top."

Susannah is breathing heavily and her face is beet red. I ask her if she wants to stop, but she shakes her head.

"Are we almost to the top," she manages to sputter.

"Yep," Sam says. "Less than five minutes."

Just when I think I can't possibly push my lungs any further; there is a sharp increase in elevation. Susannah looks at it and says, "I can't possibly do that."

"You can," Sam says. "This part is the shortest yet. It's the last push."

We all take deep breaths and bend into the last leg. Susannah leans on her stick with one hand and grabs for a tree branch with the other. From behind, I put my hand on her butt and push her up the last couple of steps. The ground flattens out and we are looking at almost the entire island from the highest point. Olivia is standing in the middle of the field, close to the lighthouse, staring out to sea. Looking over her shoulder at us as we stumble, panting and sweating into the open, she laughs. "This was so worth it."

Sam bends over for a second until she's breathing normally again. "Don't sit down, Susannah. Walk around slowly a bit until you catch your breath."

"This is unbelievable," Susannah says, after she can breathe again. "I can't believe I've never seen this before."

"It's kind of a pain to get here, that's for sure," I reply.

"We love it, though," Sam says. "Dana and I used to make a point of doing this hike twice a week. We need to get back into that."

"Agreed," I say. My breathing has returned to normal, so I spread out on the ground in the sun. It's windy up here, but it's hot and sunny, so the wind just serves to cool me off a bit. Susannah plops onto the ground next to me and rummages in her bag for some trail mix. Olivia is still wandering around, checking out the view. She actually looks kind of pretty right now. With her cheeks a bit flushed from the climb and her hair hanging loose around her shoulders instead of teased into a hair sprayed helmet, she doesn't look as phony as she usually looks. I like her face much better without the layers of makeup. And the outfit, ridiculous though it is, looks cute on her petite frame. Susannah catches me checking her out and elbows me. "Stop it."

"Stop what?" Sam looks around, smiling. She loves it up here. I think the only thing that would make it better would be if we could get some kind of pulley hook up so we could load up on beer and food. She would never want to leave.

"Dana is giving Olivia the eye," Susannah says, smugly.

Shocked, Olivia turns around, raising her eyebrow at me. "Really?"

"Well, you look really pretty today," I say.

She makes a disbelieving noise and turns back to look at the water.

"It's true, though," Sam says. "You do look pretty with your face all natural and your hair down like that."

"Well, anyway, I want to go climb into the lighthouse."

"Give me a fucking break, we just got here," Sam says, flopping down on the grass on the other side of Susannah.

"Fine, I'll wait." Olivia walks over to the other side of Sam and sits down next to her. "I didn't realize you were still recovering from the hard hike up here."

"Your false pity and harsh sarcasm haven't gone unnoticed," Sam replies.

Olivia laughs and again I'm struck by how pretty she is. Sam has obviously seen it too, as she leans close to Olivia for a moment, and pulls a leaf out of her hair.

"Olivia," Susannah says. "How the hell are you in such great shape? You don't hike, you don't swim, you don't dive, and you work in an office all day."

"Yes, but I do Jillian Michaels videos every morning," she answers. "There's not a single thing these two yahoos could have put me through that can compete with that evil bitch."

"Maybe I should start doing that," Sam says.

"Maybe," Olivia answers. "It would help you get rid of that beer belly."

"What beer belly?"

Laughing, I close my eyes, half-listening to their bickering. The wind blows across me, keeping me cool at the same time that the sun is warming my skin. I can't believe how happy I feel at this moment. Susannah and Olivia are both laughing at something Sam has said. Letting their voices flow across me without actually picking up the words, I close my eyes and soak in the warmth of the sun. If I could bottle this feeling from this moment, I could be happy for the rest of my life.

Half-aware that the other three have gone to go check out the lighthouse, I snuggle a little more comfortably into the grass. I once looked into who owns this land. I thought, if I could buy it, I'd put a tiny little hidden dirt road in for those times when I absolutely had to get supplies up here. The rest of the time, anyone who wanted to come see me would have to take the hike to get here. I'd put in a zipline down to the clearing where people park, though, so they'd have the option of leaving quickly if they want. I'm half-asleep when I hear the ladies come back from exploring the lighthouse. Propping myself up on my elbows, I open my eyes just in time to see Susannah stumble and trip. She disappears over the cliff and my heart stops in my chest. Up in a flash, I take a couple of running steps toward her when I see her sit up, laughing and rubbing her knee. Sam reaches down to help her up and Olivia brushes off her knees. I manage to stop running, but my hand is clutching my chest and I can't breathe.

"Jeeze, Dana." Susannah is still laughing as she realizes I'm standing there. "I just tripped."

For a moment, I can't speak. My body is frozen and I'm struggling to get a word out. Finally, I suck in a breath and advance on my sister, shaking my finger in her face. "Stay away from the edge," I shout. "Stay away from the fucking cliff!"

"I wasn't anywhere near..."

Sam interrupts her with a shake of her head. She puts her hand on my shoulder and gently guides me away from Susannah. "Come on, old buddy," she whispers. "Let's take a walk."

We wander off to a secondary path as Olivia and Susannah settle down onto the grass again.

"Are you okay, bud?" Sam looks concerned.

"I'm actually fine," I say, bending my head for a moment. Touching my fingers to my forehead, I close my eyes for a few deep breaths. "It scared me when she fell."

"She's fine, though."

"I know."

Sam gives me a quick one-arm hug. "You need to work through it, my friend. It's been a long time since she died."

We walk quietly back to the ladies and stretch out beside them on the grass again. Watching the clouds change shape, I bring myself back into a more peaceful place. Susannah softly sings a song that I've never heard before. Something about birds in migration. The tune is easy to pick up and within a few minutes, everyone is singing. After a while, Sam stirs. "I think it is safe to say that Dana and I have never sang a song up here."

Everyone laughs.

"See? We're good for some things," Susannah teases.

Sam reaches over to gently pull a lock of my sister's hair. "You're good for a lot of things, my almost sister."

Olivia stretches. "I think I'm ready to go."

We gather up our belongings and head to the trailhead. "Going down will be easier," Sam calls over her shoulder. "But you'll need the sticks to help keep your balance."

Susannah and Olivia follow us as we silently walk down the hill. No one speaks until we get out of the woods and onto the last stretch before the car. Then, Susannah approaches me cautiously. "Are you still mad at me?"

Turning abruptly, I put my arms around her and hug her. "I just saw you fall," I whisper. "I lost it."

"You saw me fall and your mind took you someplace else," she responds. "But it didn't really happen, so you need to let it go."

"It's just that I saw it."

Sam touches my shoulder as she walks by. "It wasn't a premonition, Dana."

"Come on," Susannah says, guiding me to her jeep. "I'll give you a ride home."

We toss our walking sticks into the back of Sam's truck and walk to the jeep. Olivia pauses, looking a little awkward. "I'm sure you two want some private time to talk, so I'll get a ride home with Sam." Glancing at Sam, she pauses again. "I mean, if that's okay."

"Uh, yeah. I guess. I mean, I don't see why not." Flustered, Sam waves goodbye to us, and gets into her truck with Olivia. Susannah gives me a look and I grin at her before hopping into the jeep.

"Well, that's interesting," she says, sliding behind the wheel.

"I'm sure it's nothing," I say. "They hate each other."

Despite Susannah's attempts to engage me in conversation, I refuse to talk about what happened at the lighthouse. Instead, I stare out the window and think about Esmé and our meeting this evening. It's time for me to get some answers, and I'm betting on her being the one to help me get them. Susannah drops me off at my doorstep and admonishes me not to wear myself out. That's not likely. The only thing on my agenda is to take a shower, change my clothes, and work on my manuscript for a few hours before dinner.

Thinking about Esmé, I toss some vegetables into a marinade and season a couple of salmon filets. I actually have no idea what she eats. If she doesn't like this, I'll make her a salad or a peanut butter and jelly sandwich.

It doesn't really matter what we eat, anyway. She's not coming here for my fine cooking and I haven't invited her to experience her scintillating company. As far as I know, we have one thing in common and that's Fran. If she can't help me sort out my head, I don't think there's anyone who can.

Chapter Seventeen

Esmé shows up promptly at six. I already have the coals going on the grill, so I offer her a drink and we step out onto the deck. The sun is starting to do its brilliant show in the western sky. My deck is the perfect place to watch it. It occurs to me that if I wasn't so fucked up, I would be a total chick magnet. I'm decent looking, I have a decent income, I cook, and I have a phenomenal house. Of course, I don't have a car, I'm middle-aged, and I'm in the midst of some sort of weird psychic meltdown. Other than that, I'm a great catch.

Perched on one of my patio chairs, Esmé is idly stroking Frank who has claimed her lap. Traitor. She smiles up at me. "So, Dana," she says. "What do you want to talk about?"

I'm fully aware that she has dressed for this evening without wanting to look as if she's dressed for the evening. She's wearing nicely shaped jeans and a peasant blouse that shows just a hint of cleavage. Her hair still has that dampish, fresh out of the shower look, and she smells amazing. She isn't wearing makeup, but her lips are shiny, like she put on lipgloss right before walking in my door. Despite myself, I feel the bit of stirring from inside that comes from being close to a pretty woman who has made an effort to make herself attractive to me.

Throwing the filets and the vegetables on the

grill, I smile at her, but don't answer. We both know why she's here, but I don't want to address it yet. We need to eat. Besides, I don't think it's going to be a pleasant conversation and I haven't completely decided if I'm ready to have it. Esmé has offered to help, but I don't need it. I'm in my element, flipping the fish and making sure the vegetables are done to a perfect texture.

"If you want to refill that glass, now's the time to do it," I tell her. She goes into the kitchen and mixes herself a drink. When she returns, she hands me a glass of water and resumes her place on the chair, apologizing to Frank for having disturbed him.

"He can't sit on your lap while you're eating dinner anyway," I say, sternly.

Frank turns his head, blinks at me, and then pointedly turns back to Esmé, launching himself back onto her lap. She laughs, delighted. "He is so obedient!"

"Cats are never obedient," I growl. "I sometimes kid myself, but we both know who's in charge of this household."

Laughing, she pets Frank until I can hear his motor across the deck. The remaining sunlight is picking up the gold flecks in Esmé's hazel eyes. When she smiles, my stomach flips a bit. Shit. Forcing my mind back to the mundane, I finish cooking our meal and set the plates on the outdoor table. There's no sense in going inside when it's still eighty degrees. Esmé divests herself of the furball and joins me at the table. She closes her eyes at the first bite of fish and makes a soft, almost inaudible moaning noise under her breath.

"This is ridiculously good," she says, smiling. "Maybe the best fish I've ever had."

Chatting lightly throughout the meal reveals next to nothing about her. She has an amazing ability to entertain without telling me a single thing about her. But two can play at that game and I can keep my cards close to my chest when I need to do so. Consequently, we spend the meal laughing and casually flirting without addressing the real reason we're together tonight. After dinner, she offers to do the dishes, so we clean up together. Coming up behind her where she's standing at the sink, I wrap an apron around her and tie it in the back. Turning her head slightly puts us eye to eye.

"Thank you," she says.

"I didn't want you to get your beautiful shirt wet," I answer.

Smiling, she turns back to the sink and resumes washing dishes. I put the leftovers away and go back out to the deck to clean up the grill area. Esmé is just finishing the dishes when I come back in to check on her.

"Shall we put these away?"

"No," I say. "They can air dry."

"Good," she says. "Then maybe we should talk about why I'm really here."

"I thought you were here for my cooking," I grin.

"Or your rugged good looks and lively conversation."

"I am pretty good looking," I grin. "But I haven't really been much of a lively conversationalist with you."

"You didn't trust me," she says. "I get that."

"To be honest, Esmé, I still don't trust you."

Bowing her head, she walks away from me. Maybe I shouldn't have said that. I have a habit of saying shitty things to women. It isn't so much that I'm a jerk. It's just that I'm stupid. It's different when I'm hanging with Sam. If I say something stupid to her, she smacks me on the head and we move on. Of course, she says stupid shit all of the time too, so maybe it's easier for her to be forgiving. The thing is, I don't trust Esmé yet. I like her, and my body is definitely telling me that she's an attractive woman, but my body can't always be trusted to do what's best for me. She's out on the deck now, petting Frank and I know that I've hurt her feelings.

"Look," I say, walking out to the deck and sitting beside her. "It isn't that I don't like you. I do. I think you're very sweet and charming. It's just that I don't really know what your motivations are and it makes me feel a little uncomfortable."

"My motivation is that I want to know what happened to Fran. I want to know why she died. I came here with the intention of hating you. Do you know that?"

"I can understand it. I hated myself for a long time."

"Sounds like you kind of still do."

Turning away, I reach across her to pet Frank. He responds by chirping his little meow and rubbing his head against my hand. For a big man, he has such a tiny little sound. Leaning against Esmé feels so nice. It's a hot night and our skin feels warm where we're touching. Part of me thinks that if I tried to kiss her right now, she would respond. Maybe we'd go to bed together and we could forget about having this conversation. Moving my mouth close to her ear, I hesitate for a few beats. Her body is responding to my breath on her ear and she leans a little closer. Pulling back a bit, I rest my forehead against the side of her face.

"Okay, so what do you want to do?"

She's dead silent for a few seconds and it occurs to me that she's having the same struggle I am. Finally, she shifts. "Let me walk you into a meditation. We can go into your mind and go to the night that Fran died."

"Look, Esmé. I don't need to delve into my subconscious to tell you what happened to Fran."

"I want to know it from Fran's side."

"You can't. You can only know what I saw and I can tell you that without any help."

"Just humor me," she says. "I know you have these visions. I know you've seen things that others can't see. I know you predicted Fran's death."

"Esmé, *Annabelle Lies* was a work of fiction. It drew from my real life, but it isn't a diary. You can't believe everything you read."

"If it wasn't for that book, I wouldn't be here on this island. All I knew of you is that you were the woman Fran was dating when she killed herself."

"That's still true. I could have saved her."

"Let's just try, Dana. That's all I'm asking. I just want to try."

She guides me to the outdoor love seat and puts a pillow under my head. Closing my eyes, I rest my head against the pillow. It feels as if my whole body is sinking into the love seat. It's too short for me, so I drape my legs over the wicker arms. Why am I so tired all of a sudden?

Esmé's voice is soft and sweet and for another moment, I think that I can end this by pulling her down here with me. The next thing I know, I'm drifting. I can feel her hands on my head, and I'm aware that it feels good, but before I can say anything about it, I'm in the other world.

I'm in Fran's apartment. Looking around, I see the thrift store furniture and the mattress on the floor. This place is depressing. I asked Fran to move in with me several times, but she said it wasn't time. I know she was right, but I hated that she lived here. The only homey touches in the places are Fran's little pieces of art. Wire sculptures, ceramics, small paintings, framed photos cover every surface in the place. She never stuck to one medium and she never mastered any of them. She was just so full of creative energy that she couldn't contain it. Picking up one of the little sculptures, I turn it in my hand. There's dust on it. I blow at the dust and it flies up into the air, making me sneeze. "Bless you," Esmé *says. I turn to face her, somehow not surprised to see her. She leans forward and kisses me lightly on the lips. When she takes my hand, I look down at our entwined fingers and I realize that I'm not myself. I'm Fran. I'd recognize those long, slim fingers and those freckled hands anywhere. "You're not really here," I whisper to Esmé.*

"I'm not really here," she whispers back.

We move around the apartment together. It looks empty and it smells moldy and unclean. I don't know how long it's been like this. Why hasn't someone cleaned everything out? She picks up a picture of me, of Dana, and holds it out to me. Like the sculpture, it's covered with dust. Taking the picture in my hands, I blow on it, again throwing up a big cloud into the air. "She saw me die," I say. "She saw me jump over the side of a cliff."

"But you're not going to die," she replies.

"I'm already dead," I whisper.

I release her hand and walk away from her. In

a moment, I'm on the cliff. I look back and see Dana sitting on the blanket. She has already told me not to get so close to the cliff, but I haven't listened. She's been over-protective since she had the vision that night in the car. Besides, the orbs are here and they want me to stay with them. They spin around me in little balls of light and heat. Dancing along the side of the cliff, I glance back at Dana again. Her face looks so tense that I relent a little and come back a few more feet from the edge. The orbs follow me gleefully. The wind lifts my skirt and my hair and suddenly I'm laughing and the whole world is filled with a brilliant gold light. The air smells delicious. Looking back at Dana again, I see that she has relaxed. "The orbs," I shout, but she shakes her head. Over the wind, I think she says that there are no orbs. She looks worried again. She worries too much. Sometimes, I push up the corners of her mouth with my fingers to force a smile. Once, when she was frowning, I bit her nose and she laughed until she cried. My heart swells when she laughs. I love her. I am filled with such a radiant love for her that sometimes it's unbearable. But my love isn't just for her. My love has to spread and grow and fill all of the dark places in the world until there is no room left for any war or violence or hunger.

Dancing in the wind, I can feel the minds and emotions of everyone in the world. If I just reach out with my mind, I can pluck the feelings of anyone and everyone. I can be the joy of the mother holding her newborn child. I can be the fear of the man sitting on death row the night before his execution. I am all of these things. I realize all at once that I can feel them all and the weight of them is pressing me down. Still spinning, I cry out for relief, but all of the feelings of everyone in the world are slamming into me and I can't escape them.

I'm the horror of a police officer at the sight of a brutal murder and I'm the terror of a woman being raped and I'm the loneliness of the teenager cringing alone in his room. Whirling, I pull the feelings in faster and faster. The orbs start dancing around me, telling me to keep spinning, to keep twirling. Their light heats my face and I know they're here to rescue me. Moving closer to the dancing orbs, I reach out for one but it skips away from me, playfully. The orbs are changing me. They're turning me into light. And I suddenly know why I feel so awkward in this world. Now, I realize why I've never fit, why I could never find my place. I've always known I was different. I've always known I didn't belong here. And I always knew that someday, my people would come to take me home.

One of the orbs, floating just on the other side of the edge of the cliff, bounces toward me. It circles my entire body, filling me with it's brilliant light. I'm not in the light anymore. I am the light. The orb moves back out over the water and starts to change again. It's becoming bigger and bigger. It's a doorway – a doorway of light. When it's bigger than I am, I turn back to look at Dana once more. She has half risen, and her face looks terrified.

"It isn't scary," I call happily over my shoulder before launching myself off the cliff and toward the door of light.

"Oh God, Oh God, Oh God!" Sitting up in a complete panic, I launch myself off the couch and land several feet away, knocking over one of the porch chairs. Sinking to my knees, I press my forehead to the deck floor, shaking and crying. I can't breathe. Trying to force air into my lungs, I breathe in hard, as hard as I can. Esmé is on her knees beside me in seconds. She rubs my back and talks to me in a soothing whisper until the weight lifts from my chest and I can breathe again.

"Es..." I start to say her name, but I can't get it out before I'm sobbing.

She lies down on the deck, pulling me down next to her. We curl around each other, crying. In a moment, my mouth is on hers and I'm kissing her through my tears. She rolls over on top of me, still crying. Our tears are mingling together as we press together in something close to panic. My hands are under her clothes and before I am even aware of what I'm doing, I'm inside of her, and she's reaching for me and we're stroking and tasting each other in a frantic effort to wash away whatever the hell just happened.

After, she pushes herself back and looks into my eyes. I'm still crying, which is funny in an odd sort of way. I didn't think I could have an orgasm while crying. After, sometimes, yes. But during? Not ever. Now I'm laughing and crying and I don't even know exactly how I feel, except drained.

Esmé stands up, gathering clothes. Her eyelashes are still wet with her tears and she looks beautiful.

"Are you leaving?" I'm not sure whether I want her to say yes or no, but I want to know so I can figure it out.

"No, but I don't want to spend the night on the deck."

Dragging myself to my feet, I grab my clothes, and bundle them under one arm. "Let's go to bed then."

Frank is already inside, so I close the door to the deck and turn off the lights.

Esmé heads to the bathroom, but turns around

to look at me when she reaches the door. "I'm going to take a shower. Do you want to take one with me?"

She doesn't say it suggestively, but sort of ambiguously, the way I had asked if she was going to leave. Shaking my head, I wave her along. "I'll go after you."

Walking into the living room, I go over to the wall of pictures and look at the faces of my friends and family. It's bizarre that I don't have any pictures of Fran on the wall. I'm still standing there staring at the wall when Esmé comes out of the bathroom wearing my robe. Her hair is wet and sticking up all over her head. She looks fresh and alive and I can't help leaning in to kiss her on the tip of her nose. She wrinkles it and smiles.

"Do you want to talk tonight?"

"No," I say. "I don't want to talk tonight."

"Then let's go to bed." Holding out her hand, Esmé looks at me and waits for me to respond. I pause for a second before slipping my hand into hers. I want to talk, but I'm so tired. I let her lead me to the bedroom and help me into bed. My last thought before drifting into sleep is that I should have asked her if she was okay.

Chapter Eighteen

The front door slamming startles me out of sleep. Frantic, I reach over to the other side of the bed to find Esmé still curled up and deeply asleep. Carefully creeping out of bed, I pull on some shorts and a tank top and stumble into the kitchen. Sam is at the coffee pot pouring herself a cup.

"Man," she grins. "It's just not like you to not have coffee waiting for me. Do you know, I had to make a pot all on my own?"

"That must have been terrible for you."

"You look like something the cat dragged in, ate, and then puked up again."

"Thanks a fucking lot, my friend." She ducks as I pick up a dish towel and throw it at her. "So why are you here?"

"Oh man, I had the craziest night," she says, smiling.

"You and me both," I sigh, sinking down onto a stool. Frank, who to this point has been sound asleep on the counter, opens one eye, looks to see that there is still food in his bowl, and goes back to sleep.

"*You* had a crazy night? What happened? Did you step on a hairball?" She chuckles at her own joke, while I roll my eyes.

"Give me a fucking cup of coffee and let's go for a walk. You can tell me all about your night."

She pours her coffee into a travel mug and takes

one down for me. While she's doing that, I go into the front room and write a note for Esmé, letting her know where I am. Taking it back to the bedroom, I tiptoe in and place it on top of the pile of folded clothes that she left on the chair.

Sam has both coffee mugs in her hand, so we walk out the door into the morning sunlight. Detouring over to the truck, I grab both of our walking sticks. I trade one of them to Sam for one of the mugs of coffee. Sam is grinning like the proverbial canary-eating cat. Gulping her coffee, she grins at me over her cup as we walk along the road and into the woods.

"So, you had a crazy night, too?" She smiles. "Did you stay up all night watching Dr. Who reruns again?"

"Oh God. Your humor is just too much for me to handle," I laugh, smacking her on the arm.

"Well, do you want to go first?"

"No, you."

We walk in silence for a few moments, and I'm about to ask her what's going on when she suddenly turns to me and smiles. "It's just...I'm not sure how to start."

Shrugging, I continue walking without looking at her. To tell the truth, I'm not sure where to start telling her about my night so the longer she takes with her story, the more time I have to think. When we crest the top of the hill, she leans against a tree and takes a sip of coffee. Perching on a stump, I follow suit. Laying my walking stick on the ground, I lean back against the tree behind me. "Well?"

"So, after the lighthouse hike, you left with Susannah."

"And?"

"And Olivia and I went out for brunch."

Shocked, I sputter a bit on a sip of coffee. "You and Olivia went out for a meal?" She could have told me that she went out to eat with Sarah Palin and I'd be less surprised.

"Well, you know, I felt like an asshole for making her cry the night before."

"She always cries."

"I know. I know it. I just felt bad this time."

Rolling my eyes, I set my coffee down on the ground in front of me. "Tell me you didn't."

Suddenly launching herself off the tree, she paces in front of me, grinning. "Yeah, I mean, as she pointed out, we've done it before. So why not?"

"Why not, indeed?"

"I sense a wee bit of sarcasm," she says in a terrible Scottish accent.

"A wee bit?" My accent is also terrible, but better than hers.

"Look, she was kind of sweet and fun on the hike. Plus, you have to admit that she's fucking adorable."

"You're right. As far as outward appearances go, she is very attractive."

"Anyway, we went back to her place after brunch and one thing led to another and next thing you know, we're on the couch and she's straddling me with her breasts in my face. What the hell was I supposed to do?"

Laughing, I collapse my head into my hands. "Sammie-Sam-Sam. Oh, Sammie, Sammie, Sammie."

"Come on." Indignant, she smacks my on the top of the head. "Stop laughing at me."

"Okay, okay. It's just, you know she's straight, right?"

Hitching her thumbs through her belt loops, she puffs her chest out. "She wasn't last night."

"Oh Jesus!" Unable to contain myself, I laugh until tears spring from my eyes. Sam stares at me in disgust for a few seconds before sitting next to me on the stump and joining me in laughter. When we manage to contain ourselves, I use the hem of my tank top to wipe the tears from my face. Sam sighs and leans against my shoulder, stretching her legs out in front of her.

"Okay, that sounded pretty ridiculous, even for me," she concedes.

"Even for you," I agree.

We pause for a few moments, staring around us at the trees and the butterflies. Sam gets up and walks over to a nearby mango tree, pulling one off. Sitting back down on the stump, she pulls out her knife and peels it, handing a slice to me before taking one for herself. We eat in silence, relishing the flavor of the luscious fruit. With juice dripping down my chin, I turn my face to the sky and let the warmth of the sun wash over me. Life isn't that bad sometimes. We finish the mango and wipe our fingers on our shorts. I think mango is a fruit best eaten on the beach. You can let the whole thing drip sinfully all over yourself and clean up by simply strolling into the seawater.

Sighing, Sam tosses the pit into the bushes. "I love mango."

"Nature's perfect fruit," I concur.

"Better than a fresh passion fruit."

"Better than papaya."

"Way better than a banana," she grins.

"So, Sam. What happens next?"

"I don't know. It's just that I kind of like her,

you know?"

"I know. You have a habit of being interested in straight women. Haven't we talked about that?"

She shakes her head. "I don't know what it is. Olivia is pretty adorable, though. Annoying as hell sometimes, yes."

"Well, you're both grown-ups. You'll figure it out."

"Besides," she adds, grinning again. "I've got to be better than porn star guy."

"My eighty-eight-year-old grandfather would be better than porn star guy."

"Is he available?"

We break into another fit of giggles. When we've recovered, Sam pokes me. "So, tell me about your crazy night."

Taking a deep breath, I decide to just bust everything out at once. "I think I've been having visions of Fran because Esmé is somewhat psychic and since we have both been wrestling with the same demons, we somehow had this connection with each other. So, she came over last night, we did this kind of mutual hypnosis thing and we went into some kind of other world or dream state where I became Fran and was inside of her body when she jumped off the cliff." Pausing for breath, I give her a sidelong glance to see if she is still with me. She's staring at me with her mouth hanging open. "So, I saw what Fran saw when she jumped, which was some kind of ethereal light sort of beings that beckoned her off the cliff. Whether they were in her head or not is irrelevant at this point. The important thing is that she jumped because she thought the aliens were taking her home that way. I came out of my trance when Fran jumped and Esmé and I cried and then made love and afterward, we both cried again and we both managed to admit that all along, we both somehow thought that I was the reason she killed herself, and Esmé even admitted that she came to the island with the idea of tormenting me or some other sort of half-baked idea of getting even with me for killing the only woman she ever loved."

Sam is still staring at me with her mouth hanging open, but on realizing that I've stopped talking, she blinks several times. Clearing her throat, she makes an attempt to speak. Her mouth opens, but nothing comes out. Clearing her throat again, she finally speaks. "So, you had sex with Esmé?"

Unable to respond, I stare at her for a second. She smiles and then we are both laughing hysterically until neither one of us can breathe. Suddenly, I can't catch my breath and Sam is hugging me while I gasp for air and cry hard on her shoulder. She rocks slightly with me in her arms, quietly holding me until I gain control of myself again. When I've regained control of myself again, I pull away, leaving a string of snot between my nose and her shirt. She looks down on it, wipes it off with her hand, and rubs her hand against the leg of her shorts.

"Sorry about that," I say, staring down at my feet.

"What's a little snot between friends?"

"You thought it was a booger, but it's snot," I grin.

"And people think I'm the immature one in this relationship," she says, rolling her eyes.

"I was drunk one night and I had a vision of Fran dying. Right there in the car, I saw the blood coming down her face and somehow, I knew that I had killed her."

"But you didn't kill her," she says, calmly.

"I know that now. Or, at least, I sort of know that. It's all jumbled up in my head. I remember her talking to me about the lights and the orbs and her people coming to take her home, but I never really took her seriously. I mean, I knew she was a little crazy, but that was part of her charm."

"Maybe she wasn't crazy."

Lifting my head, I stare at her. "What do you mean?"

"I mean, maybe she really was seeing aliens and orbs and being taken home."

Snorting, another bubble of snot comes out of my nose. I wipe it off with the back of my hand and wipe my hand on my shorts. "Sam," I say. "That's pretty rich coming from you."

"I'm just saying that there is no way of knowing whether it really happened or if it was all in her head. And, to tell you the truth, it doesn't even matter."

"Of course it matters." Grabbing my stick, I stand up and start down the path again.

She runs after me and catches up, panting. "Jeeze, I gotta quit drinking so much. I'm getting out of shape."

"Yeah, really. How can you have my back if you can't even jog a few steps?"

"You'll be all telling some bad dudes...you wanna step up? And I'll be all...hang on, hang on, let me get my breath."

Slowing down to a manageable pace, I smile at her. "I'm not really mad at you, you know."

"I know, Dana. It's a lot to handle. Maybe I didn't say it right. I just meant that regardless of where

Fran's orbs came from, they were the reason that she died. And now you know that she died happy, leaping for joy to something she believed in, even if we can't."

I'm silent for so long that Sam touches me on the shoulder. "Dana?"

"I don't know what to do next."

"Let her go?"

My house comes into view through the woods and we step off the path and onto the road. A few drops of rain are starting to fall, but like most rain in the Caribbean, it's warm. Wiping rainwater off her face, Sam looks up at the sky. "Locals say that when the rain is this warm, it means it's going to be a bad hurricane season."

"Give me a fucking break."

Opening the door, I step into the kitchen. Esmé is sitting at the counter with a cup of coffee in her hands. Roxanne is next to her.

"Esmé," I start. Momentarily at a loss for words, I look at Roxanne. "Rox," I say. "This is..."

"Awesome," Sam finishes.

She pushes me gently out of the way and heads for the coffee pot to refill her mug. Staring at Roxanne, I try to gauge how she's feeling about this situation. To be fair, I'm not sure exactly how I feel about the situation. Esmé stands and comes over to me. I let her kiss me without kissing her back. Giving her a brief hug, I look over her shoulder at Roxanne who is pointedly looking the other direction. Oblivious, Sam brings her coffee over and sits down next to Rox.

"What are you doing here?"

Roxanne gives Sam a one-arm hug. "I walked over to see if Dana wanted to hike."

Sam shrugs. "We just went for a walk, but I

wouldn't be opposed to taking another one."

"Oh, wouldn't that be fun," Esmé intones.

I suddenly realize that Sam has no idea that Roxanne and I had a little thing the other day. She stands. "Come on. We can totally do this."

Before I can open my mouth, Roxanne stands too. "No, it's fine. Now that I've had a lovely cup of coffee with Esmé, I'm ready to go home and get to work in my garden."

Sam smiles and slides back onto her stool. "Okay then." She wiggles a twist tie around the counter, catching Frank's interest.

Roxanne walks toward the door without looking at me. "Bye, Esmé. It was a pleasure talking to you this morning."

"And you," Esmé says, smiling. "We must do it again sometime."

"Bye, Dana," Roxanne says.

"Bye, Rox," I reply as she walks out the door.

"She obviously has a crush on you," Esmé says after the door closes.

"What?" Sam looks up from playing with Frank. "Roxanne has a crush on Dana?"

Esmé nods. "A woman can sense these things."

"I'm a woman and I can't sense a thing," Sam says.

"We've both always had a bit of a crush on each other," I say, twisting out of Esmé's grip and busying myself at the coffee pot. "It's nothing."

"It better be nothing," Esmé says. "I mean, she's old enough to be your grandmother."

"No she isn't," Sam says, indignant. "She's less than twenty years older than I am."

"Well, your mother then," Esmé continues.

Holding up my hand, I glare at her. "Leave it alone, Esmé." I don't want to hear any slams on Roxanne.

"Well, please," she says. "In ten years, she'll be in a nursing home and you'll still be youngish and fit."

"I said to leave it alone," I growl. "Roxanne is my friend and I don't want to hear it."

Esmé looks up at me, her eyes welling with tears. "Well, maybe I should go."

"Maybe you should."

She whirls on her heels and heads toward the bedroom. Sam looks at me questioningly. "Don't you think you should...I don't know. Do something or something?"

"Like what?"

"I said I don't know. I'm not good with women."

"Good enough to fuck straight ones."

"Hey, don't get pissed at me! I didn't do anything."

Esmé storms back out of the bedroom and heads for the front door. "You know, something pretty amazing happened last night."

"I know, I know."

"Well, you're not acting like it now," she spits. "Are you trying to be cool in front of your friend?"

Holding up her hands, Sam shakes her head. "Hey, she never has to be cool in front of me. I know she's not."

"Funny," I mouth at her before turning back to Esmé.

"I'm sorry if I hurt your feelings. I just don't want you mocking my friend."

Walking back across the room, she puts her arms around my waist. "You know, I had a pretty intense night, too."

"I know you did. But maybe our takeaway from last night is that we can finally let Fran go."

Wrenching herself away from me, she glares at me again. "Speak for yourself," she says. "I have more questions than ever."

"How can that be?" I'm flabbergasted. "We know why she killed herself. She was seeing aliens. What more do you need?"

"I need to know the truth."

"The truth is that you know everything you are ever going to know," I reply.

Glaring at me one more time, she storms out of the door, slamming it hard behind her.

Sam looks at me, shrugs, and goes back to playing with Frank.

"You sure have a way with women, my friend."

Chapter Nineteen

Frank is sitting next to my face with one paw on my nose when I open my eyes. "Frank, it's the middle of the night."

He meows and I open my eyes. It's already light. Picking up my cell to check the time, I realize I've already missed a call from Esmé. I should have called her yesterday, but I somehow never got around to it. I might as well get it over with.

"Hi Dana."

"Hey. How's it going?"

"It's good. I had a good time with you the other night."

"Yeah, yeah. I liked it. Some of it. Kind of intense in some ways."

"Well, sometimes things get a little intense when you are trying to dig deep into the dark places of the universe."

Sighing, I roll my eyes at Frank who is still sitting next to my head. "Look, we dug deep and we got the answer we've been looking for. I mean, I still feel like shit that I lost her, but I don't think I could have saved her. How could I fight her particular demons?"

"Don't you want to know the truth?"

The truth. Do I want to know the truth? Somehow, I always thought that I did. I wanted to be completely inside of Fran and know everything that she knew, feel everything that she felt. Now that

I've had a taste of it, though, I don't think I want to know more. I don't know why I find it so easy to accept that I could somehow take my mind into my dead girlfriend's head and see what she was seeing in her last moments, yet can't wrap myself around the possibility that she was truly communing with aliens. Still, I have what I needed. I had to know what I could have done differently on that day to keep her alive and I realize that there's nothing. Nothing at all.

"Dana? Did you hear my question?"

"I heard it."

"Well?"

"Esmé, I hope you find peace with yourself now that we've done everything that we are going to do to put Fran's memory to rest."

"We haven't. There's so much more we can do!"

"If you need to keep searching, please do. You're just not getting anything else out of me."

She pauses. "Well, are we going to see each other again?"

Thinking about it, I absently reach out to scratch Frank's furry head. He blerts at me before looking pointedly in the direction of the kitchen. "One minute," I mouth at him. "Esmé, of course we'll see each other again. It's a small island."

"That's shit."

"I'm sorry. I had a great time with you the other night, but that whole situation came out of our crazy experience."

"By situation, I assume you're talking about us making love with each other."

"I'm not saying it wasn't wonderful. It was. I enjoyed it a lot. I needed it and I think you did, too."

"We had a connection before the sex," she says.

"I'm not saying we didn't. I'm just saying that I'd like for us to be friends."

"Whatever."

"Look, Esmé, I'm sorry."

No answer. "Esmé?"

I turn to Frank, incredulous. "She hung up on me."

He ignores me and jumps off the bed, looking toward the kitchen again. Tossing my cell down on the bedside table, I follow him down the hall. He jumps on the counter while I fill his bowl and give him a couple of cat treats as a reward for his patience. While the coffee is brewing, I sit at the counter and watch him eat. I can hear my phone ringing in the bedroom, but the idea of talking to Esmé again suddenly has me exhausted. Besides, she's not who I really want to talk to. Filling up my mug with coffee, I say goodbye to Frank and head out the door.

Roxanne is in her garden when I approach her house.

"Hi," she says, smiling.

"Hi."

"Do you want to walk today?"

"No, I want to stand here drinking coffee and talk to you."

I set my coffee down on the top of her fence and hold my arms open. Leaning her shovel against the wall, she walks over and gives me a hug. I collapse into it, putting my arms around her and holding her tight. She feels firm, but soft and a little sweaty. Pressing my forehead against the side of her face, I breathe in deeply.

"You smell lovely," I tell her.

"Stop it." She pulls away a bit to look at me. "I

smell as if I've been working in the garden for three hours."

"So what are you working on here?"

"Replanting the coconut palms you gave me."

Whenever I find coconuts on the beach with roots starting to sprout, I bring them home and plant them. Even though it will be years before I'm getting coconuts, I still love to plant them. A few weeks ago, I brought several to Roxanne for her yard. They grow fast in the beginning. A couple of hers are already up to my knees.

"Before you know it, we'll be sitting under the shade of one of them, sharing a glass of lemonade or something."

"I don't think so," she grins. "Besides, we don't want to risk getting killed by a falling coconut."

"Life's full of risk."

Releasing herself from my arms, she reclaims her shovel and finishes digging the last hole. I bring her the coconut and we nestle half of it into the ground, patting the dirt gently in around it.

Clearing my throat, I look down at the coconut in the ground. "So, Rox..."

"Don't," she answers. "We really don't have anything to talk about."

"See, I kind of think that we do."

She leans against the shovel and rests her chin on top of her hands. "Dana, you don't owe me any explanations. Nothing has ever happened between us except a kiss in a vulnerable moment. I have never laid a claim to you and it doesn't matter who you date."

"Then why didn't you answer your phone when I called you last night?"

"I was just giving you some space."

We perch on her front steps sharing my cup of coffee. "I've been wrestling with something for a long time and I think I've finally started to get some clarity."

She doesn't answer, waiting for me to continue. "Esmé helped me with that. I think, we both needed the same answers and the only way we could get them was together."

"And did you get your answers?"

"I think I did. I'm not really sure what to believe. But I feel like I finally know enough to start putting her to rest."

"Good, Dana. I'm happy for you," she says, softly.

Leaning my head against her shoulder, I sigh. "Esmé was just part of that. What happened when we went into the corners of my mind or wherever we went was traumatic and strange and scary and what happened after just kind of followed from that."

She puts her hand on my forearm and kisses me on the forehead. "Dana, as I said, you really don't owe me any explanations."

"I feel like I do, though. I want you to understand."

"I do understand. I honestly do."

"Good." I put the coffee mug on the step next to me so I can take one of her hands in both of mine. "It's just, I've been thinking that living with the memory of Fran has been holding me back from being able to truly love. And now that I'm past it, I can move on."

"Dana..."

Interrupting her, I squeeze her hand. "Wait. Hear me out. We'd be so perfect together in so many ways. And I love you. I want to be with you. I want us to be together. As lovers."

"Dana."

"Really. I know I seem like an asshole because I slept with another woman the night before last and here I am. But I'm not asking you to have sex with me. Let's just start off with dating and see what happens. We can take it slow and let it build."

"Dana, it isn't..."

"And I know you're probably worried about the difference in our ages, but that doesn't matter to me. We're both in great shape and we love a lot of the same activities."

"That's absolutely true."

"And yes, we're friends, but isn't that the best way to start a relationship?"

"It is, however,"

"And I love you. You're beautiful. You are such an amazing woman. I can imagine holding you and dancing with you and loving you."

"Dana."

"And we kiss so beautifully together."

She holds her hand against my mouth. "Dana," she says. "Will you just listen to me?"

I mumble something against her hand. She removes it and smiles. "Yes?"

"I said I'll be quiet for a minute."

"You are a wonderful woman and I love you dearly."

"Well then."

She smiles. "I don't love you like that."

Deflated, I pull back, leaning my back against the porch railing. "You don't?"

"I don't. I'm sorry, Dana. I think you're a wonderful woman and I care about you so much. But I don't want to be your girlfriend."

Stung, I stare down at our joined hands, thinking about it. Finally, I look up at her and grin.

"How could anyone not want to be with me?"

She laughs. "It's a struggle."

"Do you think there's a chance you'll change your mind?"

She leans over to kiss me on the cheek. "You're sweet and you're very precious to me."

"So I'm guessing that means no."

"I can't foresee it changing."

Sighing again, I mime shooting myself in the head. "I guess I'm destined to be alone."

"You need to be alone. You've only just begun the process of letting go of the past. Now you need to figure out who you are in the present before you can look to the future."

"Deep."

"I amaze even myself sometimes," she says, smiling.

"Are we still going to walk together?

She stands and offers me a hand. "Of course."

"What about the Club?"

Grinning, she shakes her head. "I'll continue to hang out with you and Sam, but I don't want to continue calling ourselves The Love Sucks Club."

"I don't know what I'll tell Olivia."

"Tell her that love doesn't suck nearly as much as you and Sam have implied."

I don't know whether to be embarrassed about my outpouring or not. Looking at Roxanne's smile, I'm guessing not. I lean in to kiss her on the cheek again. "All right, I've got important things to do."

"Bye, Dana."

Walking back to my house, I kick a stone down

the lane. When I pass George's house, I spot him raking his leaves in the front yard. He waves and smiles, and I return the gesture without stopping to chat. Back at my door, I turn in circles, scoping out the yard. No particular tingles of warning, no impending panic attack, no sense of an ambush waiting for me inside. I've been complaining about my visions forever, but I don't think I'd be happy to lose them completely. What would I do if I wasn't the weird, psychic writer? I'd have to accept being just a weird writer. Imagining having this conversation with Sam, I smile to myself.

As I'm standing in my doorway, I hear Susannah's jeep coming up the road behind me. She jumps from the jeep and I throw my arms around her.

"Susannah, what do you dream about?"

"What do you mean? Like my nighttime dreams?"

"No, I mean, your dreams about your life? What do you want from it? What are your hopes? Do you want to go skydiving? Do you want to paint? Become a doctor? Travel to Europe? What is your dream?"

She pulls back from the hug and stares at me for a second. Opening my door, she walks into the kitchen and heads for the coffee pot.

I know she's thinking about it, so I don't speak. She refills my cup before pouring some for herself. When she finally pulls up a stool to the counter, Frank jumps up in front of her and bangs his head against her hand. Stroking him, she's quiet for a few minutes. Patiently drinking my coffee, I look at her, noticing the fine lines that are starting to form at the corners of her eyes. I can feel time moving in front of my eyes. Smiling at my sister across the counter, I can see her as an old woman, with a head of white hair. Her face alternates between being pinched and despairing and being open and lively, like Roxanne's. It looks like she's hovering on the edge of two futures. Reaching across the counter, I hold out my hand. Susannah looks at it for a second and then puts her hand in mine.

"Dana," she says, quietly. "All I have ever really dreamed about in my life is being happy."

Surprised, I don't know how to respond. Squeezing her hand, I smile again, trying not to show how close I am to crying.

"So, are you?"

"Not right now." She shakes her head. "Honestly, Dana, I don't know. Sometimes I think I am, and sometimes I wonder if I ever will be."

"That's most of us, Susannah."

Before she can answer, someone knocks on the door and Susannah gets up to answer it. She opens the door and Jackie walks in.

"You've got to be fucking kidding me," I say, standing with my fists clenched. "Is it going to come to this?"

Jackie holds her hands up in a gesture of peace. "I'm not here to fight."

Susannah scoffs under her breath, but doesn't say anything.

Moving out from behind the counter, I walk up to Jackie, ready to fight. "I'm done with this, you know. I'm really done."

"I'm honestly not here to fight. I swear to you, I'm not."

Crossing my arms tightly over my chest, I lean against the counter. "Well why are you here?"

"I ran into your friend Esmé. She explained to me some of the things that happened with Fran."

Irritated, I glare at her. "She had no right."

"It explains a lot."

Susannah clears her throat. "I really think you should leave."

I smile at my sister and nod my head toward the living room. "Why don't you wait in the living room or on the deck? I'll be done here in a minute."

She looks doubtful, but complies anyway. When she's gone, I turn back to Jackie. "Seriously, Jackie? I don't understand why you can't just get out of my life?"

"We were together for seven years. We lived together for five of those years. I would think there's still a connection between us that hasn't gone away just because we aren't seeing each other anymore."

"There's no connection, Jackie. We had a relationship and now we don't."

Pursing her lips, she stares down at the floor.

I don't understand what she wants from me. I don't owe her anything. Just because we were lovers doesn't mean I have a responsibility to take care of her for the rest of her life. What the hell? When do I get to be free of someone who held me back for so long? Thinking about Roxanne, I consider the possibility that it wasn't my ex who was holding me back, but my own fear.

"Do you want a cup of coffee?" I ask her.

She nods so I pour her a cup. No sugar, a dash of half and half. There used to be something comforting in knowing how she took her coffee and how she liked her eggs. As much as I profess to like excitement in my life, I did enjoy those mornings we sat in our respective chairs reading, or doing crossword puzzles, or playing Scrabble. Jackie has perched on a stool with her cup of coffee in both hands. Looking at her, I almost let the thought creep in that now that she's sober, maybe we could make another go. Laughing, I shake my head. What the hell is wrong with me?

"Why are you laughing?"

"I was thinking about why our relationship didn't work out."

"Because you weren't really in it."

Stunned, I stare at her. "It had nothing to do with your drinking problem?"

"I'm not saying I didn't have a problem. But you never even tried to help me."

"How could I help someone who wouldn't even admit that she had a problem?"

She sets her cup down on the counter. "You didn't try, Dana. Never. All you did was sink into your writing and your visions and close yourself off from me."

"That isn't true." Indignant, I point my finger at her. I'm pissed now. "All you ever did was drink and spend my money."

"And all you ever did was nag me about how much money I spent. You counted my drinks and when I got to an arbitrary number, you'd start pursing your lips and acting sanctimonious. You thought you were so much better than me because you don't drink."

Angry and somehow guilty, I lash out. "That's not true. You ruined our life together. You just drank and passed out and drank and pissed off my friends and acted like a bitch and couldn't even perform sexually because you were always at some level of drunk."

Pausing, she looks down at her coffee. Taking a deep breath, she lifts her head to make eye contact with me. "How could I make love to you when you were always judging me? You hated me. You hated my drinking. You never tried to talk to me about it in a compassionate way. You just harped and got mad and accused me of being a drunk and criticized my driving and my sexual abilities and the way I did the laundry. If I went to bed early, you implied it was because I was drunk. If I stayed up late, you said it was because I wasn't done drinking. You hated me. And I loved you. And I still don't understand why you even bothered to get involved with me when you knew I would never measure up to the one who died."

Staring at her, I open my mouth and close it again. I can't make myself speak. Our whole relationship is flashing through my head and suddenly, I can see myself through her eyes and I don't like what I see. I am an asshole.

"Wow," I finally manage to mutter.

"Yeah," she whispers. "Yeah."

"Well, I'm sorry for hurting you. I'm sorry I didn't have the strength to stand up and help you wrestle with your demon while I was still trying to wrestle with my own."

"Honestly, Dana. The only mistake that you really made was agreeing to go out with me. You should never have gone out with me. You should never have gotten involved."

Shaking my head, I blink quickly to push back the tears that are threatening to fall again. I've become such a wimp lately. It seems all I do is cry or actively work to stop myself from crying.

"You're right." I nod my head as I speak, like I've just figured it out and it all makes sense. "You're right. I should never have gotten involved with you. Who knows? Maybe you would have gotten clean sooner if you had been with someone who saw your alcoholism as a sickness to be cured and not as an irritation in her life."

"Yeah, maybe."

"When I saw you in town the other day, I had a vision that you were going to kill me."

She sighs. Pausing for a second, she takes a sip of her coffee and then looks up at me. Surprisingly, she's smiling. "I've wanted to kill you for a long time."

"Well, that's honest."

"I'm not going to. I would never kill anyone. But I can't deny that for a long time there, I wouldn't have been upset if you had died of natural causes."

We look at each other in silence for a second. She snorts and before I know it, we're both laughing hysterically. She leans her forehead on her hands and I'm holding onto the counter for support. We laugh so loud and so long that I have tears rolling down my face and she's beet red.

"So what do you want, Jackie. When all of this is said and done, what are you doing here?"

Standing, she crosses the room and pats me on the shoulder. "I wanted you to tell me you were sorry."

Nodding, I smile at her again. "Well, I'm sorry. I am sorry, Jackie. I really am."

"I'm sorry, too."

"For not helping with the housework enough?"

That sets us both off and we're laughing again until finally, I swallow my pride and put my arms around her. We cling to each other, still laughing. She gives me a last hug before pulling back.

"I am sorry, Dana. I'm sorry that I couldn't help you with your demons while I was wrestling with mine."

She pulls away and walks toward the door.

"Thanks for the coffee."

"Hey," I call. "Are you going to be all right? Money-wise, I mean."

She looks straight at me and for a second, I'm heavy with the weight of her cares. My shoulder slump and I can see the long road she's facing. Living in her car, going to AA meetings, falling off the wagon, pulling herself back onto it. There's a shadow around her future and I realize that I can't see what's going to happen to her.

"I'll be okay," she says. "I'm always okay."

She turns toward the door again.

"Jackie?"'

With her hand on the doorknob, she half turns, and pauses. "What?"

"I believe in you. I know you can do it."

Walking out the door, she raises her hand as a last goodbye, without saying another word. Still buckling under the weight of her pain, I slouch into a stool. Frank walks across the counter and head butts me. I wrap my arms around him, pulling him against me so I can bury my face in his fur. He utters a brief protest, but doesn't struggle to get away. He allows me to hold him for several minutes, as if he knows somehow that I'm seeking comfort from his very presence. Susannah tiptoes in and puts her hand on my shoulder.

"Are you all right, sis?"

Looking up at her, I smile. "Yeah, Susie. I guess I am."

"Well, good. Maybe you can help me with a problem."

Not another one. This is how life works. I get rid of one heavy weight and two more drop on me.

"What happened?"

"Thomas and I broke up."

"How come?"

"He says I'm too controlling and he doesn't want to live like that."

Nodding, I look at her seriously. "Susannah, I'm going to be painfully honest with you here in an attempt to help you save yourself."

She takes a deep breath as if to brace herself. "Okay."

"You are too controlling. When I've seen you with Thomas, I somehow see the two of you as Mom and Dad. You tell him what to do. It looks like you should be steering him around by his elbow."

Tears fill up her eyes, but she blinks to stave them off. We are stoics in this family. Never let them see you breakdown, that's our motto. She looks up at the ceiling. "I know I try to control things, Dana. I just don't want to lose myself in a relationship."

"You've got to find the balance, Sissy. Somewhere between being a controlling bitch and giving yourself completely over to his wants is a happy balance where the two of you communicate with each other and compromise to make sure that you are both comfortable and happy."

"I'm not sure that I know how to find that balance."

Wrapping my arms around her, I smile. "I don't know that any of us do, baby sister."

Chapter Twenty

Rick and Karen have canceled their end of the summer party. Apparently, the locals, who are fond of predicting hurricanes using everything from the size of the waves to the shape of the clouds were correct that hurricane season would start early this season. Still, law of averages suggests they will be right occasionally. We've been tracking Omar for a while and according to the weather reports, we are due to start getting the first bad weather from it sometime in the middle of the night. I asked my sister to come spend the night here. Her stupid apartment complex is a flimsy piece of crap and as far as I know, they haven't done anything to prepare for the oncoming storm. Sam is going to head up here after she finishes getting the resort as ready as they can be. Of course, Olivia is coming up with my sister. Whatever else happens, it will be interesting to see her and Sam together. Rolling my eyes toward the ceiling, I shake my head. I still don't get that one. Olivia is straight, for God's sake. I don't get it. I asked Sam if she and Olivia are dating now, but she danced around the answer. I'm guessing that's a yes, but it's really not any of my business. I mean, it wouldn't be my business if it didn't directly involve me. It does, however. It's bad enough I have to see her through my sister. Now, she's possibly dating my best friend.

Sam is irritated that the party is canceled. I'm

not too upset about it. Sure, there would be some people there that I would like to see, but let's face it, if I really wanted to see them, I would make an effort to do so even without the excuse of a party. Besides, the problem with a big party like that is that most of the people there are people I don't particularly want to see. Worse, it would be filled with people I don't know. I can't think of many tortures worse than being sober in a room full of people who don't know each other as they all get shit-faced together and bond over their own particular brand of drunkenness. Sam thrives in that kind of situation. Sometimes it still amazes me that we're friends.

Heading outside to pull the hurricane shutters across the glass doors to the deck, I do a quick sweep to make sure there isn't anything left outside. Oh crap. I forgot about the little setup I have on the other side of the lawn, in the grass. I don't know why it's there. I rarely sit anywhere except on the deck. Still, every once in a while when I'm working in the yard, it's nice to collapse into my huge Adirondack chairs and survey my handiwork. The stairs from the deck come out on the far side of the lawn from my little setup down below, so I'll have to cart this stuff all the way around the house. Grinning at the perfect blue sky, I run around the house to grab the first chair. By the time I manage to wrestle it around to the door, Roxanne is standing in my yard.

"Need help?"

Holding out my hand, I show her the place where I gave myself a massive splinter.

"I could use some help."

She takes my hand and looks at the cut. "We should disinfect this."

"Let's get the stuff in first."

Having a second person changes the task from an unpleasant one into a relatively simple one. Together, we bring both chairs and the little table around to the door and into the living room. Back outside, we walk the perimeter slowly, checking for any loose objects that could become projectiles during the storm. Giving it the all clear, I head back into the house to make another pot of coffee.

Roxanne, who looks kind of adorable in plaid shorts and an extremely clean t-shirt, smiles as she hands me a mug to fill for her. "So, are you completely set now?"

"I think I am. I'm stocked on canned food. The bathtub is filled with water."

Gesturing to the row of gallon jugs along the floor of the kitchen, I nod at her smugly. "Got my drinking water all separated from my non-potable water."

"Ooh, you are the hurricane whisperer."

"Yep. Rechargeable flashlights, a crank radio, battery powered fans and lights, and several board games."

"Got your chain saws prepared?"

"Of course. Two gas-powered chain saws in case we need 'em to get down the road after the storm."

"Well, let's just see to your injury and you really will be set."

After I wash my hands, Roxanne pours some hydrogen peroxide on the small hole where the splinter was. I'm gratified to watch it bubble and foam for a few seconds before she covers it with a band-aid. "I love hydrogen peroxide," I say.

"I always heard that if it bubbles, that means

there's an infection."

"Uh, actually, that's the liquid mixing with your cells, both healthy and damaged. Hydrogen peroxide kills bacteria, but it can also kill healthy skin cells which can actually slow healing and increase the likelihood of scarring."

Still holding my hand out in front of her, Roxanne glares at me. "Then why did you let me put it on you?"

I can't help laughing. She just looks so indignant. "Oh come on, Rox. It was a splinter. I don't think I have to worry about gangrene. Besides, I like watching it fizz as it eats away my skin cells."

She laughs, too. Dropping my hand, she smacks me on the shoulder. "Fine then. Get your damaged cells away from me."

"Do you need help over at your place?"

"I could. I brought in any plants that were in pots and tubs. The others will either make it or not. Already got all of my furniture in, but I haven't put up my storm shutters yet."

Roxanne has heavy wooden storm shutters that latch with giant metal latches that look like something from a medieval dungeon. They're actually kind of gorgeous, but they're huge and heavy and it's definitely a two person job.

"Why didn't you call me to come help you?"

"I figured I would find you outside taking care of your own place and I could help you in exchange for your help."

"Tit for tat?"

Grinning, she shakes her head. "No, just the storm shutters for the furniture moving."

"A girl can try."

We walk over to her house hand in hand. The day is so beautiful, it's almost impossible to believe that it will erupt into a violent storm in the next twelve hours or so. At Roxanne's house, I grab her ladder and carry it to each window to fasten the latches. One of the shutters has stuck to the side of the house, so I have to schlep back to my house for some tools to pry it from that latch and refasten it to the next one. While I'm gone, Roxanne makes a cup of tea and hands it to me on my return. Standing close to her, I take the tea, and look down into her eyes. "Thank you," I say, moving closer.

She backs away, laughing. "Are you trying to be seductive over tea? It might be easier if we weren't both so dirty and sweaty."

Denied, I roll my eyes. "Maybe I like dirty and sweaty."

Handing her my cup, I climb back up on the ladder to work on the shutter. I spray some WD-40 on the rusted catch, figuring if nothing else, maybe I can just work it loose. Wiggling the shutter back and forth, I can feel the catch starting to give. "You know, this is why you need a butch around. You really should get out here about once a month and treat these so they don't rust."

She shrugs. "I know. You told me that last hurricane season. It's just in the in-between times, I tend to forget about it."

"Well, then you need to put it on a calendar or something," I snap. I'm aware that I sound sanctimonious, but I'm irritated that I can't get the catch loose. Now I'll probably have to unscrew the entire assembly from the cement wall which will mean remounting it after the storm. Drilling into concrete is a pain in the ass, especially on a ladder.

"I'm sorry, Dana." Roxanne sounds contrite and sad, which makes me feel like a complete asshole. "If you want, I'll call a contractor. You shouldn't have to suffer for my mistakes."

Lifting my hands to the sky in a "why me?" gesture, I call out, "Why have you forsaken me?"

Roxanne laughs. I look down to smile at her. "I'm just being dramatic because this fucker is really stuck on here. It's pissing me off, not you."

"Well, you're yelling at me, not at the fastener."

"True enough," I say, laughing. "I think I'm going to have to take the whole thing apart. It's stuck on here pretty good." I give it one last yank and it jerks free, knocking my off balance. I know I'm going down and my life flashes before my eyes. Okay, technically, the image of me in a full body cast flashes before my eyes. Before I can recover my balance, I'm off the ladder and falling backward. Braced for the landing, it takes me a second to realize that I haven't hit the ground. Instead, I'm in tiny little Roxanne's arms and she's laughing. "You know, you're totally right," she says, putting me down and rubbing her arms. "This is why I need a butch around. I just can't handle this sort of thing all by my little lonesome."

Shaking my head, I glare at her for a second before bursting into laughter. "Oh God, Roxanne. You're tougher than you look."

"And you're heavier than you look."

"I guess I'm a little portly."

"Would you like me to finish the shutter?" she asks, sweetly.

"Not a chance." I climb back up the ladder and finish latching the newly released shutter into place.

When I climb back down, Roxanne puts her arms around me and kisses me on the cheek. "My hero."

"Yeah, right."

"I'm serious. That's a heavy job and I appreciate you taking care of it for me."

Wrapping my arms around her waist, I smile. "So you're admitting that I was right?"

"About what?" She grins.

"About needing a butch around."

"Isn't that kind of an antiquated notion? Like saying I need a man around?"

Ruffled, I lean back to look at her. "It's not even close to the same thing. Saying that a woman needs a man is taking away her personal identity."

"Saying a woman needs a butch is taking away her personal identity."

"Au contraire. We complement each other. I'm the Laurel to your Hardy."

"The ketchup to my mustard?"

"The salt to your vinegar."

"Gross."

We laugh for a moment before Roxanne pulls away, breaking the hug. Glancing at her watch, Roxanne says, "I better head down the hill and get some supplies."

"Are you going to the grocery store? Can I come with you?"

"I thought you were all laid in?"

"I am, but I want to get some cookies."

"If you want, I'll get some chocolate chips and make you some cookies."

"Oh, that's even better. Why don't you spend the night at my place?"

Looking at me sideways, she smiles. "Do you

really think that's a good idea?"

"Frankly, I think it's a great idea. However, Susannah and Olivia and Sam will be there, so it won't be quite the lovely intimate evening I would hope to be having with you."

She reaches into her door to retrieve her car keys.

"In that case, I would love to spend the night. I hate being alone during storms."

We get into her car and she heads down the hill. Watching her drive, I smile at her profile. She really is a beautiful woman.

At the store, we park way in the back of the lot because Roxanne isn't willing to risk getting rammed by some crazy who's trying to squeeze into the closest parking place. There are cars and people everywhere and the people leaving the stores are coming up with loaded carts full of food and bottles of water.

Looking at them, Roxanne turns to me. "Do you have enough water to share?"

"I have enough water for twenty people for three weeks," I answer. "Don't worry."

Since there are no carts left, I grab a basket. Trying to maneuver down the aisle is like playing a big and impatient game of Frogger. One woman runs over my toe with her cart and doesn't bother to apologize. "Excuse me," I say, loudly.

She turns to glare at me over her shoulder before moving on.

Roxanne pokes my arm. "Just keep your cool, Dana."

"I am cool."

Reaching for a bag of flour, I feel an elbow in my back that knocks me into the display. A hand reaches past me to grab the flour from my hand. Tucking it against my body, I turn around with my other hand curled into a fist. A woman who looks to be about ninety is standing behind me. Realizing the she can't get the flour I've already picked up, she pushes me aside to grab another. Before I can say a word, she's off, darting around an oncoming cart. Roxanne looks after her, appalled.

"Really?" I'm dumbfounded. "Did I just get body slammed by a ninety-year-old?"

Laughing, Rox takes the flour from me and puts it into the basket. "I didn't realize there would be such a demand for flour."

Jumping aside to make way for a guy who is running through the aisle with four gallon jugs of water, I knock back into the flour display again. This is ridiculous. I raise my voice as high as I can. "The storm isn't due to hit for another ten hours. Everyone calm the fuck down!" Silence descends on the aisle for a moment. A mother with a toddler in the cart gives me a dirty look before pushing her child away from me. Everyone else looks at me for a second before looking away. They go back to pushing each other and snapping at each other as if there hadn't been an interruption. Roxanne puts her hand on my forearm. "Maybe you should go wait in the car."

"No way. You need someone to protect you."

We make it to the end of the aisle. Continuing to dodge and dive to avoid the angry mob, we manage to finally make it through the store. Almost everything is decimated, but we are able to gather the ingredients we need for chocolate chip, peanut butter, and oatmeal raisin cookies. Roxanne has promised to bake them all before the storm hits so that we have them when the power goes out. Standing in the long line, I lament out loud about the lack of cashiers. "Maybe they were given the time off to prepare their own homes," Roxanne says.

"Doubt it. The store just wants us to wait in this long, horrible line."

"I'm sure that's it," she replies.

"Excuse me." The lady behind me pokes me in the back. Turning around, I see the old lady who knocked me into the flour. "Can I go in front of you? I have to get back to make sure my cats are okay."

She has an entire loaded grocery cart, piled so high it's overflowing the sides. "Are you kidding me? I only have a basket full of stuff."

"Really, Dana?" Roxanne gapes at me. "We can't just let her go first?"

I'm almost to the front of the line by now and I'm not in a great mood. There is no way I'm letting someone with an overstuffed cart in front of me, no matter how old she is. Ignoring both of them, I turn back to the front. Roxanne comes up close behind me.

Whispering, she says, "Are you really not going to let her go in front of us?"

"Why would I?"

"Because she's really old."

"I don't care how old she is. She has a million items and she's probably paying with pennies."

Roxanne laughs. The line moves forward. Another cashier opens next to us and says, "I'll take the next person in line."

The old lady rushes toward to new cashier, but I'm quicker. Diving in front of her, I knock the front of her cart into the candy display, spilling Peppermint Patties and Reese's all over the place. She tries to block my path with the front of her cart and manages to smash the front of it into my hip, but by then, I'm already into the line. Skidding across the spilled candy, I practically fall onto the belt, slamming my basket down in front of the cashier. She pulls back, looking at me like I'm the crazy one. I dump my groceries out of the basket and turn around to look for Roxanne. She's still standing behind the old lady, looking flabbergasted. "Come on," I call to her.

As I turn back to the cashier, I can't resist throwing down a smug look at the old lady with the cart. She feints like she's going to ram her cart into me and I back up. Cackling like an evil witch, she pulls back to let Roxanne into the line. As I pay for the groceries, Roxanne helps the old lady load hers onto the belt. Finally, I'm done and I tug on Roxanne's sleeve. "Let's go."

Back in the car, I stow the groceries in the trunk and Roxanne gets behind the wheel. Staring straight ahead, she says, "What the hell happened back there?"

"I stood up to a bully."

"A ninety-something year old bully?"

"A person's age has nothing to do with their personality flaws."

"Dana, she weighed eighty pounds soaking wet."

"Yeah, well, I'll probably have a bruise on my hip for weeks."

She's shaking her head, but I can see the laugh lines at the side of her mouth. Silently, she pulls out of the parking lot and we head back through town and back up the hill.

"Anyway," I say, rubbing at my hip, "Are you still going to make me cookies?"

She finally laughs. Reaching across the car, she

slaps me on the thigh, hard. "You should be ashamed of yourself."

"No way. Life's too short to let old people take advantage of me."

She laughs softly, and we drive the rest of the way in silence. Thinking about the store, I envision telling the story to Sam. She'll probably be pissed that she wasn't there. It would have been an entirely differently situation if she had been. She would have been blocking for me while I slid into the new line. And I never would have gotten the elbow to the back if Sam had been there. Women are different from buddies. Sometimes, you have to be on better behavior with them.

When we get to my house, I note that my sister's car is already in the driveway.

Roxanne pulls up to the door and Susannah comes running out.

"Hey, I wondered where you were." She runs over to give me a hug.

"I went down the hill with Roxanne to get groceries."

"We brought pre-popped popcorn, cut veggies, and several bags of ice in the world's best cooler."

Coming around the side of the car, Roxanne raises her eyebrow. "We?"

Susannah manages to look smug and sheepish at the same time. "Thomas came with me."

"I thought you two were..." Interrupted by Thomas coming out the front door, I make a note to get my sister aside later and find out what's going on.

Thomas smiles as he approaches the car. "Hey, Dana. Hi Roxanne. Can I help carry in your groceries?"

"Please do," I say.

We get all of the bags in one trip and then Thomas and I go back out to Susannah's jeep to move in some water he brought. "You can never have too much."

Since the storm is coming from the southeast, we move both Roxanne's car and Susannah's jeep to the other side of the house, making sure to position them as far away from any hanging tree branches that we can. Thomas looks up at the closest tree. "How sturdy are they?"

"It's the best we can do."

Back in the house, Susannah and Roxanne have started mixing cookie batter. Leaning over the bowl Roxanne is stirring gets me a whack on the hand. "What? I was just looking!"

"You were hoping to score some cookie dough and that isn't going to happen."

"You're a hard woman, Roxanne."

Susannah snaps me with a dish towel. "Shouldn't you be walking around the house securing the perimeter or something?"

"I did that already? What did you do to secure your place?"

She shrugs. "I put everything I could think of into waterproof containers or Ziplocs and elevated everything off the floor. The sensitive stuff is here." She gestures toward a pile of her belongings on the floor.

"You had better find a place for all of that," I cautioned. "Once the storm starts, we're likely to have water coming in under the sliders, even with the shutters on."

Thomas walks over. "Where can we put this?"

"Best place will be the spare bedroom on top of

the bed or dressers. I moved everything to the center of the room and have all of the potential leakage areas in the windows stopped up, but you can never tell. Best we can do is be as prepared as possible."

Susannah and Thomas start moving her stuff to the other room. The skies have just opened up and the rain is starting to pound against the roof. It will still be several hours or more until the actual storm gets here. These rain bands will cause a lot of mud on my road, though. I should call Sam and tell her to hurry up. I'm pacing like an expectant father. The storm is projected to be a category two when it hits us, which is not too bad. However, you can never tell if it is going to pick up and if the wind is bad enough, it will take out the power lines and block the roads. Plus, with sideways rain, we're looking at the possibility of flooding. My hilltop house is perfect to avoid surge and flash flooding, but we won't be as safe up here from the high winds if the storm becomes really bad. Still, I've made a lot of improvements on this house over the past several years and I think it's pretty hearty in a moderate to severe storm.

Roxanne has taken a couple of trays of cookies out of the oven already. Frank is sitting on one of the bar stools behind her, watching her every move. "Don't forget that he can't have chocolate," I warn.

They both turn to give me haughty looks. "Please," Roxanne sneers. Frank doesn't bother to respond at all. He merely blinks imperiously and turns back to Roxanne.

"Well, jeeze. I was just reminding you."

Muttering to myself, I grab my cell phone and plug it into the charger. That reminds me. "Anyone who hasn't charged their phone should do so now.

The power company will shut down if they look to get hit hard."

Looking up from her own phone, Roxanne nods. "NOAA is now saying that it looks to hit us directly as a Cat three. Do you think we need to do anything else at my house?"

"I think we're set at your place, Rox, unless you want to bring over anything from the fridge or freezer to put in the coolers after the fridge starts getting warm."

"No, I cleaned out everything already. Last big storm, we lost power for a month and I had a freezer full of leftovers."

"I remember. I ate like royalty for about a week."

Someone knocks on the door and Roxanne goes to answer it. Expecting Sam, I blink several times before realizing it's Esmé.

"Come in," Roxanne says. "Do you want a cookie?"

"No, thank you. I brought some honey, tea, and water." She holds up her bags, looking awkward.

My mouth opens at least three times, but I can't formulate any words. Roxanne relieves Esmé of her bags, and offers her a seat. Still looking at me, Esmé slides onto the stool not occupied by Frank. He ignores her as he's still staring in the direction of the cookies.

"I left a message earlier, but you didn't call back," Esmé says.

That's true. She called earlier and I ignored the call. Then I decided I didn't want to listen to the voice mail. I guess I'm an asshole, but I was busy all day. Shrugging, I turn away toward the kitchen windows so I can check the seals.

"Dana?"

"What do you want me to say? You're here. It's already raining and you have a shitty car. It looks like you're here for the duration."

"Wow, Dana," Susannah says, walking into the room. "Bitchy much?"

"Speaking of which, where is Olivia?"

Susannah walks past me to take a cookie from the tray. "She parked her car at the resort. Sam is going to bring her up after work. Hopefully they'll get here soon." She pauses to hug Esmé. "I'm glad you're here. This is a safe space."

"From the storm, at least," Roxanne mutters.

I can't tell if she's irritated at Esmé's presence or at my rude behavior. I'm guessing it's the latter. Stomping off into the other room, I check and recheck all of the windows and doors. I debate about going outside to check the hurricane shutters again, but I decide against it. I know I fastened them all securely. When I come back to the kitchen, Thomas is coming back through the front door, soaking wet. I hand him a towel from a pile on the table as he hands Esmé her car keys.

"I moved her car over by Roxanne's and Susannah's."

"Good thinking. I really think we're as set as we're going to get."

Walking past Esmé, I stop for a second. "I'm happy you're safe."

"I didn't know where else to go," she says.

"It's fine."

She looks up at me, smiling. "Maybe we can talk later," she says, touching my arm.

"Probably not," I reply.

Roxanne is putting the last of the cookie sheets

in the oven. The wind is picking up a bit and the rain is coming down a lot harder. I can hear it rattling against the storm shutters. Walking up behind Roxanne, I put my arms around her waist and rest my chin on her shoulder. She leans back against me for a second. "The cookies will be done in twelve minutes," she says.

"I saw you give a piece to Frank."

"He loves peanut butter," she says, smiling.

"I apologized to Esmé for being an asshole," I whisper in her ear.

"Good," she says. "Because you really were one."

Turning from Roxanne, I notice Esmé staring at us, but I don't stop to answer any questions. The door slams open and Olivia walks in carrying a pet carrier. Oh great. I forgot she has that little freakish dog. Frank has moved into a sitting position and is eying the carrier with interest. Thomas runs over to close the door behind Olivia, but before he can get it closed, the whole floor in front of the door is soaked. Susannah grabs another towel and throws it on the ground. Before she can wipe up the water, the door is open again, and Sam comes in, slamming the door shut behind her. "Damn," she says, wiping water out of her eyes. "It's wet out there!"

"Hey, look, the master of the painfully obvious has arrived," I laugh, moving forward to hug her.

Susannah starts to tuck one of the towels under the slight space between the door and the floor, but I ask her to stop. Now that everyone is here, I can shove some rolled up plastic grocery bags into the space to repel some of the water. The rolled up towel can go behind that. Sam is vigorously toweling off her short hair while Olivia opens the carrier and brings out her little mutt. I'm not sure what kind of dog it is, though

I'm pretty sure it has some Chihuahua and perhaps some rat in it. It's small and yippy and it shakes all of the time. Frank is staring down at the dog with disdain. He looks at me as if to say, "Really?"

"I know. Right?" I pat his head as I walk past, but he turns his back on all of us. Climbing up onto the counter, he walks over to the wall and lies down facing it.

Olivia's dog is running around at her feet, whining. The wind is continuing to pound the rain against the shutters.

Roxanne takes the last of the cookies out of the oven and turns it off. Sam looks pensive. "Do you think we should disconnect the propane tanks?"

"No, I don't. They're sheltered pretty well in their little shed. And I want to have access to the stove after the storm."

"Fair enough." She drags her cooler across the floor to set it next to the other coolers. "More ice," she explains. "Can't have too much, in my opinion."

"Especially in those super solid cold coolers."

"Totally. Should we put this in the freezer until the power goes out?"

"Without a doubt."

Thomas and Sam and I load all of the ice into my drop down freezer. I've already frozen several gallons of potable water. I figure we can use them to cool food and as they melt, we can drink them.

"What else?" Thomas is looking to move around.

"Well, I thought it would be best if we hung out in here. The windows are solid. I have the radio and the cases of flashlights and portable lanterns in here. The coolers are here and there isn't a lot of crap to trip over. Plus, we're close to the bathroom. So, maybe we could drag in the couch and a couple of the chairs from the living room."

"Solid." Thomas and Sam head off to start doing that.

"In the meantime, Olivia, pick up your dog and let's make sure the doors to the other rooms are all closed. That way when the storm gets going, we'll know the animals are in here with us."

"I'm pretty sure Muffin won't leave my side," she says.

Muffin. Roxanne and I exchange glances and smile. Olivia and Esmé move to close the bedroom and bathroom doors. Sam smiles as she and Thomas bring the couch in. "Anyone that has to poop better do so now!"

"Classy, Sam," Roxanne says.

"All the way, baby."

The door slams open again, scattering plastic bags everywhere. The wind whips through the house, carrying water across the counters.

"Close the door," Roxanne yells, as I scramble for the plastic bags. Looking up from the floor, I freeze in a squatting position, staring at the new arrival. "Hey Karen," I yell over the wind.

She wrestles the door shut as Roxanne comes over with a mop to soak up some of the water.

Karen is standing in the doorway, soaking wet. I get up from the floor and drape a towel around her. "What on earth?"

"Rick and I are right on the beach," she says. "When the news changed the prediction to a cat three, we figured we better head up here. I tried to call, but there was no answer."

"I probably didn't hear my phone over the rain

and wind," I say.

The doorknob turns and Roxanne opens the door quickly, closing it as soon as Rick gets in the door. Grabbing a couple extra towels, I toss one to him, and throw one on the floor. He towels his head, smiling at me. "I'm sorry for busting in. We brought supplies, though." He holds up two big reusable grocery bags. "I'll take them," Roxanne says. She places them on the counter and starts digging through, looking for perishables.

"Do either of you want dry clothes?'"

"Yes, please," Karen answers.

Esmé stands up. "Do you have something in particular you're offering them, or just anything in your closet?"

"I have a bunch of extra shorts, t-shirts, and sweatshirts in the spare bedroom," I tell her. "Anyone can help themselves."

"You're the best hurricane party thrower ever," Sam chirps as she drags in another chair. Thomas is right behind her with another.

"It's just a bunch of stuff that I haven't gotten around to taking to the thrift store," I say, smiling.

Sam notices Rick and Karen moving toward the spare bedroom with Esmé. She waves at all of them. When they close themselves in the spare bedroom, Sam turns to me. "Is it me or is that a little weird?"

"I guess it makes sense. They do live really close to the water and I'd rather be here than one of the crowded and probably not too clean temporary shelters."

"I meant Esmé being here."

"It's a little weird."

"I'm sure she must have other friends than you."

"What does it matter, Sam?" Roxanne is perplexed. "We have plenty of food and water. Why not offer a safe space to anyone who needs it?"

A loud pounding at the door makes me jump. "Seriously? What the fuck?"

Sam walks over to the door and opens it. My ex slides in with Mandy right behind her. They're both soaking wet. Standing there dripping water all over my floor, my ex spreads her arms and shrugs. "We didn't have anywhere else to go?"

"You could have gone to The Pit," I snarl.

"They're shut down," Mandy pouts.

Catching movement out of the corner of my eye, I see Roxanne smiling to herself. I'm so glad someone is getting a kick out of my misery.

The wind roars over the house, slamming what sounds like small branches and pebbles against the walls. "You still have time to make it down the hill before the storm starts."

"Dana," Jackie pleads. "Your road is already a mud pit. We almost went over the side of the hill twice on our way up here."

"How is that my problem? I don't recall inviting you here!"

Mandy sniffs. "Trust me. I don't want to be here anymore than you want me here. Jackie insisted this would be the safest place for us to spend the storm."

"Jackie was wrong." Irritated as I am at their presence, I'm even more irritated by the fact that I won't really send them out to die in the storm.

Roxanne puts her hand on my arm and looks into my eyes. "Dana, I know you're upset and you have every right to be. But a compassionate person cannot send them back out into the storm. What if they drove off the road and died?"

"I'd send flowers to the funeral home," I say, though I'm smiling.

"Dana." Roxanne whispers. "I'd feel horrible for the rest of my life."

Still smiling, I put my arms around her. "Even if the world would be better without either of them?"

"Even then," she answers, grinning up at me.

"Fine," I say, turning to Jackie and Mandy. "Dry off and then clean up the water you left all over my floor."

Esmé comes into the kitchen, carrying another stack of towels. "I grabbed these from the laundry room."

"Let's run a load of towels while we still have power," I say. "We've already gone through a lot."

"Should I just put them in the dryer?"

"Yeah, let's do that. Leave that stack here. There's a few clean ones in the bathroom that we should try to save for use on people, rather than floors."

Esmé gathers up a bunch of wet towels, nodding to Mandy and smiling at Jackie. Drying off as best they can, Jackie takes both of their towels and starts trying to mop up the floor with them. "Just go in the spare bedroom for dry clothes. Take a towel with you."

"Thanks, Dana," Jackie says. She sounds almost sincere. Mandy curls her lip at me as they walk past me to the hallway.

"What a douche," I mutter just loud enough for her to hear me.

Turning her head, she glares at me over her shoulder before flouncing off down the hall. Looking at Roxanne, I whisper, "I'm pretty sure she won't find anything of mine to fit over that rack."

"Dana, be nice," she says.

"Why do I have to be the bigger person?"

"Because you're just so wonderful," she smiles.

"Whatever."

Walking through to the living room, I help Sam and Thomas move the last of the furniture. Everything is lifted from the floor of this room. If there's going to be leakage, I'm pretty sure it will come from underneath the sliders. I sealed them as best as I could and have shoved towels into the tracks, so it's as secure as it's going to get. I'll still have to check on it every so often to see if I need to bring in a mop.

Coming back into the kitchen and dining area, I slide the partition between the living room and the kitchen closed. I don't want Frank running in there in terror. I'd rather have him sitting on my lap in terror. I don't think I'll have to worry about him, though. Roxanne is sitting cross-legged on one of the arm chairs and Frank is on her lap. He's licking his lips and she's finishing a cookie, so I can only assume they've been sharing. I give her a warning look, but she just smiles back at me.

Olivia and Sam are standing at the kitchen counter, giggling together. Sam is actually holding Muffin. Really? I mouth "Ass" at her before turning back to the dining area. Rick and Karen have taken seats at opposite sides of the couch, so I slide into the chair next to Roxanne. Esmé comes back from the laundry and takes the chair on the other side of me. Standing, I push two of the empty chairs to the other side of the couch so that Mandy and Jackie will be as far away from my chair as possible. Roxanne raises an eyebrow but doesn't say anything. Speak of the devil, here they come. Jackie's just wearing a t-shirt and some sweats that I got at the thrift store. Mandy has crammed herself into a pair of shorts and a tank top.

"If she bends over too fast, someone's gonna get a black eye," Esmé whispers in my ear. Snorting in answer, I direct them to the chairs furthest away from me. Not that I'll be sitting all that much.

"What happens when people need to sleep?" Mandy asks.

"There are air mattresses in the living room area, along with some battery powered pumps. Someone should go ahead and get those filled now so that when people want to sleep, they don't have to worry about it."

"I'll do it," Thomas says.

"I'll help," my ex offers.

They slide open the partition and disappear into the living room. Sam follows, closing it behind her.

"If anyone does need to sleep, there is a stack of blankets in the living room. I didn't provide sheets. You'll have to rough it."

Mandy sniffs.

Turning to glare at her, Esmé says, "You should consider being grateful."

"What business is it of yours?" Mandy stands up, throwing her shoulders back. Esmé jumps out of her chair as well. Stepping in between them, I hold up my hands, trying not to laugh. "There will be no chick fighting here, no matter how much you piss each other off."

"Just as well," Esmé mutters under her breath. "She'd kill me with one swipe of her boob."

"There will also be no insulting people based on their appearance," Roxanne says, loudly.

Huffing, Esmé and Mandy both slam back into

their chairs. Roxanne sighs and Olivia makes a tutting sound from the other side of the kitchen.

The wind is really picking up now. I can hear the branches slamming against the house. There is a little bit of water coming in under the kitchen door. Kneeling to mop some of it up, I hear someone rummaging in the beer cooler. Looking around, expecting to see Sam, I see Mandy instead.

"That's Sam's beer, buddy. You might consider asking before you dive into it."

"What? You're going to let us stay at your party without letting us drink or eat anything?"

"You can eat or drink anything you want. I'm just letting you know that it might be polite to ask before you take, especially considering you didn't bring anything to contribute."

"I didn't ask to be here. I was dragged here by Jackie."

Turning my back on her, I continue mopping up the water. She's still standing behind me and it's irritating. "If you're just going to stand there, get a towel and help me replace the wet ones!"

Sighing, she bends down and hands me several dry towels, relieving me of the wet ones that I have taken from the crack under the door.

She asks Esmé about putting the towels in the dryer. Putting them out of my mind, I concentrate on rolling up the new towels and shoving them in under the door. Roxanne leans over beside me. "Want some more plastic bags?"

"Maybe."

While she grabs the bags from the counter, I remove the towels that I've already placed. She kneels next to me to squeeze the bags under the door. "If we pack them in as tightly as possible, less water will get through," she says.

"Really? I hadn't thought of that."

She elbows me in the ribs. Laughing, I lean in to kiss her on the cheek. We work quietly together packing every square inch of space with plastic bags.

"Where else could we have gone, Karen?" I hear Rick say loudly, over the wind.

"I don't know. We should have stayed at our house."

"Our house is going to be flooded," he responds.

"I'd rather be there dealing with the flood than here with you."

Pretending I can't hear them, I continue poking towels in along the door. Roxanne catches my eye and I smile at her. "I'm glad you're here," I whisper.

Whispering back, she says, "Are you?"

"Yes. You're the one beacon of normalcy in this group."

Laughing, she stands up before offering me a hand. Dragging me to my feet, she smiles. "If I'm your beacon of normalcy, you've set your bar pretty low."

Sam, Jackie, and Thomas come back from the living room singing, "Row, Row, Row Your Boat" at the top of their lungs. Looking back at Roxanne, I grin. "I've set my bar pretty low."

Something slams against the side of the house, making me jump. Roxanne takes my hand. "Oh, don't worry, Dana. I'll protect you."

"Funny."

"Oh, you must need a femme around to keep you safe," she grins.

Shaking my head at her, I walk away, laughing.

She follows me, stopping in the kitchen to grab a tray of cookies. Sam heads for her beer cooler. Turning to Thomas and Jackie, she offers them a beer. Thomas takes one, but Jackie refuses.

Back to my chair, I pick up Frank and deposit him on my lap. He lets out an indignant meow before settling in. Rick and Karen are about as far away on the couch as two people can get. Obvious as usual, Sam comes in and plops down between them. "Hey, Karen," she says in an overly jovial voice. "What's shaking?"

Karen glares at her. "Grow up, Sam."

Unperturbed, Sam shakes her head. "Never. I'm perfect the way I am."

"Hardly," Olivia scoffs, coming into the dining area with a plate of food.

That reminds me. "If anyone gets hungry, there is all sort of food in the fridge and all over the counters. Once the power goes out, we want to make sure to open the fridge as little as possible. It will probably keep the food good for about twenty-four hours. After that, we'll put stuff on ice in the coolers. And hopefully after that, we'll be able to get down the hill."

"God, let us hope," Esmé says.

"You didn't have to be here," Sam reminds her. "In fact, if I remember correctly, you weren't invited."

"There's a lot of that going around," I say, laughing.

"Fine," Karen says, standing. "Sorry for busting in on you. We can go."

The whole house shakes as something crashes into one of the walls. Rick takes Karen by the hand and pulls her down next to him. "We aren't going anywhere in this."

"No one is going anywhere in this," I state. "I'm pretty sure no one is going to be going anywhere for at least twenty-four hours, so we might all try to pretend that we like each other."

Jackie grins. "One year we had a hurricane party for fifteen. Everyone except Dana got trashed. There was a leak in one of the windows and it was shooting water in right where I was sleeping. When she woke me up, I was soaking wet from head to toe. Good times."

Smiling at her, I shrug my shoulders. "They weren't all bad times."

Something else crashes hard against the house, causing everyone to jump.

"That was a big one," my sister says, walking past on her way to the kitchen.

Sam gets off the couch and sits on the ground in front of Olivia. Running her fingers over Sam's short hair, Olivia bends down and kisses Sam on the ear. Leaning over to press my face against Roxanne's shoulder, I fake shudder. "I can't believe I couldn't avert my eyes in time to miss that."

Mandy moves her chair closer to Jackie so she can put her arm around her. She's on her third or fourth beer and I can tell Jackie is getting upset. I don't think that relationship will last long. It's hard to recover while still dealing with someone who drinks like that. Jackie stretches her long legs out onto a side table, leaning away from Mandy as she does. Roxanne squeezes my hand. "Want a cookie?"

"Yeah, I do." Taking a couple of chocolate chip cookies, I lean back in my chair, surveying the room. I should probably get up and walk the house again. Shoving both cookies into my mouth, I stand and motion to Sam. "Everyone else stay put. We're going to check the house."

Back in the spare bedroom, everything looks good. There is a little water seepage under one of the windows, but other than that, things are holding up well. The house is shaking like crazy by now and it sounds like a freight train outside. Glancing at her phone, Sam says, "We aren't in the worst of it yet. According to the satellite, we're still in the outer bands."

Leaning over to look at it, I point out the movement of the storm. "Look at the update. We're getting close to the hardest part."

She pulls some duct tape out of the pocket of her cargo shorts. Pulling off a piece, she hands the end to me so she can reach in her pocket for a knife. After she cuts the piece off, I tape it across the bottom of the window.

She puts the tape back in her pocket. Reaching for her phone again, she looks at the satellite image one more time. "The biggest convection is one the other side of the eye and that's what will be over us in a couple of hours."

"It's moving fast. Won't stick around."

"That's a good thing," she says.

There's a crash from the other room and someone screams. Looking down the hall, I call, "Do we need to come back there?"

"Everything's fine," Roxanne calls back.

"Good."

Sam and I check the bathroom, but it's sealed up tight. In my bedroom, everything looks good. Everything that can fit into a plastic container is in one. My books are all in waterproof bags and containers, just to be safe. As we're standing there, something slams outside of the house, and water starts spraying into my room. Sam gets hit with it, but she doesn't flinch. Running to the window, she slams her hand against the new crack. I go back to the bathroom for a towel. Bringing it back to the bedroom, I see what's happened. The hurricane shutter has come off the fastening on the wall side and is slamming against the window. Something obviously hit the window hard enough to crack it. Standing here, watching Sam hold the towel against the crack, I'm stunned by the way the window itself is moving in and out. The glass is bowing with each huge gust. With the roar of the wind over our heads, I'm torn about whether to brave the storm to fix the shutter, or risk more damage by letting it go.

Putting my mouth next to Sam's ear, I yell over the roar of the storm. "Do we need to go fix this?"

"We need to do something," she yells back. "I don't want this glass breaking all over the room."

"Tape the glass." Running back to the kitchen for a cardboard box from the storage closet, I stop for a second to see what had made the crash.

"It's nothing," Roxanne assures me. "Mandy tripped over the cooler and fell."

Mandy is sitting in a chair with her leg elevated on a stool. Jackie is holding an ice pack over the woman's ankle. Rolling my eyes toward the ceiling, I turn away without comment. Rummaging in the closet until I find a box, I smile at Roxanne. "Hold down the fort, gorgeous. Sam and I are taking care of business."

"My heroes," she says.

"Was that sarcasm?" I call back over my shoulder as I walk back down the hall.

The towel in Sam's hands is soaked through.

She takes it off and water immediately starts pouring into the room again. It looks as if someone is standing directly outside the crack with a fire hose.

"Horizontal rain," Sam says. "Cool."

"Cool if it isn't your bedroom," I reply.

I slam a plastic bag over the crack, holding it against the window. The window shudders under my hand. It feels like it will break at any moment. "Damn, weren't you scared you were going to get a face full of glass?"

We both jump as the storm shutter slams back into the window. I have both hands on the window now and it's shaking so hard, I can feel it jarring my shoulders. Sam whips her duct tape out again and tapes the plastic against the window. Once that's done, we both back away. It's visibly shimmying, but I think it will hold. Another slam of the shutter and we hear another cracking noise.

"Help me get this box torn up," I tell Sam.

We tear off a big piece of cardboard and put it against the window. While I hold it, Sam carefully surrounds the entire thing with duct tape. Once that's in place, I feel a little better. The whole assembly is still blowing in and out, but at least the cardboard should contain the glass.

"We're probably going to have to secure that shutter," Sam says as it bangs up against the window again.

"Secure it or take it down, whichever is faster."

There's a click, and a kind of whooshing noise. "Here it comes," Sam says.

All of the lights go off. "There it goes," Sam says, laughing. "I don't suppose you brought any of those flashlights in here with you."

"There's a whole shitload of them in the crate in the kitchen."

"Perfect, oh Master of Preparedness."

"That's not even a word."

"It is." I can hear her shuffling around in the dark. "And lucky for you, I am uber-prepared."

A light shines in my face. Sam has a tiny flashlight in her hand. Directing the beam at the window, she says, "I think that's the best we can do for now."

"Me too. Let's go into the kitchen and get a real flashlight."

"Don't mock it," she replies. "It's saving your bacon right now."

"Bacon sounds good right about now," I say.

"Mmmm. Bacon."

We walk back down the hallway toward the glow from the kitchen and dining room area. Roxanne and Susannah already have all of the battery powered lights scattered around. Esmé is handing out flashlights to everyone.

"Don't use them now," I caution. "We have plenty of light in here. Just take one if you need to go in the other room."

"And don't flush the toilet without making sure there's water in the back of the tank," Sam says.

"Yeah, in fact, whenever you flush, pour more water in the tank afterward," I counter.

"Thank you," Susannah says. "Because none of the rest of us have been in a hurricane before."

"Or lost power on a sunny day," Rick says, smiling.

"For utterly no reason," Thomas agrees.

"Okay, okay. I was reminding everyone," I reply. "Jeeze. Sue me."

Susannah stands. "On that note, let me be the first to pee."

Everyone laughs.

"Do you want me to come with you?" Thomas asks.

"No, I have my trusty mag light. If there's something scary in the bathroom, I'll handle it."

"That's my amazon," Thomas laughs.

Susannah hefts the mag light, making an exaggerated flexing gesture.

"I think we want to leave when the eye hits," Karen says.

"You've got to be kidding," Sam laughs. "Have you been listening to the storm?"

"The road will be washed out, Karen. And I'd be surprised if there weren't trees down all up and down the road. You aren't going anywhere."

"Settle down, Karen. What's wrong with you?" Rick is exasperated.

"What's wrong with me? We haven't spoken to each other in weeks. We haven't had sex in months. And now I'm cooped up in here with you and all of your friends."

"Well, technically we're *your* friends, Karen," Sam says.

She screeches and storms down the hall in the dark, slamming the door of my spare room. Rick looks at us helplessly. Sam hands him a flashlight.

"I'd recommend going after her," she says.

"I don't know what good I can do. I've been trying to figure out what's going on for weeks."

Mandy slides down in her chair, waving a beer bottle in Rick's direction. "Don't bother, Ricky old boy. Women are crazy. You'll never understand them."

"Pretty," I whisper sidelong to Sam.

Breaking one of my own rules, I open the fridge, reaching for a pound of bacon, a hunk of cheese, and some eggs.

"Oh yeah," Sam yells. "Bacon and eggs, baby."

Roxanne joins me in the kitchen. "Want hash browns, too?"

"Totally."

Grabbing a cutting board and a knife, Roxanne starts dicing potatoes. Sam chops an onion while I crack some eggs into a bowl. Thomas jumps up, offering to fry the bacon. Before I can light the stove, I realize that the sound has died down. Sam looks at me.

"The eye?"

"Yeah. We gotta go."

"I'll take over here," Roxanne says. She lights one of the burners with a match. "Thank God for propane."

"We'll be back in a few. We have to take care of that shutter."

"It will take a while for the potatoes," she says, smiling. "I'll wait on the eggs until you get back."

"Do you need help?" Jackie says, standing.

Sam doesn't even look at her. "We can handle it."

"We could use an extra set of hands," I tell Sam.

"Not hers."

Thomas steps forward. "I'll help."

The three of us head out into the rain. Looking up, I can see a bit of sky through the clouds. Mesmerized for a minute by the swirling clouds, I stop dead. Sam and Thomas stop too, and we all stand there staring at the sky.

"Amazing, isn't it?" Thomas says.

"Amazing and horrifying." Sam replies, turning to smile at him.

"Come on."

The yard is littered with branches and leaves. There are several decorative shutters down, but the rest of the storm shutters look good. Sam and Thomas go around to look at the broken shutter while I run through the yard picking up debris and securing it in the shed. Sam jogs back, grabbing a handful of nails.

"We're just going to secure it for now," she says. "We can fix it after the storm."

"Good idea."

"And you should check out Roxanne's car," she calls as she trots away.

Walking around to the other side of the other, I look around the corner. All of the cars are covered with sticks, but Roxanne's car is smashed under a huge tree limb. It has flattened the roof, broken the windshield, and caved in half of the hood. "Shit."

Continuing around the house, I spy Sam and Thomas hammering the shutter back together. They have it under control, so I continue patrolling. There's an awful lot of debris, but the wind is starting to pick up again and I doubt I can get it all cleaned up before the other side of the storm kicks in. Someone's grill is in my yard. Dragging it along, I decide to shove it under the deck. That should brace it enough to keep it from moving. Kicking it under the deck, I look at the sky again. The little patch of visible sky is gone and the wind is whipping through the trees again. The remaining leaves are starting to drop from the trees. Thomas and Sam meet me at the corner.

"We've got it as secure as it's going to get,"

Thomas says.

"All right, let's go."

A gust of wind picks up as we run around the house. Stopping at Roxanne's car, we look at the damage together. Sam puts a hand on the branch. "Should we try to pull it off?"

"Maybe, but where will we put it?"

She shrugs. "Under the deck?"

"Okay."

Thomas and I grab one end and Sam gets on the other. Lifting it from the car, we heft it over to the side yard. As we drag it over the yard toward the deck, the wind knocks us around, and Thomas almost falls.

"Auntie Em," Sam screams, laughing wildly.

We get the branch to the deck and shove it underneath next to the grill. Lying down on the ground, I slam my foot against the branch wedging it in as far as it will go. Sam hauls me to my feet and we run for the door.

"Come on, Thomas," I yell, as the wind nearly knocks him off his feet again. Sam reaches back to take his hand. Turning back toward the house, she takes a tree branch to the face.

"Fuck," she yells, grabbing her eye.

Yanking her by the elbow, I pull her around the house and into the door. Thomas slams it shut behind us. Olivia comes tearing over to Sam. "What happened, sweetie?"

"I'm fine. I think. I just got hit in the face."

Olivia takes Sam out of my hands and walks her into the kitchen. "Help me, Susannah."

Roxanne looks up as the two other women coo over Sam's head. "Is she going to be okay?"

"She'll be fine," Susannah says, holding one of

the lamps near the wound.

"It's okay," Olivia concurs. "We just need to wash it out and pour some hydrogen peroxide on it."

"Don't put hydrogen peroxide on it," Roxanne laughs. "It will kill the good cells."

Smiling across the counter at her, I shake my head. She smiles back at me as she turns back to the stove.

"Food smells good," Sam says.

"Hold still," Olivia tells her.

The wind is back at full force. I'm glad that we decided to move that large branch, but I doubt it will make much of a difference. Hopefully the cars will be all right. Which reminds me, I should probably tell Roxanne about her car.

"There's been some damage outside," I tell her.

"We can assess it all after the storm," she says, leaning over the counter to put a finger to my lips.

Susannah and Olivia get Sam's wound cleaned and bandaged while Roxanne finishes cooking breakfast. I wipe my hands down with a couple of wet wipes before pouring some water over them from one of the jugs.

Roxanne dishes food out and everyone digs in. Mandy, barely able to stand, manages to dump her entire plate on the floor after one bite. Muffin who had been shaking in the corner of the chair, jumps down and starts snarfing up bacon as fast as he can. Mandy, tries to shoo him out of the way, pushing the dog with one hand, while trying to cram eggs and bacon back onto her plate with the other. Jackie, continuing to shovel food in her own mouth, ignores her. I try to catch Sam's eye, but she's busy feeding bites of potatoes to Olivia. Karen and Rick, still sitting on opposite sides of the couch, eat in silence. Susannah and Thomas are laughing together. Catching Susannah's eye, I motion toward Mandy who is now on the ground, holding the dog back with one hand. She shakes her head, laughing. Finally taking pity on the woman, I reach down to pick up Muffin. Taking him over to Olivia, I push him into her arms.

"He's being a pain," I say.

Now that he's not actively trying to eat bacon, Muffin is trembling like a baby again.

"Poor thing," Olivia murmurs. "He's not a pain, Dana. He's just scared."

"Whatever."

Roxanne starts to say something to me, but I can't hear any sound. A screeching boom shakes the whole house. Looking around wildly, I don't see any interior problems. The wind sounds horrible, though. It sounds as if a bulldozer is being dragged across my roof. Everyone is one their feet, looking nervous. Roxanne tells everyone to stack their dishes in a plastic bin, which she then stashes under the sink.

"We can worry about washing them after the storm," she yells in my ear.

"Yeah, what kind of jackass decides to have bacon when there's no hot running water?" I grin.

The noise on top of the roof is getting louder. Sam reaches over and tugs at my shirt. She's pointing at a corner of the roof where water is starting to shoot through. Great. If we lose the roof, we're fucked.

Roxanne has already thrown towels over everything that's under the spray of water, but it isn't doing much good.

"Just get everyone into the bathroom," I yell. I look around for Frank, but Susannah already has him in her arms.

Trusting Roxanne to take care of everyone else, I grab Sam's arm and pull her over toward the roof. Olivia, clutching Muffin, runs toward the bathroom.

"Do you think we should try to stabilize it?" I scream.

Jumping up on the counter, she reaches up toward the ceiling. "Hand me some plastic," she yells.

I grab several bags and heft myself up onto the counter next to her. "You make it look so easy," I yell.

Laughing, she shakes her head. "Must be all of those years of ballet lessons."

She's taller than I am, so I have to stand on my toes to hold the bags. The roof is shimmying as wildly as the window. "I think we should take cover," I holler in her ear.

She shakes her head again. "Let's get it taped up at least. We'll feel it if it starts to give."

"It's starting to give now," I yell.

"Just hold the fucking bags."

Both of us are soaking wet. The rain is gushing in around the bags. Sam starts to plaster the bags and the ceiling with tape, but it isn't sticking very well to the wet plaster. The crack between the roof and the wall widens and we're blasted with a hard sheet of water. With water stinging my eyes, I can't see anything for a second. The force of the wind coming in through the hole almost knocks me off the counter. A knot of anxiety starts to form in my stomach and I reach for Sam, though she suddenly seems far away. I can see the entire roof tearing away from the house and with it, I see Sam being sucked into the storm. Paralyzed, I stand on the counter being pelted by small rocks and driving rain. A leaf blows in on the wind and slashes against my face. Dimly, I'm aware that my entire kitchen is getting wet, but I can't move to try to save anything. My vision darkens and then I'm looking at Sam, lying dead in the yard, thrown to the ground by the force of the wind. My heart stops and I drop to my knees on the counter. Swaying dangerously, I realize that I'm about to pass out. Suddenly, Sam's face is in my line of vision. She yanks me off the counter into her arms and half-drags me down the hall to the bathroom. Crowding into the small space with nine other people, we fall through the door. Roxanne is sitting on the side of the tub next to Jackie and Mandy. Karen is sitting on the closed toilet. Olivia is on the floor with both Muffin and Frank curled up in her arms. Everyone else is standing. Sam lowers me to the floor next to Olivia and squats in front of me, scared.

"Hey, buddy." Sam tries to smile. "Hey. Dana. Hi."

Blinking at her, I try to return the smile. "I thought I saw you sucked out through the roof," I whisper.

She leans forward, unable to hear me over the wind. "What did you say?"

"I said I guess I'm not as healed as I thought I was," I answer, still whispering.

Grimly, she shakes her head. "I'm sorry, I still can't hear you."

"I said I think I'm fucked up," I yell over the noise. Bursting into tears, I put both of my hands over my face, shaking with the effort of not losing it. Sam pats me awkwardly on the shoulder. I can feel everyone in the room looking at me, even though I can't see them. The wind noise is screaming through the house and now, all I can see is a vision of Sam jumping off the same cliff that took Fran. I can hear Esmé yelling something, but I can't make out what she's saying. Shaking and crying, I press my hands tight against my face, trying to stem the tide. Suddenly, Roxanne is kneeling in front of me. She reaches around me and pulls me into her arms. Collapsing against her, I press my face into her chest, letting go of everything. Her hands feel warm on my body. I know she's whispering things in my ear, but I can't tell what she's saying. It doesn't really matter. It has the necessary effect. With my tears subsiding, I lean back against the wall and open my eyes. Sam is looking terrified. I give her a wink and she relaxes a bit. Roxanne turns around and sits between my legs, resting her back against my chest. My arms move naturally against her waist. I can't help noticing a look from Esmé that I can't quite decipher. I give her a quick smile, but she doesn't smile back.

"I'm fine," I yell. "I'm perfectly fine. Everyone can stop staring at me."

"It's not a problem," Rick yells back. "We've all been there."

"Really?" Karen is speaking loudly, but I can only just hear her over the noise of the wind. "I didn't think you ever lose control."

"No shit," Mandy slurs. "Like Jackie. She's a robot."

"Excuse me," Jackie yells back. "I'm trying to get my life under control. I have to keep a tight lid on myself."

"That doesn't mean you have to be cold and unfeeling," Karen yells.

Rick squats in front of Karen. "I'm not cold and unfeeling. I just don't understand why you're always complaining."

"Because I never feel like you love me enough," she yells, tearing up.

Mandy nods and pats Karen's shoulder. "I know exactly what you mean."

"How can you know what she means?" My ex looks livid. "You're never sober enough to recognize love." Jackie turns to look at me. "I get it, you know. I get it now."

Nodding at her, I look back at Esmé who is watching the argument with a pained expression. I remember her telling me that she never felt like Fran loved her as much as she loved Fran. This time when I smile at her, she smiles back. Tightening my arms around Roxanne, I turn back to look at Jackie. "I know. I know it."

Mandy waves her hands around, almost knocking herself off balance. A vision of her falling into the tub full of water gives me a bit of a laugh. Reading my thoughts, Roxanne laughs too.

"Karen," Rick tries again. "We can talk about this more when we go home. I do love you. I just don't know what else I can do to show it."

"You can try hugging me and kissing me and being affectionate with me even when we aren't having sex."

"Yeah," Mandy yells again, waving her hand toward Jackie.

Ignoring her, Rick looks at his wife. "Well, I feel like when I try, you get mad."

"Because it's already been so long that I'm frustrated when you even try."

Rick throws his arms up in exasperation. "Then what can I do? I feel like I'm always trying. I check your tire pressure every day. I take your car in for servicing. I get up every night and walk around the house checking the locks. I do everything I can to keep you safe."

"I don't want to just feel safe," Karen says, starting to cry. "I want to feel desired."

Rick reaches out to touch her hair. "Sometimes it's hard to desire you when you're always angry at me."

"I know," she replies.

Mandy leans back, almost falling into the tub again and again I chuckle. "Shut the hell up, Dana," she yells.

Oblivious to the screams of the roof and the storm, she pops open another beer and chugs half of it. "You let go of Jackie and I got her. Who's the loser now?"

"You will be," I yell across the room, "when she comes to the realization that someone in recovery can't be with someone who's drunk all of the time."

Jackie looks away, staring at the wall. Karen is still softly crying, but she's letting Rick hold her. Sam clears her throat. "Well, as long as we're all in couple's counseling," she yells, boisterously. "Susannah, Thomas. Anything you want to tell us?"

"Well, for a while there, I thought I might have to join your club," Susannah begins.

"Oh, that stupid thing," Roxanne breaks in. "Why on earth did I ever agree to be a part of something so ridiculous?"

"Because you're secretly in love with me and you thought it was the best way to get my attention?" I offer.

"Excuse me," Susannah interrupts. "I believe I have the floor."

We all wait while a particularly loud crash shakes the house again. Roxanne reaches over for Frank and hugs him in close to her body. "At least he gets cuddled," I call in her ear.

"I'm pressed against you and you're complaining?"

"Anyway," Susannah says, loudly. "Thomas is wonderful."

"Really?" He smiles at her.

"Really," she says. "Truly wonderful."

"Oh, good for you," Mandy says, waving her beer in the air in some kind of sloppy toast. "So glad to hear the breeders are happy."

"Can it, Mandy," Jackie warns.

"Or what?"

"Wow," Olivia says. "What a drama queen."

Sam and I both bust out laughing. "That's pretty rich coming from you," I say, slapping my hand against my knee.

Olivia looks furious for a second. She opens her mouth to say something, but closes it again. Smiling, she nods at me. "You're right. I am a drama queen. But I'm working on it."

Roxanne takes her hand and the two of them smile affectionately at each other.

"So, Olivia," I say. "Are you still straight?"

"Does everyone have to have a label in your world, Dana?"

"Pretty much," I say, grinning.

Roxanne rolls her eyes. "Dana is very much into the butch and femme thing. She considers herself an old school butch."

"What's that mean?" Olivia asks.

"Oh you know. She holds open the car door,

makes sure to get to the door to an establishment first so she can open it, takes a woman's coat or sweater, and pays for everything."

"Hmm." Olivia looks up at Sam.

"Hey, don't look at me. I'm new school."

Everyone on our side of the bathroom laughs. Mandy and Jackie still seem to be having an argument, but I can't hear a word they're saying. Squeezing Roxanne, I rest my head on her shoulder. She presses her cheek against my face. "So, what do you think, Roxanne?"

"I already told you what I think," she says.

"I thought maybe you had changed your mind."

"I think you still need some time to heal," she replies.

"That's probably true."

Leaning my head back against the wall, I listen to the screaming sounds of the storm against my house. Roxanne drifts off with her head on my shoulder. Aware that Esmé is squeezing my toe, I look up at her and smile.

"How are you faring?"

She smiles. "I'll survive. I'm sorry for the things I said about Roxanne. She's really a stellar woman."

"She is."

"Are you two a couple now?"

"No, we're not."

"There's not a chance of anything happening with us, is there?" Esmé asks, though she's already smiling a little sadly, and I know she knows how I'm going to answer.

"We'll always have a bond because of Fran."

"I still feel like I failed her. Like, if only I could have been better for her, she would have stayed and gotten better and lived."

"The only thing that I've learned for sure, Esmé, is that we can't ever change anyone."

She laughs. "We can only change ourselves."

"And that takes a shitload of effort."

We both laugh. Maneuvering a bit, I manage to reach down toward my feet and squeeze her hand. Leaning my head back against the wall, I give in to the heaviness that's filling my head.

Startled, I open my eyes, aware that I had been sleeping. There's only one battery powered lamp on now in the bathroom. In the dim glow, I see that everyone has managed to squeeze onto a spot on the floor. Looking at Karen and Rick sitting on the floor next to the toilet, I send up a small prayer of thanks that I had the house cleaned right before the storm. Jackie and Mandy are mashed together next to the tub, with their legs draped over Rick's. Esmé is still perched on the sink, wide awake. Meeting her eyes, I smile, and she raises her hand toward me, palm forward. Susannah and Thomas are both asleep, propped up against my laundry hamper. Olivia and Sam are snoozing next to me. Roxanne is still pressed up against my chest and my right arm has gone to sleep. Frank is sound asleep across her lap and she has her hands twined into his coat. Looking over her shoulder, I blert softly at him. He lifts his head to blink slowly at me. Aware that the storm has passed, I start to work on maneuvering myself out from behind Roxanne. She wakes as I push her gently forward. As she stretches her legs out, I hear loud popping from both of her knees.

"The thrill of getting old," she says.

"Oh yeah, check this out." I straighten both arms over my head, causing my shoulders to pop.

"Ew."

"I know."

Sam opens her eyes. "What are you two jabbering about?"

"Storm is over," I tell her.

After setting Frank down on top of Susannah, Roxanne is able to get to her feet. She takes my hand and hauls me up. Squeezing around the bodies on the floor, I open the bathroom door. Roxanne follows me out. We haven't even made it down the hallway and I can see the damage. There are pieces of debris all over the floor. Giant holes in the roof along the hallway spill beams of light in random spots. Poking my head back into the bathroom, I catch Sam's eye.

"If you come out, shut the door. I don't want the animals out here," I say, softly.

Backing back out of the room, I brace myself. Roxanne takes my hand as we walk down the hall together. The floor is damp, even all the way back here. When we get to the kitchen, I see why. The entire roof over the kitchen and dining room has blown off. The partition between this area and the living room has been wrenched off the track. All of the furniture has been knocked over or blown across the room. There are nails and screws everywhere. A piece of jagged wood is stuck through the kitchen window, and there is shattered glass everywhere. Glancing past the now broken partition toward the deck, I see that the entire roof and the glass wall of the living room is smashed to bits. Picking my way over the shards of wood and glass, I glance down at Roxanne's feet. She's wearing heavy duty shoes. She catches me checking and smiles. "It isn't my first rodeo," she says.

Reaching down, I pull up a soaked and ruined

copy of Annabelle Lies from the floor. Holding it in my hands, I look down at the cover with the shadowy woman standing near the edge of a cliff. Maybe it's time to write the sequel. Smiling at Roxanne, I fling the ruined book to where the kitchen garbage can would be if it hadn't blown away.

"Dana," Roxanna says. "You look like a woman who has found all the answers."

"Oh, Roxanne. I'm a woman who realizes I have none of the answers."

Sam and Olivia come out of the bathroom and make their way cautiously down the hall. Turning at the sound of crunching glass, I catch Sam's eye and smile. "Looks like my roof is gone," I say, shrugging.

"Walls too," she answers, deadpan.

For a few minutes, none of us can move. Standing in a line in the kitchen, staring at the sky through what used to be my ceiling, we're all silent. I'm struck by an insane desire to laugh. I don't know why. I must be making a strange noise while trying to choke down the laughter because the other three are staring at me.

"Are you all right?" Roxanne asks.

"Actually, I am."

"It's just...I know it can be upsetting. Your house is destroyed."

"You should see your car." Hysterical laughter wells up from my stomach and has me bent double. Roxanne starts laughing with me and then Sam and Olivia are laughing, too. Standing under the ruins of my roof, all I can do is laugh, deep, beautiful belly laughter. A ray of light is shining through the hole in my house, and I turn my face to the sky to feel the warmth.

Looking at the sun, I realize that maybe I'm a

little more healed than I thought I was.

Roxanne, smiling next to me, takes my hand. "You've come a long way, baby."

I have come a long way. Looking down at her beautiful smile, I'm suddenly filled with an inexplicable joy. Maybe we aren't meant to be together. Or maybe we're just not meant to be together right now. Whatever else happens, whatever other trials I go through, I know I can count on her to hold my hand on the journey.

Putting her arm around Olivia, Sam smiles at me over Roxanne's head. "What are you thinking, my friend?"

"I'm thinking we're going to have to change the name of our club."

The End

About the Author:

Beth Burnett believes in creating her own reality. To that end, before she gets out of bed every morning, she says, "I am awesome!" Beth is a full-time student, a full-time writer and a somewhat reluctant corporate employee. (For the record, she does not wear pantyhose...ever.) When she isn't writing or working, Beth plays the banjo badly, hangs out with her soul mate dog, and chases warm weather. Obsessed with traveling, if she isn't actively on the road, she's in the middle of planning her next trip. The Love Sucks Club is Beth's third novel.

Other *Author's* titles available at Sapphire Books

Man Enough ISBN - 978-1-939062-09-3

Things are going well for Davey Carter. She loves her job and she has a comfortable bed. Granted, her love life is non-existent, her pot-smoking mother is wreaking havoc in her apartment, and she is starting to suspect that her lesbian best friend might be secretly in love with her. But none of that matters when Davey meets Danny, a kind, loving, intelligent man who just may be the love of Davey's life. Until it turns out that Danny is harboring a secret of his own.

Andy's Song ISBN - 978-1939062-14-7

Is there more to life than sex? Andy Ericksson is trying to find out. She's had a pretty easy life. She's sexy, she's tough, and she has a trust fund that ensures she will never have to work a "normal" job. She has a circle of adoring friends and all of the hot, casual sex she could want. It's a recipe for a great time. However, lately, Andy has started to feel that something is missing. Casual sex isn't cutting through the loneliness. Her best friend falls in love with someone else, her ex-girlfriend makes an appearance, and she meets someone who isn't willing to be a one-night stand. Andy's world is changing and she's not sure that she's changing with it. In the midst of Andy's turmoil, everyone in her life suddenly seems to be spouting new age wisdom and finding inner peace. Through the changing of one relationship and the beginning of another, Andy struggles to open her heart without sacrificing her freedom or alienating those she loves the most.

CPSIA information can be obtained at www.ICGtesting.com
Printed in the USA
BVOW08s0325291115

428750BV00004B/208/P

9 781939 062505